I0590194

Swamp Gum

Swamp Gum

Rowan Sylva

99% Press

Published by 99% Press,
an imprint of Lasavia Publishing Ltd.
Auckland, New Zealand
www.lasaviapublishing.com

ISBN: 978-0-473-36196-9

To The Wilderness Society

Acknowledgements

I would like to give a big shout out to my friend Shane Clarence for all the stories he told me, providing inspiration for the novel. A special thanks to my partner Daniela Gast for constant motivation, helping with revision and the cover design. Thank you to Ida Mitrani for the cover art. Thanks to James George for helping me with the writing process. Thanks to Linus Norman and Jacek Maliszweski for feedback and proof reading. Thanks to Tania White for support in the early stages of writing. Big thank you to Mike, Odette, Mahina, Jenn and the whole team at Lasavia Publishing for making this book a reality. Thank you also to Still Wild Still Threatened and The Wilderness Society for continuing the fight for Australia's forests.

'It is most extraordinary to see that these dense forests, ancient daughters of nature and time, where the noise of the axe is never heard and where the vegetation is richer every day from its own products, can extend unimpeded everywhere; and when at the other end of the world, one happens to see forests exclusively composed of trees unknown in Europe, of plants strange in form and various in their productions, one's interest becomes more keen and more pronounced.'

Nicolas Baudin, French explorer, January 1802

'Getting that 74,000 hectares out of World Heritage Listing, it's still going to leave half of Tasmania protected forever, but that will be an important sign to you, to Tasmanians, to the world, that we support the timber industry.'

Tony Abbot, Prime Minister of Australia, March 2014

Chapter 1: Tuesday

It was springtime in the Balloong Valley, and Jane walked slowly through the lush temperate rainforest. The midday sun trickled down through the evergreen canopy, illuminating the glades in a soft light. The forest was not dense and scrubby like on the highlands, nor was it sparse, dry and thorny like the stringy bark forests on the coast. It was like walking through a cathedral of bright moss. The moss covered the floor, caked the tree trunks and hung in great tufts from the branches.

Jane stopped, stroked the lens cap of her camera and looked around her. Myrtles, sassafras and celery-top pines grew into twisted shapes that formed the lower storey. Native laurels exploded into white bell-shaped flowers, tinged with pink. Tiny sprigs of golden rosemary shone in the dim light, and orange fungi blossomed from the rotting logs. Towering above all this were the huge ninety-metre-tall swamp gums, the second tallest trees on earth. They grew sporadically among the rainforest, and their trunks were the pillars of the Green Cathedral.

A native pink-breasted robin flitted onto a branch above her, singing a high pitched, warbling song. Holding her camera, Jane zoomed in on the robin, and clicked. Tiny birds, turquoise fairy wrens and silvereyes, darted through the grove. A brown, long-limbed huntsman spider showed itself, just long enough to be caught on camera before slipping under the leaves.

Jane paused as she heard a rustling in the ferns. She crouched and held her camera ready. An echidna crept slowly and cautiously into the light. Its long snout searched for insects, while the barbs covering its back, ruffled as it moved. It paused and went still as it became aware of Jane who clicked her camera. It was rare to see mammals in the daytime; it was at night that the woods came alive with possums, bats, wombats and wallabies.

Jane continued to walk through the Green Cathedral until she came to Old Gnarly, the oldest and tallest tree in the Balloong Valley. He rose above the canopy, twisted like a corkscrew, his roots extending out from the base of his trunk in long buttresses. Placing her camera beside her, Jane lay down between the roots of the tree, stared up at the canopy, and felt the forest lull her into a state of rest. The moss was damp but it didn't bother her and the sounds soothed her – the creaking of Old Gnarly above and the chirping of insects below. She felt that she could almost hear the forest talking. She lay staring at the sky for a long time, and it was late afternoon when she returned to camp.

The camp blockaded a short, gravelled logging road. A swamp gum had fallen the previous year and its huge trunk formed the natural basis of the blockade. Behind the fallen trunk, the activists had constructed a yurt out of tarps, canvas and materials from the bush, while tree sits, built in the crowns of the swamp gums, formed a semi-circular ring at the end of the road. Camp Balloong was strategically important because the logging road was scheduled to be extended and the forest clear felled.

It was warm and dry inside the yurt, elevated from the road with a wooden floor made from pallets, and covered with cushions and blankets, and in the middle there was a brick fireplace, and kneeling beside it was a young man. He had short brown hair, a stubbly narrow face and was dressed in oversized blue thermals and gumboots. He was silent and thoughtful, and it seemed to Jane that he was a fixture of Camp Balloong like the yurt he had helped to build. His name was Lui and he was making tea, concentrating on the fire, adding small sticks and blowing upon it.

A shaven haired girl, Nails, sat on a cushion, chewing a celery stick. She wore tight black jeans, covered in stencilled patches and a black singlet. She was a lawyer with a sharp tongue, single-mindedly dedicated to the forests, and the unofficial leader of the campaign. In the dark, on the edge of the yurt, Old Mad Mark sipped some cheap wine.

Nails smiled as Jane entered. It was a very slight, tight smile that cut across her thin lips. 'I was wondering where you were. Get any nice shots today?'

'Yeah I got a beauty of an echidna.' Jane flicked through the shots on her camera and handed it to Nails. 'What's the news from the big smoke?'

Nails hesitated. 'Awful. The federal government's gone crazy trying to sell the country to China, and the state government is licking their arses. They're amping up for a summer of clearfelling and burnoffs. I've heard some contractors logged a coupe down the Balloong River, close to Dead Miners Ford. I suspect that'll be a breach of their agreement. Lui and I wanna go down and check it out. I was hoping you'd come and take some shots.'

Lui lifted the big, cast iron kettle off the fire and poured the tea into tin mugs. A horned beetle ponderously crawled across the gravel.

'Sure, I'll come,' said Jane.

The scouting mission was joined by Lauren. She was tall and had a tattoo on her left shoulder, depicting a forest goblin holding a pair of bolt cutters and a spotted mushroom. They took Nails' beat-up and bumper-sticker-covered hatchback and drove south toward Dead Miners Ford. When they turned off the main road, they found that their way was blocked by a steel padlocked gate. Jane and Nails kept watch while Lui and Lauren took turns at sawing through the chain with a hacksaw. Eventually the chain clanged free, the gate swung open and they drove through a maze of logging roads. Nails parked the car in an overgrown dead end road, where it was unlikely to be noticed, and the group of four trekked toward the coupe.

The area of logged forest was a rectangular scar the size of a football field, and the red light of the early evening illuminated the pale mottled flesh of the swamp gums on its edge. The coupe stretched out before them, an obliterated landscape of crushed rainforest, while smashed heaps of myrtles and sassafras rose above them in great pyres. The trunks of the gums had begun to be stacked ready for removal to the woodchipping plant. Next to these was parked a grappler, a vehicle resembling a digger with a crane like neck and a large claw designed for gripping logs. To Jane it looked like a sleeping monster.

Two white cockatoos flew overhead, swooping and gliding. Lovers, thought Jane. They alighted on a lone habitat tree, left to sway gently in the middle of the destruction. They began to scream and their strange shrieking echoed through the still valley. It was breeding season. Cockatoos could live until the age of eighty, forming long term partnerships and taking years to raise chicks. The parrots must have lost family in the destruction. Jane zoomed in on them, capturing the pair on her camera.

The activists walked through the coupe. They moved slowly, scrambling along the slippery fallen logs, and clambering over piles of sawn vegetation. Nails was noting the corners of the coupe on a GPS. It was an arduous process and Jane constantly shot stills of the destruction as they clambered from one end to the other. The light began to fade and the shadows of the trees grew long. Somewhere off in the distance a possum screeched.

Lauren spat out a mouthful of sassafras leaves, a mild stimulant. 'Let's get out of here. We've got the shots. This place is depressing.'

'One minute,' said Nails, 'we've nearly finished. They're pushing too far north. They're not supposed to come this far.'

Jane, who had seated herself on a stump, wondered if the lawyer took a masochistic joy from lingering in logging coupes.

Lui stood behind Jane, staring toward the distant, bush clad mountains, hazy in the twilight.

The roar of a vehicle moving up the road became audible, and the activists froze.

'Quick,' said Lauren, 'get down.'

Lui and Jane slithered off the stump and nestled themselves behind a mound of debris. Lauren and Nails joined them, and they huddled together, smelling of damp polypropylene and watching the road below. Jane knew that getting caught in a coupe wasn't good. They could be charged with trespass, but violence from the contractors was a more tangible threat, and Jane felt a rush of adrenaline. She didn't like to admit it but she was an activist, not just for the forest, but also for the illicit thrill – the constant threat of violence or arrest.

'Why's there a truck at this hour?' asked Nails to no one in particular. 'From our camp? Na can't be.'

'Maybe they like to come gloat over their work,' said Lauren.

'Logging trucks do pickups at all hours,' said Jane.

'It's not the sound of a logging truck,' said Lui.

There was still enough light to see, and Jane, holding her camera with a steady hand, shot stills of the yellow dump truck, as it pulled up at the end of the road. Her camera had a powerful zoom lens and she could see two men wearing hard hats exit the truck.

'Here'll be right.' The occa accent of the contractor was just audible above the rumble of the engine in the still evening. The men worked in silence as the dump truck backed toward the edge of the coupe. They pulled off the edge of the trailer and Jane heard it clang. The trailer began to tilt up and its load clattered as it slid off into the coupe.

'Let's get a beer.' Jane heard a contractor say before the doors slammed shut and the dump truck roared off into the night.

It was dark and the activists turned on their torches before they made their way, zigzagging down, to the location of the dumped rubbish. When they arrived they flashed their torches across it.

It appeared to be a pile of industrial waste, rusted rolls of razor wire, some steel drums, and a large number of broken asbestos panels, while the glossy sheen of black rubbish sacks reflected the light of the waxing moon as it rose over the swamp gums.

'Dumping rubbish,' said Lauren. 'The bastards, do you reckon we can get them for that?'

'Depends,' said Nails, 'we don't even know who dumped it.' She turned to Jane. 'You got this on camera, hun?'

'Yip'

'Well, let's get out of here,' said Lauren. 'It's dark, I'm hungry, and we've got all the evidence we need.'

'Hang on a minute,' said Lui. 'There might be something useful down there. We might have a purpose for razor wire, and we can always do with more drums.'

'Assuming they're not filled with radioactive waste,' said Lauren.

'I think we should have a closer look at what's in there,' said Nails.

Jane felt that she agreed more with Lauren but said nothing, and so the activists slithered down the slope to investigate. Lui swore as his trousers caught on some razor wire and it sliced into his leg.

'Hope ya got ya tetanus shots,' said Lauren.

Jane skirted around the waste, photographing it. Her nostrils were filled with a pungent chemical stench, and looking down, she noticed that a lid had come off a drum and liquid had spilled onto the ground. It seeped through the sticks and dripped off the corrugated asbestos. She photographed it. Nails had come to join her and stared at the spill.

'What do you reckon it is?' asked Jane.

The lawyer shrugged. 'Don't know.'

Lui had clambered on top of the pile of trash and was kicking a piece of asbestos out of the way. 'These drums are filled with shit,' he remarked and pushed one. 'Look out,' he shouted as it smashed through more asbestos and rolled toward Jane and Nails.

They scrambled out of the way and watched as it hit a log. Its lid came loose and the top of a plastic rubbish sack slid out from inside the drum.

'Come on, Lui, we don't need any of this shit, let's get out of here,' said Lauren who stood back from the scene, her arms folded.

'Hang on,' said Lui, 'I want to see what's in that plastic bag. It felt solid.' He climbed down to stand beside Jane and Nails. 'Come on then, give us a hand.' He seemed to be enjoying himself.

Jane helped Lui pull the plastic bag out of the drum. It was heavy but slid out easily. Lui took out his pocket knife, levered open the blade, sliced through the plastic and pulled it open.

Jane screamed and dropped her torch. Lui stepped back while Lauren and Nails came forward to shine their torches onto the sack. Jane shivered, a creeping fear seeping over her body. She broke into a cold sweat, but she focused her camera and shot a still of the body, seeing it through the digital screen.

The girl's face was white, though covered in dark blue bruises, the skin peeling away from the flesh near the cheeks. Her thin lips were blue and cracked; her eyes were sunken pits. The head and torso were framed by hair, which, though matted, tangled, and stained with dried blood, still had a pale sheen that reflected the light of the torches. Her bloated torso had broken open and her naked skin was blistered and covered in black veins. The stench of decaying meat filled Jane's nose, overpowering the scent of chemicals. She shuddered with repulsion and fought to control her queasy stomach as she photographed the corpse.

Lui vomited. An owl hooted. A possum shrieked.

'You got this on camera?' asked Nails.

'Let's go,' said Lauren, and Jane could hear fear in her tone, a shaky urgency.

This time nobody argued, and the activists ran back to where the car was hidden. They drove in silence, the trees looming over them as they dodged the wallabies that ran along the edges of the forest. Nails slammed on the brakes as a wombat, its eyes reflecting the headlights, shambled across the road.

Back at camp, hot hippy-slop was poured into bowls, and the smouldering fire filled the yurt with an orange glow. Outside, the snarls of fighting possums and the melodic calls of black currawongs filled the night. The people in the yurt were silent as the camera was passed from hand to hand.

Nails spoke, raising her voice above the hubbub of the yurt. 'We need to stay calm people. We need to look at the facts. What do we know? We know that somebody dumped rubbish several hours ago in a coupe. We know that inside a drum among that rubbish is the corpse of a girl, at least a few days dead.'

Could it be an accident, somebody wanted to know.

'Of course it wasn't a fucken accident,' Lui shouted. 'You think she just climbed into a drum and drowned herself in Roundup for the fun of it. What a stupid question.'

Was it the contractors that killed her, another person was asking, and no one had an answer to that.

'Piss poor place to hide a body, anywhere in the bush would be better!' cut in Tom, a self-proclaimed anarchist.

'People,' Nails banged with a teaspoon on her tin camping cup, 'we simply don't know how, why or at whose hands this happened. What we need to decide is what we are going to do about it.'

Goldy, a first year science student, who was usually quiet and reserved, and who had been sitting tensely by the fire, burst out, 'It's obvious what we have to do, call the police immediately. Warwick can drive into satellite reception, now, and we can alert the authorities.'

Tom spat into the fire and held his hand up. 'Fuck the cops, they'll probably just cover it up. We ought to go straight to the media, blow the whole thing up underneath them before they've time to act. Imagine the headline: Logging Contractors Kill Virgin. Meanwhile we launch our own investigation into what happened.'

'You're being ridiculous,' said Lui and he pointed at Goldy, giving her the thumbs up. 'Goldy's right. Not reporting the crime suggests complicity in it. We call the cops now, wash our hands of the whole damn thing, clean, neat, lawful.' Lui seemed to shiver and went back to looking at the fire, and Jane knew that he, like her, was recalling the appearance of the dead body, the stench, the sunken eyes, the open torso.

'You think the pigs are gonna help us?' said Tom. 'The pigs are a gang, they'll probably use the thing as a pretext to lock us all up and shut down the camp, I block that motion.' The anarchist crossed his arms, forming an X. He sounded angsty and Jane suspected that he was bitter that he'd not come on the scouting mission.

'This isn't a discussion over camp process.' The volume of Lui's voice rose. He stood and waved a stick ending in a glowing ember in Tom's direction. 'It's a fucken murder. We're going to the cops and that's the end of it.'

Up until this point Old Mad Mark had been gently plucking his guitar, his jar of cheap red goon never far from his hand. He was the oldest member of the campaign. His dreadlocks were grey and wispy, in some places hanging to his scalp by only a few threads. His eyes were bloodshot, and his gaunt, ruddy face showed years of alcoholism. His glass fell from his shaking hand, and he began to weep and splutter through his few blackened teeth.

'She's so beautiful,' he wept, 'she's so beautiful. The bastards, look what they've done! They've taken her soul!' His voice rose to a howl and his hands shook more violently. 'It's demonic! Think of what we've done. What we did to the black fellas. What we did to the American Indians. What we're doing to our land.' Mad Mark collapsed on the floor in a fit of weeping, drunken emotion.

Lauren moved to comfort him.

Jane closed her eyes and pictured the girl, her white skin marbled with black veins, the torso opened from the gasses of her organs, her matted hair. She remembered the last bust, the sneering faces of the police as they cut her out of her lock-on and dragged her by her hair across the gravel while the sound of chainsaws cut through the forest she loved. She remembered the pain, the violence and her anger. They had kicked her in the stomach so that they could break her and make her move, and when she had told them that she needed medical attention, that she thought her rib might be broken, that handcuffs were too tight and bit into her skin, they'd laughed at her. When it went to court she was the one found guilty. Her brutal treatment warranted no mention. She was a trouble maker, she had resisted arrest, and she had put lives in dangers. The police prosecutor had smirked while the judge delivered his verdict.

That was what she knew of the police and those were the memories that slid through her mind as she thought of the murdered girl. Old Mad Mark's weeping subsided. She agreed with Tom. Fuck the cops. 'I took this footage. It's on my camera. I'll decide what to do with it.' She glared at the people around the yurt. 'I say we see what we can find out before we take any action. I'll get a lift into town tomorrow and have a dig around. There must be something. Somebody must have filed a missing person report.'

Lui gave Jane a hard look. 'For god sakes, Jane, this is a matter for the cops. Don't be a bloody idiot.'

'Watch your mouth, Lui,' said Nails.

Warwick flicked his honey-coloured hair out of his round youthful face and moved to warm his hands by the fire. He hadn't taken part in the debate and he didn't really care. He looked at Jane. She was pretty in a tomboyish kind of way. She wore a bush shirt, shorts and black long johns. She had green eyes and her small face was framed by thick dirty-blond dreadlocks. Warwick looked away. It wasn't that he disagreed with the sentiment of forest protection it was just that he knew it was hopeless. Didn't these ferals get it? Government and forestry would do what they wanted anyway. They simply didn't give a shit.

And Warwick didn't really care either. That was the way capitalism operated. If you didn't like it – move to Bolivia. Really, the nerve of these people, if this was Borneo, or Sumatra, they would quickly disappear in the night. But because they came from white Australia they believed they had rights. This was the real world and in the real world money had the say. Civil disobedience was a bourgeois luxury for wankers who wanted to feel important. But Warwick had a job to do, because he wasn't just a cynic, he was a paid informant – a spy for forestry.

The meeting had ended and the ferals were washing up and possum proofing the kitchen before sleep time. Warwick moved over to where Jane was sitting, staring at the fire. He crouched beside her.

She looked over. 'Oh hi, Warwick.'

Warwick smiled at her. 'I was wondering if I could get a lift into town with you. There's some stuff I need to do there. I liked your speech by the way.'

'Right, thanks,' replied Jane. 'Yeah I'm getting a lift with Nails. I'm sure it'll be fine if you come. I think she wants to leave super early though.' She smiled at him, and Warwick felt a flash of guilt at his plan, but it was only a flash. Forestry had to be told about the photographs, or given the camera if he had the chance. He moved off, heading for his tent that he shared with Goldy. She'd been waiting for him by the exit and once they were outside she grasped his hand with affection and kissed his throat. He smelled the scent of her curls and felt the brush of her breasts against his chest and her warm breath on his neck. The job certainly had its perks.

'You think we should've gone to the cops don't you, hun?' She said.

'Of course I do, of course.'

Johnno slurped back a pint as he sat around a table with his mates at the local. The pub had a wooden bar, VB on tap, a row of pokies and a flat screen TV that beamed horse races from one end of the bar. He winked at the barmaid as she filled his jug with VB. Johnno appreciated his job, cutting down trees. There was something satisfying about destroying in five minutes what Mother Nature had taken a thousand years to create, all to the whir of a chainsaw. It was underpaid and dangerous, but it was what he knew. He was good at it and it was in his blood.

'There's nothing I'd rather be doing,' Johnno remarked to his work buddy Hank. 'Trees are made to be cut down just as pussies are made to be fucked. The earth loves it. That's what it's there for. It wants to be drilled.' He slapped his hand on the table and took a slug of his beer. But despite his joviality a shadow hung over the contractor on that cool Tuesday night. The company was slashing jobs. There was pressure to lay off the old growth, and the Japanese had terminated their contract with Woodchips Ltd. The long recession had also taken its toll on the logging industry with a reduced number of coupes, layoffs, shorter hours, and no bloody pay rise, after ten years of ripping up the earth.

Johnno's drink-clouded eyes met with his fellow contractors, Pete and Hank, both reasonably tough blokes in their early forties. Hank had a lazy eye and a quick mouth on him, while Pete, Johnno was fond of saying, was thick as pig shit. Young Trev, Pete's son, was also drinking with them. He was a young bloke, but a good cunt, recently returned from working down a bauxite hole in The Territory.

Trev was telling a joke. 'There's a bloke, right, and he's driving through The Territory and his car breaks down and he doesn't know what he's gonna do. He's next to a paddock, he is, and miraculously a horse jumps over the fence and the horse talks. The horse tells him how to fix his engine. Then the horse leaps back over the fence and keeps eating grass. He's so amazed at what's happened he needs a drink. So he drives to the nearest pub and orders a scotch on the rocks.

'"You won't believe what just happened to me!" He says to the bartender.

"This bloody horse told me how to fix me car, it did."

'The bartender asks him, "Was it a black horse or a white horse?"

'"Well," he says, "it's funny you should ask that cos it was as white as me bare arse."

'The bartender says, "Well, ain't that lucky cos a black horse wouldn't know fuck all about engines!" Ya get it?' Trev, who had laboured through the joke, grinned at his mates.

Johnno snorted into his drink. 'I got one for ya. What do ya say to a lesbian feminist with no arms and no legs, on a beach?'

'What?'

'Nice tits.'

The boys at the table laughed. Nice tits, Johnno repeated the punch line under his breath and chuckled. Damn fine yarn that one, damn fine yarn.

'So,' Hank interrupted the pleasant flow of his thoughts. 'That young fella, Mat, he's been given the sack. Who'll be next do ya reckon, Johnno? Probably be you, with ya stupid expression, always staring off into space. I saw ol' Johnston with his slick suit, out in the coupe, giving ya the quiet word yesterday. We'd hate t' lose ya now, Johnno, being such a joker, wouldn't be the same without ya!'

'Call me stupid again and I'll drop ya like a sack of shit.'

Johnno slurped his beer. 'It's the greenies Hank, always slinking around, poking their noses in where they're not wanted, hanging banners, protesting, like they've got nothing better to do then make it difficult for a man to make an honest living.' He lowered his voice. 'I've heard the pollies are going soft. Shit mates, we could all be out of work. Now I've been thinking —'

'God never ceases to amaze.'

'Shut ya pie hole, Hank, or you'll get a fist in it. Now, as I was saying, if the pollies are going weak at the knees, it's about time we took matters into our own hands. I think we'd better soften them up a bit. If they're gonna mess with a man's work, show them that they're gonna get a decent hiding.'

While Johnno had been talking, a drunken gambler had been swilling a schooner, watching the television. He stepped back in an awkward attempt to get perspective on the race and knocked the table at which the contractors were seated. Johnno's beer splashed across the front of his shirt.

Johnno stood up, walked over to the gambler and poured the remainder of the pint glass over his head. Rage flared in the gambler's eyes and he launched a clumsy punch at the contractor. Johnno dodged and responded with a swift jab to the man's nose, breaking it, and sending blood splattering over the beer stain. The gambler went down, knocking stools as he fell. Johnno then began to kick his victim in the ribs, while the injured man groaned, clutching his damaged face. It was a good ten seconds before his mates pulled him away, and out the door before the police arrived.

Chapter 2: Wednesday Morning

Nails drove, Jane looked out the window of the passenger seat and Warwick slouched in the back as they headed to Port Town. At first they followed windy roads through the old growth forests of the highlands, and the cool air blew in through the windows. They forded streams, red with the tannins of tea tree, drove past glistening wetlands, and over rocky tussock-covered hills, but soon they came to pine and eucalypt plantations, planted in straight rows, all the same height, with only a smattering of tree ferns. As they descended to the lowland they passed through a small town; a bank, a teahouse, an op shop, and, that sign of civilisation in Australia - a horse racing track, mown, maintained, but never used.

They sped through flat land used for dairy and beef farming. The land, thought Jane, would once have been wetland, but over the years the settlers had drained it, driven away the wildlife, and now it was a desert of effluent filled ponds and ditches, wind breaks and lone eucalypts. They drove past a cow paddock and Jane watched as one of them lifted its tail and let loose a wet stream of poo. They got stuck for a while behind a logging truck and that slowed their progress, but eventually they came to the outskirts of the historic city of Port Town, where the new infill housing suburbs sprawled along the edges of the highway. Jane picked at a blob of Blu-Tack, which held a spiral shell to the dashboard.

'Nails?' Jane asked.

'Yip?'

'You know a bit about the people involved in forestry, don't you?'

'Unfortunately I've had to deal with some of them, yes.'

'Who are they?'

'Arseholes.'

'No, but really.'

Nails clicked her tongue. 'The actual contracting company operating in the Balloong is a pretty small scale operation. It's a private company, subcontracted by the government, receiving subsidies. A man runs it,' she paused searching for the name, 'Collin, he's at least a million dollars in debt. But he's only small fry. The big bucks are with Woodchips Ltd. Their head honcho is the one person you can't contact no matter how many secretaries you talk to. They buy the logs dirt cheap from the contractors, chip them and sell them for a profit to the toilet paper companies. The woodchipping companies give kickbacks to the pollies. That's why he ends up on the receiving end of all those government subsidies.'

'If we know they've been giving kickbacks, can't we get them done for corruption?'

Nails made a farting noise by blowing air through her tight lips. 'Not so simple. There's a whole group of major shareholders, including politicians. The kickbacks probably go through some kind of slush fund, which make them difficult to trace.'

'I'm sorry for sounding so dumb but what's a slush fund?'

'It's a special account,' Warwick cut in from the backseat, 'for people who want to be discreet about where their dosh goes. Sorry,' he added, 'I couldn't help hearing your conversation, sounds interesting.'

'All good, join in,' Nails waved away Warwick's apology. 'Where do you want me to drop you, hun?'

'Oh, at my place if you can.'

They had made good time, leaving Camp Balloong at six and it was nearly ten when they pulled up at Jane's house on the hill.

Lui sat outside on a wooden crate by the entrance of the yurt, sharpening the camp axe on a whetstone. It was a clear morning and the sound of chirping insects and silvereyes filled the air. He ran the camp chores through his head, water containers filled, kitchen clean, food secured from possums, Front Watch occupied, firewood collected, sawdust for the composting toilet. Everything should be fine, but something was seriously wrong. Somewhere out there was the body of a dead girl, a girl whose death was going unreported because of the madness of their photographer.

The rhythmic scraping of stone on steel calmed him as he pondered what to do. If he alerted the police now he would break trust with Nails and Jane. They could possibly end up in custody. On the other hand the idea of not reporting the murder, and simply doing nothing went against his instincts. He shivered as he remembered the smell of rotting flesh and the taste of bile in his mouth. Lui loved the cops no more than the next activist. He remembered the last bust, kicks, abuse, arrest. He had fought for years on the other side of the line. But a murder had been committed, a girl was dead, Jane was a smart chick, but she wasn't a detective. The cops may not be good guys but if ever they had a purpose it was for this, and the sooner they were informed the cleaner, and the better.

Lauren appeared from the kitchen – a rough structure made of tarps and sticks, situated behind the yurt. 'Coffee, Lui?'

'Yeah that'd be great, thanks.'

'Black, soy or rape juice?'

'Milk.'

'Rape juice it is.'

Lauren had her own coffee black and crouched down beside Lui. They sat in silence, drinking their coffees, and watching the sun rise over the forest. The air was cool and clean.

'Nice day,' said Lauren cheerfully, but Lui sensed that the comment was contrived and he suspected that her thoughts lingered, like his own, on something far from nice.

'We have to call the cops,' he said.

'Well, your call. I want no part in it. It'll be on your head if Jane gets arrested for withholding evidence.' Lauren stood up and tipped out the dregs of her coffee.

'I've thought it through. I won't have a clear conscience unless I act.' Lui didn't meet Lauren's eyes but looked out over the rainforest.

'Just make sure you can find the coupe again. Nails was pretty good with maps. It was a maze getting in there.'

'I can find it.'

'All I'm saying is, you better be sure before you call the cops.'

Lui tested the axe blade against his thumb – sharp as a razor. 'I guess you're right,' he said.

The small house that Jane shared with her cousin Sky was built in the wooden colonial style of the 1890's. It was painted light blue and perched on a high hill with a balcony overlooking town and beyond that, the Pacific Ocean. Dry, crackly, stringy barks and blue gums covered the steep hills and their pale blue leaves shimmered in the afternoon sun. Sky was out, probably working at the Purring Kitten. She slotted her key into the door, pushed it open and headed for the kitchen. She made a black coffee and peanut butter on toast, before making her way to her room.

It was a simple square with one window facing the trees. Her walls were covered with photographs of wildlife, mostly ones she had taken herself. A framed picture of a quoll hung above her single bed – the shot of the little marsupial carnivore had won her a prize in the Australian Geographic and sparked her desire to become a professional. She took a bite of her toast and sat down at her workstation: a second-hand desk, a computer and a messy pile of photos and documents.

She pushed the papers out of the way, booted up her computer and uploaded the photographs from her camera. She scrolled past the shots of the huntsman and the echidna, and brought up the images of the incident. Even with the high resolution zoom lens, the lack of light made it impossible to discern the features of the men, and the rim of the hill hid the truck's number plate. No help there. She flicked forward to the shots of the girl and zoomed into the face, pale, bilious and webbed with black veins. She stared for several moments at the sunken eyes. It was disgusting, yet fascinating. Jane drummed her fingers on the desk and fiddled with the contrast of the shot. How do we begin investigating? she asked herself. Missing person reports, I guess.

Jane gulped down some coffee and took another bite of her toast. The Port Town Times' archives had been helpfully digitalised. And she scrolled through different issues looking at missing person reports – typing in key words to bring up related articles. It seemed like a hopeless task. She tried missing person, and the first hit was some feel-good story about a boy who had gone missing and was then returned to his mother. Another story was from the international section, something about a girl kidnapped by gypsies. Then there was a story about a group of people missing at sea.

Jane picked up a pen and began to click and unclick it impulsively as she thought. The list of articles was long, and she supposed she could probably scroll through them all day without finding what she was searching for. She changed the parameter of her search to order articles by date. The body after all didn't look like it had been dead that long. As she scrolled through the articles she found something – a simple notice, two sentences.

A fourteen-year-old, Anya Ivanova, was reported missing on Friday. Anybody with information regarding the whereabouts of the girl should contact the police.

It was the closest she'd come so far. She typed Anya Ivanova into Google, and was bombarded by a torrent of irrelevant hits. Sounds Russian, thought Jane, I bet she lives on North Side. She typed Ivanova into a Port Town phone book. The site returned several hits, all on North Side. She downed the last of her coffee, scribbled the addresses onto a scrap of paper and checked the time. It was one in the afternoon. Time enough, she reckoned, for a mission.

The bus to North Side was not very crowded, and Jane stood close to the exit, holding her bicycle in front of her. On a seat nearby, an Eastern European woman, her head covered in a shawl, chanted as she rolled prayer beads through her fingers. When they neared the river a man in baggy tracksuit pants, greased-back hair, and stinking of chemical cologne approached her and tried to sell her a collection of stolen DVDs. She politely declined, and the bus clattered over the bridge.

North Side was poor and run down. State housing, built in the fifties and never properly maintained, hugged the hillsides. Immigrants from Eastern Europe and Africa, as well as poor whites lived here. The streets of North Side were also home to packs of stray dogs, starving cats and large rats. In winter, a chilling fog washed up from the river, causing outbreaks of influenza and pneumonia to spread through the overcrowded and under insulated homes, while in summer the immigrant children ran half naked through the streets.

North Side was a hub of crime, and illegal gambling dens pushed out onto the streets and alleyways, while drug dealers touted from street corners, and smacked-out junkies huddled in doorways. Suburban houses had been converted into brothels from where busty brown women and narrow faced, short-skirted Russian girls sold their assets.

Jane exited the bus and mounted her bike. She rode past several two-dollar-shops, loan shark outlets, fruit sellers, and grog shops. People clustered outside a Salvation Army outlet, smoking cigarettes while waiting for food hand-outs. She bought an apple from a toothless fruit seller. It was powdery but sweet.

The first house she went to was unhelpful. A woman answered the door and shouted at her in Russian. Eventually, she went and got her son who spoke a little English and told Jane that no one called Anya lived there. The door was promptly slammed in her face. At the second house, a man dressed in nothing but his underwear, with a large hairy gut and muscular arms tried to invite her in for a beer. At the third house, she was nearly torn apart by a pair of aggressive German Shepherds. An African woman hanging out washing on the neighbouring section gave her an odd look as she cycled off.

Jane felt exhausted and dispirited by the time she came to the fourth house on her list. It was large, like it had been a wealthy mansion or possibly a convent, years ago, and now it seemed to be rotting and dilapidated, its lawn unkempt. When she knocked, a short, thin, old man answered the door. He looked like he could have been Greek or maybe Croatian. His face was covered in thick white hairs that stabbed from his chin and leathery cheeks. He smoked a long wooden tobacco pipe, the smell of which was overwhelming, and every part of him seemed to be stained with nicotine.

'Hello girly, wadda ya want?' The old man stared rudely at Jane. 'Ya need t' brush ya hair.'

Jane smiled, 'I was looking for Miss Ivanova.'

'Ya were, was ya,' said the man and he licked his nicotine stained lips. 'She ain't live here no more.' He moved to close the door.

'Wait,' she said, placing her foot in the door, 'I'm a journalist.' She held up her camera. 'I'm doing a story on Anya's disappearance, if I could just have a quick look at her room, take a few shots, I'll be on my way.' The bluff worked; a rather odd discussion and twenty bucks later she walked through a hallway and up a flight of stairs. The old wallpaper was peeling, the walls were mouldy and the carpet covering the stairs was dirty and worn to nothing.

They stopped in front of a door with a plastic butterfly tacked to the front, and the pipe smoker pushed it open. The room had a grey carpet and a grimy window that overlooked the street. Clothes were strewn on the floor and cheap jewellery collected dust on the windowsill. The room had a scent of apricot flavoured perfume, and Jane photographed it. She moved over to the windowsill. A solitary photograph lay underneath a pile of plastic jewellery. She picked it up and wiped the dust off it. The photo showed two women, mother and daughter, she supposed. It was a glossy card, one of those ones you get from booths in Asian arcades, and had a background of stars, with cute kitten faces at the corners. The photograph gave the two women a smooth, air brushed quality, both with long light blond hair and elegant faces, smiling at the camera. It could be the girl from the coupe thought Jane, though it was hard to equate the smooth happy face with the rotting corpse. She turned the card over and on the back side somebody had scribbled a series of numbers – 9, 3, 5, 5, 3, 2. Jane photographed the back and front of the card.

'Why are all her things still here?' Jane said to the pipe smoker.

The old man grinned revealing yellow teeth. 'You're a right smart wee nipper. You just need t' brush that hair of yours, eh? Miss Anya didn't move out. The Devil took them both. Young girl shouldn't be going out late all dressed like that. No good can come of it.' He paused to stuff a pinch of tobacco into his pipe and light it with a match, blowing a cloud of smoke into the room. 'The Devil walks about the city all dressed in black, and a handsome young man, all the young ladies they want to dance with him.' He gestured. 'But if they're not careful he'll whisk them up and carry them off to hell. That's what happened to Miss Anya, when that week back she disappeared. I know she was gone with the Devil. For all know that every so often a wee girl in Port Town goes a missing, and is taken by the Devil to be his bride.' The old man made the sign of the cross and lifted a Greek style silver cross from under his shirt and kissed it.

'I know it was the Devil who take her 'cause I seen him once come out

34

of that very door you standing in front of now. He was young, dressed all in black and he smiles to Missy Anya and he gives her some chocolate and she eats the chocolate. And then I knows that she is damned, 'cause she ate the food of the Devil. And then,' he snapped his fingers. 'Don't go poking into the affairs of the Devil.'

'What did he look like?'

The man tutted, blew smoke and wagged his finger at her. 'Ain't none of your business, nor mine.'

Jane wanted to search the room for clues. But the old man was scowling at her, and she felt her welcome was wearing thin. 'Earlier, you said "a young woman like that." What did you mean?'

The old man grinned again and blew another cloud of smoke in her direction 'Anya was a working girl.'

Warwick sat on the balcony of the expensive restaurant on Waterloo Street and surveyed the yachts in the marina. He sipped his Sauvignon Blanc and looked down at his plate. The googly eyed crayfish looked back. He'd ordered it because it was the most expensive thing on the menu. One of the benefits of meeting with David Johnston was that he was able to order whatever he wished, allowing for those sensuous luxuries that made the job worth it. Warwick had dreams of affluence and a palate for the sumptuous.

Despite its delectable reputation, Warwick was having second thoughts about the cray. It looked too much like an actual animal staring up at him, a weird kind of giant sea spider, and he was unsure about how to attack it with his cutlery; he was never really a fan of seafood anyway. Were they being overfished, he wondered as he ripped off a leg, snapped it and sucked out the flesh. That was the problem with hanging out with greenies; you couldn't eat anything without wondering where it came from.

David Johnston smiled indulgently at Warwick. Johnston was a shadowy figure who ran campaigns for conservative politicians. A lobbyist for the logging industry, his current hobby was a job for government forestry ensuring that nobody messed with the flow of cash to private hands. He was a man used to getting his way and his fleshy face had an exuberant charm. He always dressed to impress. He was tall and his presence was at once intimidating yet warm. Johnston had only a strong black coffee and watched as Warwick struggled with the crayfish.

'Here are all the pics of the camp.' Warwick pushed the USB drive across the table with one hand while with the other broke off another crayfish leg.

Johnston pushed the USB drive into his tablet and began to thumb through the photographs. 'Organised, these greenies,' he offered after a minute, without expecting a reply. 'Tell me about the camp.'

'Well, Dave, they're organised, they know a bust is coming.' Warwick told Johnston about the scouting missions, the organisation of the camp and their plans for responding to a bust. The lobbyist just nodded, and ordered another white wine for the young spy. Warwick finished his report with a rundown of the major troublemakers and leaders in the campaign. The one remaining eye of the half demolished cray gazed resentfully up at Warwick.

'Anything else to report?'

'Last night some of the greenies were scouting a coupe. They witnessed a couple of contractors dumping a load of trash. They found the body of a murdered girl in the trash. They got shots of it,' Warwick said through a mouthful of wine and cray.

Chapter 3: Wednesday Evening

Lui and Tom the anarchist drove toward Dead Miners Ford. They found a place to park by the side of the road and set off to find the coupe. It took more than an hour of hiking along dirt roads, and they'd had to dive periodically into bushes to avoid vehicles. They'd sneaked past workers using grapplers to load logs onto a double trailer truck. At one point Lui took a wrong turn and led them into a maze of very old coupes, thick with eucalypt regrowth. They encountered few animals apart from bull ants, blood sucking horseflies and a pair of magpies. By the time they reached their destination, they were tired and hungry.

Lui sat down on the verge at the edge of the coupe, threw down his backpack, took a swig from his water bottle, and took out his lunch: cold rice, soy sauce and grated cheese, east meets west in a lunchbox.

'So this is the coupe?' said Tom. The skinny anarchist was dressed in full black, with a bandana around his neck, in case he needed to instantly hide his features. He'd vehemently disapproved of calling the cops. But his curiosity at seeing the body had led him to accompany Lui. Tom pulled out of his pack a slice of gluten-free bread, which he ate with a thick slab of vegan cheese.

Lui put down his rice for minute to survey the coupe. Rainforest and swamp gums lined its edge, and a lone habitat tree, left in the middle, swayed in the breeze. The ground was steep and uneven and the trash was visible, a pile of rusting tin and broken asbestos.

'Yeah, this is the one. That shit,' Lui pointed to the vegan cheese, 'it's expensive innit?'

'Yeah, I guess, I got my mum to buy it for me. It's nearly gone. Ya want some?'

'Na, I'm all good. I heard processed soy is hard on the body.'

'Says the cunt who smothers his shit in dairy. So where's the body?'

'Somewhere down there.' Lui pointed toward the trash and pushed a forkful of rice into his mouth.

They picked their way toward the trash, past the razor wire and bits of tin to where Lui could see the fallen drum, from which the plastic bag and the body had emerged. He slapped at the horse flies, which buzzed around his face. As he approached he realised something was wrong. The plastic bag was still there, but it was empty and the wind had blown the torn piece of black plastic into a pile of sticks and razor wire. The body was gone. He pushed the empty drum with his foot and slapped at another horse fly, which landed on his hand.

'What's the story mate?' asked Tom.

'The body's gone.'

'What do ya mean the body's gone?' Tom stood on the massive stump of a swamp gum, surveying the rubbish from above.

'I mean it's gone, disappeared, somebody's taken it.'

Lui and Tom scoured the coupe and dumped rubbish for any sign of the body but they found nothing. Lui felt confused, frustrated and unnerved. 'I don't believe it,' he said.

'No point in calling the cops then,' said Tom as if he had scored a point. 'What would you tell them, "I illegally broke into a logging coupe last night. There was a body there but now it's gone. There are photos but you'll have to arrest my friend to get them." They'll just arrest you for cutting open a gate.'

Lui kicked a drum. 'I guess you're right.'

'Let's get out of here, mate. I was planning on doing some scouting tonight, see what they're up to down the river. It's going to take us long enough to get back to camp as it is.'

Lui didn't object, grey cloud covered the sky, and he was sure he could smell rain. Smell rain, it was a funny saying, but there was something to it, a faint yet distinctive scent of breaking ozone.

Jane cycled back toward the centre of North Side, past grim concrete apartment blocks. Her journey, she supposed, had been worth it. She'd found out the dead girl's name and where she'd lived, but what now? She was tired, hungry and also felt the need to share with someone; it had been a lonely day. She turned the corner onto the main road and stopped outside a Vietnamese bakery with a Buddhist shrine in the window, surrounded by fruits, fake money, and incense. She locked up her bike on a street lamp, and bells tinkled as she entered the bakery. She ordered a chicken salad roll for three dollars. The woman who served her smiled widely and said something in Vietnamese when Jane placed a two-dollar coin in the shrine and offered a quick prayer. She stood outside by her bike and watched the street while she ate. The roll was delicious, stuffed with coriander, chicken, pate and salad.

'Jane.'

She turned quickly to face the voice.

'You right there? You're on the wrong side of the river.'

'Sorry, you gave me a fright,' said Jane. It was Chris, a guy with a rough appearance, thick dreadlocks and torn clothing. He lived somewhere on North Side, she knew him from activist circles, and he was a vague friend.

He smiled at her, and began rolling a cigarette. 'What're ya doing up here? Ya better be careful with that camera. It'll get nicked.'

'Somewhere round here that we can chill?' asked Jane.

It was cold by the river among the wandering jew, but the joint they smoked was comforting.

'Devil's Bride, it's called,' said Chris, referring to the old man's story about girls disappearing. 'All the uncles and aunties use it, scare their girls from getting their cherries popped too early.' He stubbed out the spliff and made a popping sound with his cheeks.

'Cherries popped?'

'Well, you know what I mean, the story goes: the Devil is a handsome white man who wears black. He seduces a girl from the ghetto who's out on the town. They dance into a frenzy and he takes her off to hell. Just Christian bullshit, I reckon. Christians eh, they worship a tortured emaciated god, ritualistically drink his blood and eat his flesh, and they think other religions are weird. I can't stand them. But whether Muslim or a Christian everybody on North Side loves God. At least the Muslims don't push it on you.'

'But do you reckon there could be something to it? I mean this girl really did disappear, obviously not the whole Devil thing, but maybe there is some rich weirdo who, well, ya know, kidnaps people.'

'Yeah, but the Devil's Bride story's really old. Maybe there was some guy back in history that did it, but old mate's probably a bit crazy.' Chris waved away some of the first mosquitoes of the season.

'Yeah, I suppose you're right.' Jane stretched. It really was getting cold and the shadows were lengthening. 'I better get going.' She stood up.

'Before you go,' Chris lounged back among the lush dark leaves, 'how is it going with all those wankers out in the bush?'

'Well, you're a member of Ecology First. When was the last time you've actually done something? Why don't you come up to camp instead of hanging out down here talking about it?' Jane picked up her pack.

'Wow, chill out. I do lots of stuff you don't know about, and as for going up there, I just start hating people. It starts off with real small things, but soon I think you're just all wankers and want power. Nah, not for me, cuz.'

'Sorry, I didn't mean to offend you.' She let her pack drop back onto the ground. 'You should come up though, seriously. It'd be good. Things are pretty different from when you were there. We've got a lot more people now, things have really up-scaled, and it's good to get out of town. You may hate people but people like you, and you're brave. Remember the last bust?'

Chris grinned, clearly chuffed from the compliment. 'I'll make you a deal. I'll come to camp, if you come for a drink with me.'

Jane considered his offer, 'I don't drink, but I guess we could go for a coffee or something.'

'And I don't drink coffee, especially not in cafes, but come round to my place on Friday, I'm having a gathering, bring a friend, and you can smoke as much choof as you like.' Chris stood up and Jane put on her pack.

'All right then. I'll see you there.'

'Hug before you go?'

'No.'

'One last thing. I'll keep an ear out for any information about this chick, Anya. I'll chuck ya a bell if I hear anything. Ya got a number?'

Nails' warehouse was one of the well-established squats in Port Town and had everything from running water to electricity. The walls were covered with maps, banners and posters of native wildlife. Stacks of placards and unfolded flyers covered the tables. People were seated on an eclectic collection of couches, chairs and cushions. Soup and bread were served from the kitchen, and a projector had been set up to beam onto an old sheet.

Nails had spoken at length about the forests, the logging, the subsidies, the revolving door between forestry and local government and had finished with outlining her plans to hold a rally in Parliament Square that weekend.

Nails enjoyed public speaking; she knew how to run through her points quickly and with clarity. She had always been the outspoken one in high school, throwing her hand up and arguing with the teacher. She had always looked forward to the school speech competition while her peers were dreading it. Nails had always known she would go to law school and be a lawyer. She was a fighter, that's what her father had called her, a fighter, and he was right. It was injustice that drove her and she compiled mental lists of injustices great and small. Lists that she would work to right. Right and wrong, those were two emotions that Nails felt most strongly. She detested the moral philosophising that some in the campaign indulged in. There were no grey areas for her. She knew in her heart what was wrong and that propelled her to action, and she was confident that the surety of her conviction would bring others to her cause.

The meeting had broken down into informal discussions and Nails watched as she stood by the kitchen bench and compulsively ate celery sticks. A short, broad shouldered man filled a glass with red cask wine and approached her.

'Line in the sand, eh?' he said, 'nice speech.'

'What are you doing here, Herb?' she replied. 'I didn't think conservation was your thing.'

'Let's just say I've a found a new appreciation for the dangers that climate change poses for the working classes.' The socialist sipped his wine.

'Really?' Nails doubted whether Herb's comment was sincere. She disliked him, particularly as he tended to hijack any action by turning it into a platform for, what Nails viewed as out dated and irrelevant, rhetoric.

'What did Lenin say, my enemy's enemy —'

'What do you want, Herb?'

The socialist gulped some wine. 'I want you to meet someone.' He motioned to a figure standing near the door and beckoned him to come over. The man was tall and he looked African. He was dressed in a pressed suit and black dress shoes. 'I would like you to meet Mateen, community organiser and activist working for the immigrant communities north of the river. Mateen, this is Nalia Hunter.'

The African took Nails' hand, 'pleasure to meet you,' he said.

'Pleasure to meet you, too. Help yourself to some food. Would you like anything to drink?'

'No, thank you.'

'Mateen,' said Herb swilling back the last of his glass and moving to refill it, 'has been lobbying unsuccessfully for housing improvements in North Side, needless to say neither the landlords nor the government give a shit.'

'Most of the families,' added Mateen, 'spend all their money on rent and still get sick because they have no money to heat their homes and there's no insulation.'

'In other news,' put in Herb, 'the cops shot an unarmed kid up in North Side last week, and nothing's been done about it.'

'No one seems to care about dead kids from North Side,' explained Mateen.

Nails understood the plight of the poor immigrant suburbs, and had worked with refugees as part of her degree. The situation was heartbreaking, but battles had to be picked, and for Nails that battle was for the forests. 'What do you want me to do?'

'We're interested,' replied Herb, 'in your rally. The environmental movement,' he waved his hand around the room, 'has a great appeal to the bourgeois classes and the white liberals. You're expecting many people to turn up?'

'Sure we are,' Nails had moved on to the raw carrot sticks, dipping them in homemade hummus. Sceptical though she was of Herb's intentions, she was intrigued with where he was going and wished he would get to the point.

'It's a pity,' he continued, 'that the environmental movement has never made solid inroads into the working class, or, immigrants.' Herb paused, obviously relishing the chance to have a dig. 'We reckon this weekend is a great opportunity to join forces, support for immigrant housing and protection of the forests.'

'What's the link?'

Herb grinned. 'Climate change. The three of us could pull together some pretty serious numbers, the unions, the immigrants, the greenies —'

'What do you get out of it, Herb?' asked Nails.

'Furthering the revolution.'

The three of them shook hands again and Herb and Mateen moved off to mingle.

Nails bit into another carrot stick. The commie was up to something but she wasn't sure what. Her thoughts flicked to the previous night and she shuddered inwardly as she chewed on the raw carrot. She thought of Mateen's words, 'no one seems to care about dead kids from North Side.' Jane was right, they needed more information and she had the perfect mind for that investigation. She could be a little terrier once she got onto something, and whoever killed that girl deserved to rot in hell.

Chris cycled through the night, the wind flushed his face beneath his drooping beanie, as he rode south across the river to the suburb of Bluebottle Point, his backpack stuffed with green bags. He locked his bike to a lamppost, and walked, weaving his way through back alleys, where fading stencils spattered the walls, a banksy copycat of a girl hugging a bomb, the prime minister's face merged with Hitler, the words NO WAR underneath, the white stencils contrasting with the colourful zigzagging tags of the hood rats.

'Oi you, dirty rope head.' Leaning against the alleyway was Johnny Vegas, a fourteen-year-old crusty punk. He wore dirty tight black jeans, a studded leather jacket and a short pink mohawk. This American was surrounded by a gaggle of admiring, juvenile local punks. They were a menagerie of torn fishnet stockings, fluorescent hair with shaved patches, leather boots, tartan skirts and immodestly torn jeans. They had multi coloured shoelaces, safety pins and rat tails. One girl had a large patch pinned to her bosom, a swastika with a red line through it proudly declared – Nazi Punks Fuck Off. They were handing around a silver goon bag, already half empty. Chris pulled out his pouch of tobacco and began rolling a cigarette.

'I see you finished doing your make up, Johnny,' he said.

'Got a smoke?' demanded the young punk.

'Got an ID?'

Vegas fished from his dirty pocket a faded student ID.

Chris glanced at the photo. 'Where did you steal this one?' He handed his tobacco pouch to Vegas. He'd wanted to smoke too when he was that age. 'Hey kid, you probably know most of the nippers in the city your age.'

'What if I do, bro?' Vegas drew out the word bro with a long American O.

'Do you know a girl called Anya Ivanova?

'What's it to you, man?'

'Do you want a copy of the dumpster key or not?'

'Ok bro, no problem, yeah I know a girl, called Anya, she's from North Side, her mom was like a crazy crack whore, died of an overdose.'

Johnny's consorts giggled.

'She's always kinda quiet, you know, bit strange, but hot, she can drink too man, must be the Russian in her. She lives by herself, totally hates her life, wants to get out of this town. Last time I saw her she was like real rich. She had all this money, dude. I just assumed she stole it from somewhere, but Amber reckons she's selling her ass like her mom.'

'When was the last time you saw her?'

'Bout a week and half ago, we were just hanging and then she got a text, left in a total hurry dude.'

'Did she say where she was going?'

'Not really man... I think she said something about some club or some shit.'

'Vitoria Club,' said the girl with the big antifascist patch, through a mouth filled with chewing gum. 'I asked her where she was going and she just said Vitoria Club. Can I have a ciggy too?'

Chris sighed and passed over his tobacco. 'What's the Victoria Club?'

'No, not Victoria, Vitoria.'

'Sorry, Vitoria, but what's the story with it?'

The girl shrugged and blew a bubble with her chewing gum. 'Dunno.'

Chris, followed by the young punks, confidently walked to the loading zone at the back of the supermarket where the two large industrial bins were located. He leapt up onto the loading bay, slipped the key into the padlock, and flicked up the lids. A couple of the kids held green bags and others kept watch, while Chris jumped inside.

'You guys like ice cream?'

He passed out semi-melted tubs of Neapolitan. As he dug deeper he revealed more food – fresh fruit and vegetables, an excessive amount of fresh watermelon, breads, muesli bars, two litres of iced coffee covered in slimy chicken grease, and dozens of eggs. The punks and Chris grinned with glee.

'Hey, Johnny?' Chris handed out a bag of bread rolls.

'Yeah bro?'

'Do you ever hang out at the warehouse on Broomfield Street, you know the one that chick, Nails, runs?'

'Oh yeah, sometimes, dude, they got food and movie nights and shit.'

'If you're around there just keep an eye out on what's going on, and let me know.'

'Sure thing, dude. This yoghurt is good to go, man.'

Jane sat at her computer, scrolling and googling her way through the Port Town Times. She sucked in her breath and tapped the desk. After several fruitless hours, she had found what she was looking for – an article related to the Devil's Bride story. The headline read: Story of Missing Teenager Revives Local Legend. The article explained how Margo Jenkins, a fourteen-year-old girl had disappeared in the spring of 2003. The article went on to describe the story and explained how Margo was last seen with a handsome man with a black jacket. The article quoted her single father, Mark, urging anyone with information to come forward.

Jane yawned and slumped back into her chair. It had been a long day and she should catch some sleep. Her phone vibrated, informing her that she'd received a text. The message was from Chris. It read: 'Hey possum face (: Found some information about little ruskia. Before it happened she was headed to the Vitoria Club. Hope that means something to u. Keep it real.'

'Thanks Chris. You're a star. Sleep well.'

'You're my star (:' the text shot back.

Cheeky bastard, thought Jane, and she chose not to reply.

Chapter 4: Thursday

Rain drizzled down as Lui gathered wood for the fire. He loved the simple life of camp, the daily tasks, the clean air, the night unpolluted by lights of houses, the sounds of the birds and animals. It wasn't always an easy life, it could be bitterly cold in winter, and in July it had snowed. All water had to be heated either from the fire or the limited gas supplies. When visitors were few the food supplies ran low, and of course there was the danger of arrest.

Lui watched the small, colourful turquoise birds – fairy wrens – as they scampered across the wet ground. He was originally from upper Ruhr Valley, Germany, and, sometimes, he missed it. Though it was one of the most industrialised regions in Europe, it was nevertheless rich with forests, and he had a garden in a village where he would sit and drink tea under an old rowan tree and watch the land and sky. Sometimes he missed the banks of nettles, the changing seasons. He missed the dark pine groves where the trunks of the trees were covered in blue-green ivy. He missed the insects, the birds, the flowers and the autumn leaves. He missed the smooth-trunked beeches that overshadowed the sharp-leaved holly. But nothing in Germany had ever been far from the activity of people. Even in his garden he would hear the autobahn, and steam from power plants spewed clouds into the sky, and even in the forest, wood was placed in neat piles. Everywhere the wilderness grew on layers of civilisation and industry. He had caught a flight to Australia on a working holiday visa and he'd stayed, always searching for the elusive dream of untouched nature, and here he had come close. This was his home now, the lawless wilderness. He couldn't imagine any place more beautiful – from the rich moss to the giant eucalypts. He chewed on a sassafras leaf. It had a slight taste of aniseed.

As he walked back toward camp he picked up pieces of wood for the fire and skinks darted out of his way. He stopped and breathed in the cool mountain air and observed the wilderness around him. If left for a few more hundred years without fire, the giant eucalypts would crash to the ground and the ancient Gondwanaland rainforest would grow up around them: a remnant of earth's geological past. He thought again of the dead girl, of her stench, and he felt bile in his mouth. A white butterfly alighted on his hand.

There were four people in the yurt when Lui returned, Tom, and his two friends, who had a penchant for wearing black and advocating vandalism, and Old Mad Mark, sipping goon. The anarchist was playing chess with one of his mates and all three were eating bread and cucumber. Lui broke the sticks he'd gathered and pressed them onto the coals allowing them to flare up. He placed a log on top of that and filled the old cast iron kettle with the red water from the streams, before heating it for tea.

'How'd the scout go?' Lui asked Tom.

Tom looked up from the chess game. 'The loggers will get a shock.' The group of three laughed. 'Their grapplers won't be going very far.'

'You've broken the truce, haven't ya?' said Lui. 'The cops will be down on us now for breaking the law. Nails'll be pissed.'

'Fuck the truce,' said Tom.

Lui watched as he moved his black bishop to put the white king in check.

'They haven't kept their end of the bargain. At least this way we stop them from working and cost them money, besides, we're breaking the law just being here.'

Lui didn't respond but watched the flames curl around the logs. He heard the hum of what sounded like a car in the distance. He listened as the hum grew nearer and then he heard the car pull into the parking bay. They had visitors. The activists were alert, but no alarm had been sounded, and, Lui reasoned, it was probably just tourists. He rested the kettle on the fire, and walked down to the main blockade gate.

In the pullover zone, Lauren, who had been occupying Front Watch, was talking to two young women, standing in front of a sleek hire car. One had dark brown hair pinned into a Japanese topknot and wore a silky flowing blue dress, which displayed her willowy figure. Her tall, blond companion, dressed in red, lounged back on the bonnet of the car and fingered a camera with a long scope-like lens. Lauren stopped talking to the women as Lui approached. She rolled her eyes at him, one of her favourite gestures.

'Get a load of these two,' she said.

If the women took offence at Lauren's comment they gave no sign. The brunette held out her hand, which Lui took.

'My name's Jeanette, I'm a freelance journalist, and this is a photographer, Holly.'

Holly smiled and waved.

'We thought we would go for a nice little story on the logging issue.' The camera went click. 'Isn't it beautiful here?' Jeanette leaned forward, subtly revealing her cleavage. 'I've been living in the big ugly city, it's so good to be in the country. It feels so liberating to be out here in the bush. The air's so clean. Gosh, they're not really going to cut these trees down are they, how horrid. How are you for food? Because we brought a lot. I hope you enjoy freshly ground organic coffee. What a gorgeous little camp you have. Do you mind if I take a photo with you?'

Jeanette had a manner of flirting ever so slightly as she spoke and displaying her figure in a way which made Lui feel uncomfortable, but she had sweetness, combined with an element of class and her perfume was subtle and tasteful above the smell of damp soil.

'We were thinking of staying for a few days,' said Jeanette, 'do you mind?'

'It's government land. You're welcome. Just make sure you write a good column,' said Lui.

A brief silence followed.

'Don't just stare at my tits. Help me with my things.'

Jane woke to the sound of Sky thrashing the radio in the kitchen. She rolled out of bed, and still in her pyjamas, walked bleary eyed toward the bathroom. Her cousin had the day off work, and the two girls shared a breakfast of coffee and thick American style pancakes, cooked with slices of banana. Sky wore a long dress that was covered in patterns like old wallpaper. She dug her toes into the coat of her border collie, Roofus, who was curled under the table, and Jane shared the events of the past few days. Her cousin listened, intrigued.

'You know who'd be able to help you figure it out?'

'Who?'

'Lizzy Leavitt.'

'Who's that?'

'She's a psychic... No, Jane, don't look at me like that. She's really good. She's amazing. You know Katie?'

'Ah ha.'

'She had her motorbike stolen and went to Lizzy and Lizzy saw it in a vision and told her exactly where it had been dumped, and Katie got it back. It was really trashed though. And you remember Sarah? She was all upset 'cause Billy got lost at sea. Remember that? So she went to Lizzy and Lizzy told her that he was safe and she'd hear news of him the next day and the next day they found him. He'd made it to Jellyfish Island and was living off oysters. Come on, Jane, don't be a sourpuss. We'll go today. I'll pay for you, and she's totally confidential.'

Jane seriously doubted whether the magical powers of the mysterious Lizzy Leavitt would yield results, but Sky was obviously so excited about the idea, that she agreed to visit the woman, if only to placate her cousin. So Sky found her number, made an appointment for that morning and they left the blue house on the hill, got into Sky's old Toyota and went in search of Lizzy Leavitt.

The psychic lived in an old city flat overlooking the historic Fitzroy Street. The apartment had been renovated in a tasteful open plan style and was appropriately decorated with prayer flags, wind chimes, silks, candles and cushions. A sign directed them to remove their shoes at the door, and, Jane noted as she entered, there was a bookshelf filled with titles such as A Journey into the Esoteric, or The Teachings of a Modern Day Shaman.

The psychic was a thin woman with short brown hair, big green eyes and a long bent nose. She wore a flowing purple dress, her fingers were covered in a variety of rings and a large bone pendant with an indigenous design hung around her neck. She hugged both Jane and Sky as a greeting, kissing them both on the cheeks.

'Welcome, welcome,' she said, and ushered them to sit on a pair of embroidered cushions, which, Jane appreciatively noticed, were placed next to a cast iron fireplace in which a fire burned. In front of this was a low table covered in a purple cloth. Once the two girls had seated themselves on one side of the table Lizzy Leavitt took her place opposite them.

'Peppermint tea?' she asked.

'Yes, please,' answered Sky.

The psychic poured tea from a Japanese style teapot into three ceramic cups. 'Now, how may I help you?' she asked when everybody had a tea in hand.

'We want information about a girl,' explained Sky.

'Oh, a friend of yours?' She peered across at the two girls. 'Somebody who's got herself into a bit of trouble?'

'Not exactly,' said Jane.

The two girls looked awkwardly at each other.

'Ah, I see,' said the psychic. 'You don't want to tell me. Well don't worry I'm not a prying, nasty, little psychotherapist.' She lifted up her arms displaying the rings on her fingers so that the long sleeves of her dress fell down past her elbows. 'I practice the much more ancient, revered and spiritual path, channelling the wisdom of the ancestors and the animal spirits, the elementals.' She lowered her hands to the table. 'Now, which of you will be the medium?'

'I will,' said Jane.

The psychic directed Jane to lie face up on the carpet. She placed a pillow under her head. And covered her body with a light knitted blanket. She pulled the curtains closed, turned off the lights, and lit several long blue candles so that the room was filled with an ambient light. The psychic took a drum from the wall; it was a simple piece of hide stretched over a thin hoop, and painted with a buffalo motif. She seated herself beside Jane.

'Now close your eyes, and relax your body.'

Jane felt the tension seep out of her body, as she lay on the cushions and her scattered, busy thoughts streamed through her mind.

'Now,' she heard the voice of the psychic, 'I will beat the drum and visions may come to you. But I want you to visualise the girl as you knew her.'

Jane heard the beat of the drum. It was slow and steady and she thought of Anya. She pictured the night at the logging coupe, the sound of the animals in the night, the pale, peeling face, and mangled torso. She pictured the photo she had found at the house on North Side, the shiny elegant airbrushed features, the cheap jewellery, the smell of perfume in the room. The words of the old pipe smoking man: Ivanova was a working girl. His voice echoed through her mind, a working girl, a working girl, and the vision in her mind began to spiral, darken and change.

The dark world lurched back and forward, and gradually she realised that there was a rhythm to it and she saw that she was onboard an old sailing ship, rolling on ocean swells, whipped by the wind into foaming crests. Men chanted as they bailed water, pulled down the sails and secured cargo. Jane walked among them, invisible, and ethereal, though she could smell the salt spray and feel the wind on her face. Like a spirit she passed along the ship, coming to the stern, and, as she entered the hold she could smell sweat and urine and hear the moaning and crying of men and women.

When her eyes adjusted she saw that she was in a cramped space at the bottom of the ship, where people were chained row on row. They were white men and women dressed in rags. Their faces were sallow, their bodies were thin and vomit sloshed with the bilge water around their feet. One woman looked right at Jane, and she was different. Her skin was brown, her face was tattooed with blue-green swirls and she was bare breasted. She chanted rhythmically as the ship rolled, and she was beautiful, even among the misery.

The vision changed and she heard men shouting to each other and seagulls shrieking. She was in Port Town, at the docks, and the harbour was filled with old sailing ships. A group of men drank grog and gambled, as they squatted on coils of rope. Women with low cut dresses called out to passers-by. Two sailors reeled past, and she caught snippets of the song that they sang in their loud, drink sodden voices. 'Haul haul away, haul away for Rosie oh.'

A tall man with blond hair, a top hat, leather gloves, and a black riding coat hurried past her, making his way along one of the wooden piers. There was something about him that caught Jane's attention and she followed him. He came to a large warehouse and banged on the door with his gloved fist.

A fleshy man with a cauliflower nose pulled open the door, the tall wealthy man slipped inside, and Jane, invisible, followed. The building was high, long and cold. Men and women lay huddled in blankets, talking quietly to one another, while sailors nuzzled women in alcoves, cordoned off with scraps of sailcloth. Rats squeaked under the creaking boards, and Jane followed the well-dressed man down the hall. People fell silent and watched suspiciously as he passed. He walked to the end of the hall, where he pushed open a wooden door, through which Jane also passed.

In the dim light she could see that it was a crowded warehouse. Here, arrayed for inspection, were the men and women that she had seen on the convict ship. The richly dressed man exchanged whispered words with another man who wore a three pointed hat. The two men then began to walk up and down the row of human traffic, feeling their arms and inspecting their teeth.

'Half of them are sick with fever.' The richly dressed man remarked.

'It was a rough passage.'

The man in the top hat tutted. 'There's much work to be done in the colony and this is what I get, the sick dregs of London?'

'They'll work,' replied the man in the three pointed hat, 'much less trouble than free labourers.'

The man in the top hat stopped in front of the woman with the facial tattoo. 'Good morning,' he addressed her, 'a New Zealander. What are you doing here?'

The woman said something in her own language.

'Ain't she a beauty? And she's in good health.' The man in the three pointed hat cupped her breast in his hand.

The woman didn't move.

'She's a high born, prisoner of war, I bought her off a chief for a musket, en route. She came quite willingly, but she's a spirited animal. Special gift to you, Sir Grey. To speak frankly, I'll be glad to be rid of the wench. We encountered a freak storm on our passage south. The men think her a witch, and they won't sail with her on board, though she has a voice like an angel.'

'Foolish superstitions,' said the man called Grey.

The vision faded, the world swirled in front of her, and the words of the richly dressed man echoed through her head, foolish superstitions, foolish superstitions. Then she heard the voice of the old Greek, it was the Devil what took her. The Devil what took her. Jane woke. She was back in the room with Sky and Lizzy Leavitt next to her.

'Did you see anything? What happened?' Sky was grasping her hand urgently. 'You've been out for ages. You were muttering in your sleep.'

Lizzy Leavitt handed Jane a glass of water, and she noticed that the blue candles had burned low.

Johnno clenched his fists and spat. The greenies had fucked the grapplers, sugar in the tanks. No grapplers meant no work. Those greenies were gonna get it. Getting on the backs of the pollies was one thing; fucking with Johnno's grapplers was another. He pictured his fist connecting with a greenie skull. That'd be satisfying, hearing the little faggots moan for mummy. He'd teach them a lesson. Do them some good to be knocked around, probably hadn't been beaten enough as children.

'What we gonna do, Johnno?' asked Pete.

'Give those greenies a bashing, is what we're gonna do, but first let's get a drink. It's thirsty Thursday and it'll be thirsty work.'

'You're always thirsty, Johnno,' said Hank, 'ya fat fucken fish.'

Hank ducked as Johnno swung a punch at him. 'Think you're a smart arse do ya, Hank? Well ya won't be sounding so smug when your pissing blood out your jap eye, ya piece of pig shit.'

'Johnno, mate,' said Pete, 'don't ya think we should let sleeping dogs lie?' Collin will pick up the insurance on the grapplers, we'll take a week off...'

'And let the greenies win?' Johnno mopped the sweat off his forehead with the back of his hand. 'Are ya afraid, Pete? Ya scared o' some fagball greenies and some hairy hippy bitches? What happened to ya balls, mate? Ya missus got 'em in a jar in the kitchen? Toughen up.' Johnno spotted a huntsman creeping over the gravel, lashing out with his boot he pulverised the big spider.

'Why do ya hate the greenies so much, Johnno?' said Pete. 'I mean, I'm not saying I like them, just —'

'You mean, why do I hate them other than that they're sneaking, cowardly meddling pricks?' Johnno pulled off his singlet, showing his muscular upper body, and jabbed his finger toward his chest where a long pale scar ran from his shoulder to his belly. 'You know how I got that, Pete? I was working a coupe up Cockatoo River way. What I didn't know was that the greenies had nailed metal into some of the trees about the height you cut them.' Johnno demonstrated the height by holding his hand to the level of his chest. 'The chain saw bit into the metal. The chain snapped and lashed back, nearly bloody killed me, sent me to hospital, scarred me for life and cost me a fortune in medical bills. That's the problem with the greenies, Pete, they care about the trees more then they care about people. They're fucked in the head. Now are ya in, or are ya out?'

Warwick was hanging out at Nails' warehouse, helping to make the placards for the rally on Saturday. He placed the stencil on the placard and sprayed it with black spray paint, Forests for Climate, it read. Other people worked on a long cloth banner carrying the same slogan. They were decorating it with colourful pictures of stick figure animals. A young punk with a pink mohawk had been hanging around, and it annoyed Warwick how he kept painting anarchy symbols on the placards. What kind of message was that sending out to the public? Another group worked folding leaflets. Warwick held out the placard he had just finished. The paint ran a little but it looked pretty good. He placed it with the others and began stencilling the next.

Nails, he'd noticed, had spent most of the day on the computer at the other end of the room, and when he saw Jane and another girl with a black and white dog enter the warehouse, he pricked up his ears. Nails went over to greet them and they stood around in the kitchen talking. Warwick got up on the pretext of getting a glass of water so he could listen to what was said.

Nails was crouching down rubbing the dog's ears. 'Yeah,' she was saying, 'I had a look into the Vitoria Club, called and emailed a bunch of my lawyer and government mates, and, thanks for putting me onto it. It's basically a high class brothel, pretty exclusive by the sound of things.'

'That is interesting,' said Jane, filling a glass of water for herself.

'Sure is,' said Nails, 'and you reckon the Vitoria Club has something to do with you know... the night in the coupe?'

'Well, you remember Chris... Chris, North Side, Chris, dreads.'

'Yeah right, dready Chris.'

'Yeah, yeah, him. Well anyway I was in North Side, just found the house of that girl Anya, fits the description of the girl, and I ran into Chris, and he must've had some contact 'cause he texted me last night to say that Anya was going to the Vitoria Club shortly before she disappeared. It was the best lead I had. Anyway, I'm gonna see him again tomorrow; he's invited me to some kind of party. Maybe I'll find out more about his source. Could you try and find out for me what their address is?' asked Jane. 'I'd like to pay the Vitoria Club a visit. Banners are looking nice by the way.'

Warwick took that as his cue to leave. Johnston had to be told about these developments. He pushed open the door to the warehouse, walked onto the street, flicked open his phone and dialled his boss. An unkindness of Australian ravens landed on the rusting tin roof.

'So there you have it,' said Lui. 'That's camp Balloong.' Lui had finished his tour of the camp and sat with Jeanette and Holly on a wooden bench in the forest on the west side of the logging road. A well-built hut was nestled among the tree ferns in front of them.

'It's amazing,' said Jeanette, 'all those little details and everything with its own story. It's like living on the frontier in the old time.'

'It's beautiful,' said Holly as she photographed the hut.

'You can set up camp wherever you like,' said Lui. 'You're also more than welcome to stay in the yurt if you prefer.'

'What about there?' said Jeanette, pointing to the hut in front of them. 'It looks really comfortable, is anybody staying in it?'

Lui shook his head.

The hut was exceptional. Not a tarp and stick lean-to, like most of the other structures, it had a proper wooden floor, a high triangular roof and an elevated sleeping platform. It also had a wooden bench outside for sitting on.

'It's very nice,' said Holly. 'Who built it?'

'A man built it,' Lui paused, 'for a girl.'

'Oh,' Jeanette looked inquisitively at Lui, 'did he love her?'

'Yes, she was a very free spirit, bubbly, energetic, laughed a lot. Plenty of people loved her. There was something about her.'

'What happened in the end? Did she love him? Did they make love in the shack he built for her?' Jeanette ran her fingers through her hair and glanced at the shifting light of the canopy.

'No, she went off with somebody else.' Lui had picked up a piece of eucalypt bark and began to tear it into strips.

'What a sad story. The poor man. He must have been heartbroken.'

'He was.' Lui stood up and threw the strips of bark on the ground. 'But it was his own fault. He invested so much emotion in the girl and never told her how he felt. He was an idiot.'

Jeanette looked at Lui through discerning eyes. 'You seem to have a strong opinion on the matter.'

Lui felt himself blush and his muscles tense. Why had he brought them here? It was a place in the forest that held painful memories. He remembered how he'd felt that day when he saw Chris holding hands with Aliya. Her face flushed and happy, Chris whispering in her ear. The pain, the bitter jealousy, it'd hurt physically like a knife in the gut. Lui cringed as he remembered his love sick self and the things he'd said. 'I built it.' The words caught in his throat. 'I'm sorry. I've got to go.'

Chapter 5: Friday

Warwick stopped eating the tasty balls of hazelnut chocolate, rolled between the thighs of Swiss milkmaids – well, he thought, it'd be cool if they were. He watched the two girls leave the house and walk to their car. He watched them enter the cream coloured Toyota while the black and white dog jumped into the back seat. He sat in his car, a large cap covered his face and he was parked in the shade. He didn't really have to observe Jane's house, but Johnston had told him to keep a close eye on her and monitor her movements, and, he admitted to himself, he got a kind of thrill out of it.

The two girls started up their car, pulled out of the driveway, and began to roll down the street. Warwick was about to leave too, when it occurred to him that he wasn't the only person monitoring the house. Looking into his rear view mirror, Warwick could see a white van with Harry's Furniture Removal painted on the side. The van had been parked there since he had arrived, but what raised his suspicions was that it had tinted windows – an unnecessary feature for a furniture removal company.

Warwick popped another chocolate into his mouth and watched as two large men got out of the van, dressed in suits and wearing black gloves. They walked quickly up the steps to the door. One of them punched the stain glass window, breaking it, and pushing his arm inside to unlock the door. They shoved it open and walked inside.

Warwick called Johnston.

'Hey, Dave, it's Warwick. I'm at Jane Thistle's house. Two big guys just broke in. What should I do?'

'What are you doing there?' Johnston sounded angry.

'Well, you told me to keep a close eye on her.'

'Just let them do their damn work, and keep your mouth shut.' Johnston hung up.

Warwick sat in his car and waited. A few minutes later the men exited the house. They took with them a computer and a box of papers, which they threw in the back of the van before driving off. Warwick hesitated for a moment, and then decided to follow the van. He followed it through the winding suburban streets. It was travelling fast but it couldn't take the corners as quickly as Warwick's little car and he followed it into the bustle of the city where he lost it at a set of lights, cut off by a rattling tram.

'We're ready,' said Jeanette and she spun around theatrically. Jeanette and Holly were smothered in sunscreen and insect repellent. Both wore top and bottom thermals, short shorts, T shirts, hiking boots and snake protective leggings. They had backpacks with water and emergency kits, and they held expensive hiking sticks.

'Ready to climb Mount Kilimanjaro,' said Lauren as she gulped her tea before heading to the edge of the yurt. 'Hope you've got the right sorts of anti-venom. The snakes out here are airborne. They leap from the trees and attack the face. Those snake protectors you've got are good for ground snakes but you've got to be prepared for the aerial attack.'

'Really?' said Jeanette, looking shocked.

'Yeah – ya better be careful. We call them hoop snakes because when they drop from the branches they put their tail in their mouth and roll down the hill.' Lauren rolled her eyes.

'Oh, I get it, it's a joke,' said Jeanette.

They hiked through the rainforest, heading for the high ground of the West Sister, one of the high hills that overlooked the Balloong valley. Light rain blew across the hills, as Lui, who was scouting ahead, pushed through the tea tree, which marked the change of altitude. The tea tree became smaller, stunted, and more windswept as he ascended the rocky path. Their narrow leaves were covered with drops of water, which collected into pools and ran down the trunks before forming into miniature streams that trickled down the hill or gathered into puddles, surrounded by clumps of button grass. The tea tree were covered in pink and white spring blossoms, and Lui knew that if the day had been clear, tiny native wasps and bees would be buzzing between the flowers. He rested on a grey, lichen covered rock, took water from his pack, and surveyed the landscape.

Jeanette, who had not been far behind, joined Lui by the rock. 'Mind if I sit with you?'

Lui shuffled over, and the dainty journalist pulled herself up to join him.

'Gosh it's beautiful up here,' she said. 'You can see for miles.'

And despite the rain, they could.

'Yeah, that there,' Lui pointed to a winding grey line below them, 'Is the headwaters of the Balloong River. It cuts the valley in half. And over there,' he pointed toward the hazy green forest on the far side of the river, 'is the abandoned gold mining town, Croydon, and the old mining trail.'

'All I can see is trees.' Jeanette peered into the distance as more sheets of rain blew in from the south.

'Even on a clear day you wouldn't see it. Croydon was abandoned over a hundred years ago. The forest has reclaimed it.'

'Oh,' said Jeanette. 'What's that smoke?'

Lui's eyes followed where she was pointing, south. He saw a plume of dark smoke rising into the sky and felt a foreboding sensation in the pit of his stomach.

'Is it a wild fire?' asked Jeanette.

'No. It's a burnoff.'

'A what?'

'A burnoff. Once forestry logs a coupe, they burn it with napalm to clear the debris, the rainforest, and prepare the ground for planting plantations.'

'You're kidding?'

'Nah ah, they used to drop the napalm from the air, just like Vietnam. Now, they do it by hand.'

'That's unbelievable.'

'They also bait the fresh plantations with 1080 to kill any native animals which might feed on the young plants. I've seen it myself. So,' Lui changed the subject, 'You're a journalist?'

'Oh – you know, I just travel around covering things that seem interesting, try and get it published.'

'So what sort of things have you published?'

'Well, I've spent a bit of time travelling in Europe, and I wrote articles about food that I managed to sell to some women's magazines. It was pretty exciting getting something published and getting paid.'

'Wow, that sounds amazing. You must have had some exciting adventures.'

The journalist grinned. 'Well, not really. I just ate lots of random food, frog legs, cheese with worms, that kind of thing. But there was one time where things got a bit more exciting. I was in Greece doing research on seafood when all of a sudden there was all this violence going on. It was leftists on fascists, lots of people got hurt, and a couple got killed. But it turned out to be a blessing in disguise. I got some pictures of the violence and did a write-up and a magazine bought it. I cashed up and came back to Australia, maybe get a story about,' she swept her arm over the forest, 'this place. But what about you, Lui? I mean what do you do for a crust?'

'I do this.'

'You mean you're on the dole?'

'No, I wish. The dole would never pay me to live up here. No, I live on the donations to the campaign. But I don't need much you know. I've got a home here and as long as people bring up food, medical stuff and the odd pair of second hand clothes, I'm sorted. In return I try and do my best to save the bush. Most of the time it's actually a pretty boring life.'

Jeanette leaned close to Lui so that he could smell her perfume. Her small face, flushed from the wind, looked up into his. 'I think you're very brave,' she said.

The activist experienced butterflies in his stomach. He felt flustered, uncomfortable and didn't know what to say. The rest of the hiking group joined them, but his gaze lingered on the plume of smoke rising from the south.

Jane and Sky had driven to North Side, and made their way back to the house where she had talked to the pipe smoking Greek man and seen Anya's room. They turned the car onto the street with the house, and Sky swore.

'Holy fuck.'

Black smoke rose from the old mansion. Bright red flames licked the air through the windows on the left hand side of the upper storey, and Jane could see the waves of heat rising in the cool spring day. A crowd of people had gathered to watch the blaze, and a fire engine was parked on the street, its lights flashing, and two fire fighters fired water at the building from handheld hoses.

'Pull over.'

Sky parked the car on the side of the street. Jane jumped out, and ran to join the crowd. Sky followed behind with the dog. Jane tapped the elbow of an African man wearing a hoody.

'What's happened?'

The man shrugged. 'I saw the smoke from across the street. By the time I got here the place was on fire.'

A beam cracked and a mass of burning cladding crashed to the ground where it was quickly quenched by the fire fighters.

'The people inside, did they get out?'

'Some of them did. Some of them went off in the meat wagon.'

Jane gazed once more at the burning building. She was sure it was Anya's room, which had crashed to the ground. She wondered what had happened to the old Greek man. It seemed so strange. Just the day before yesterday she had been in that room and now whatever clues had been there floated through the air in particles of black ash. Sky had come up to stand beside her, and Roofus sat on the ground next to them wagging his tail, oblivious to the disaster.

Jane photographed the fire.

'Come on,' said Sky, 'There's nothing more to see here. Let's go.'

Neither girl spoke as they drove through a neighbourhood of abandoned houses. Their windows were smashed or boarded up and the panels were covered in tagging. They passed an area fenced off with razor wire. It looked like a building had been demolished, but the plans to rebuild never enacted, and tall weeds grew through the rocks. Only after they had crossed the bridge, and were waiting at a set of lights in the city, did they talk.

'Will you be able to sell the shots of the fire to the paper?' asked Sky.

'They probably won't be interested in the story.' Jane was shaking. 'Nobody cares what happens on North Side. I can't believe it. It was only two days ago I was there, and now this.' She held her head in her hands. 'It's sick.'

Sky stroked Jane's arm. 'It's ok, hun. It was probably an accident. You know, old houses. You can't blame yourself. I've never really thought much about North Side. It's funny. I've lived in this town all my life and this is first time I've actually been there.'

'I quite like it. There's something kind of real about it, people are really friendly, and the food is cheap. When I was biking around the other day, going to random houses, I didn't actually feel like I was in danger at any time.'

'Hey, Jane?'

'Yip.'

'You know how we went to see Lizzy Leavitt?'

'Yes?'

The car leapt forward. 'What happened? You seemed like you were in a real intensive state and then you just got up and left and didn't want to talk about it.'

'Well, yeah it was strange. I did have a kind of – well I guess you could call it a vision. It was real vivid and I could hear sounds. It freaked me out a bit. In the vision I was there, present, but invisible. The thing is the vision had nothing to do with Anya Ivanova. It was like I was seeing something back in colonial times. I was on a ship, a convict ship, and I saw this woman. And there was a man in a top hat and he bought convicts.'

'What do you reckon it means?'

'I don't know, maybe it was just something in my subconscious, which, you know, came out.'

They drove on up the hill through winding suburban streets to the blue house. Roofus bounded up the steps and began barking at the front door. When they got there they saw that it was open and its window had been smashed. They walked through the ransacked house, and Jane photographed the destruction. Everything from the kitchen cupboards had been thrown onto the floor, their clothes had been pulled from their draws and were scattered on the ground. Jane's computer was gone.

'They took my dirty knickers, the sickos,' said Sky. 'I'm calling the cops.'

'Please don't,' Jane began to rub Roofus behind the ears. 'This happened because of me. I don't want to get the cops involved, not yet.'

'You're crazy.' Sky was screaming. 'You find some fucked up dead body in the bush, and decide to investigate it yourself and now sickos are trashing our place, and probably spying on us when we're in the shower, and you won't even let me call the cops. Pull your head in, girl.'

'How do you know it isn't the cops that did this? If we get the cops involved they'll ask a lot of questions, and I don't trust what they'll do with the answers.'

'That's not my problem.'

'I'm sorry. You're right. I can't endanger you. It's not fair. I'll go.' Jane picked up a hoody from the floor and stuffed it into her backpack. She felt a lump in her throat. Things were happening so quickly, the visions, the fire, now this. And the person she was closest to blaming her.

'Where are you going?' asked Sky.

'North Side.' Jane headed for the door and tried to choke back the tears, but the words had brought them out and she began to cry.

'Wait,' the anger went out of Sky's voice, 'really we're going back there? Jesus, I didn't think we'd be going twice in one day.'

Jane turned to look at her cousin, her wet face broke out into a smile and she wiped her eyes on her sleeve. 'You mean you're coming with me?'

Sky came forward and hugged Jane. 'Of course I'm coming with you. You can't go back to North Side by yourself. People carry guns.'

Sky drove them to North Side, down from the hill, through the old town and west up the river, before crossing it.

'Do you think that van is following us?' asked Jane as she stared at the rear-view mirror. 'It's been more or less behind us since we were heading into town.'

'I've noticed it, too,' said Sky, 'but it's been with us longer than that. I remember it was behind us when we were driving back from North Side. I keep on thinking it's disappeared, then it turns up again.'

The white van followed them across the river, but they seemed to lose it as they followed the Balloong on the north bank, and when they arrived at Chris's house there was no sign of it.

The house was small, wooden, had once been white. It leaned out into the willows and brambles along the river and newly sown garden beds took up most of the available yard space. Chris met them at the door, dressed lazily in a baggy T shirt and combat pants, a half smoked spliff hanging out of his mouth. Reggae sounded from within. 'You mob are early,' he said, then peered at them more closely, 'are you lot all right?'

'We're fine,' said Jane.

Sun spilled through the dusty windows of the lounge. It had two couches; one was grey and so saggy in the middle that Jane had to struggle to avoid being sucked into it. The other couch was blue, hard and totally threadbare. The two couches formed an L shape around a coffee table that was in fact an old real estate sign placed on top of a cardboard box. But the most striking feature of the space was a large hole in the middle of it, which had been repaired with an odd collection of different scraps of wood and nails.

'I would offer you a drink,' said Chris, 'But —'

'It's all right,' said Sky, 'I felt like I needed a drink, so I brought some vodka. You got glasses?'

Chris grinned, 'I like you already. No glasses, but I got jars.'

'Got any teas?' asked Jane, staring at the hole in the floor. 'And it's a nice little place you got here, Chris, by the river.'

'Yeah, me and my house mates found it abandoned. We did it up. I've got no idea who actually owns it.'

Two vodkas and a cup of black tea later, Jane filled Chris in on the events of the day and her conversation with Nails.

'So you think this fire was arson, possibly connected to your house being burgled? Don't you think you might be getting a bit paranoid? How would anybody know to connect you with this girl? Couldn't it all be a coincidence?'

'It's not a coincidence. What about the van following us? Somebody wanted to destroy all the evidence in that house, and send a strong message to me to shut up.'

'They're also sickos,' added Sky, stroking the neck of her dog. 'They took my dirty knickers.'

'That's weird,' said Chris. 'Maybe it's time to go to the pigs.'

'Chris, if even you don't believe me that it's a conspiracy, you think the cops will? At best it'd be a waste of my time.'

'I do believe you, but what do you want to do about it?' Chris was pouring another jar of vodka for himself and Sky.

Jane stood up and paced around the room. 'I don't know. I'm kind of scared, scared for you too, Sky. I think I need to keep under the radar for a bit. I wanna go back to the bush. But I feel I'm close to finding out something here.'

'Well, you're welcome to crash on the couch here for as long as you like.'

Jane stared down at the grey saggy couch. 'Thanks, Chris.'

Jane's phone bleeped, message received. She pulled out her phone. The message was from Nails.

'Hey hun,' it read, '(: some information you might want, 56 Sea View Road, Man-O-War Bay.'

They sat out in the yard and shared a spliff. Sky and Chris drank more vodka. When afternoon became evening Chris lit a fire in a brazier in the back yard, and slowly people began to arrive – a crew of boys dressed in hoodies, bottles clinking in their packs, a group of punky looking girls wearing band T shirts, and Herb the commie with his Greek girlfriend. Jane was polite, but she wasn't feeling talkative, so she sat in the plastic chair, watched the fire, and thought about her vision – the man in the top hat and the tattooed New Zealander.

Sky seemed to be enjoying the party. Her voice slurred slightly as she talked. She was a good storyteller, and had a sassy manner that endeared her to people. She was telling the story of the raid on their house to three boys. They were listening, interested, laughing.

Sky bludged a cigarette.

Jane wished she'd shut up and then felt bad for the unkind thought. Political Hip Hop blared from the lounge, and she wished it would all just be quiet so she could sleep, sleep and maybe dream. A guy with a rat tail offered her a beer.

'Nah thanks, I don't drink.' Jane kept staring at the fire.

She heard the sound of yelling and confrontation at the front of the house. People fell silent. Somebody killed the music. Another person yelled, 'cops.' Clangs from the kitchen indicated that people were hiding drug paraphernalia.

'What, noise control already, that's a bit extreme, should tell the cops to go find some criminals,' said one of the guys who had been listening to Sky.

'We should invite them in for a beer,' said another. 'They must be thirsty. Officer... oi,' he acted out, 'would you like a drink officer?' Jane felt the creeping feeling of fear beginning in her stomach and travelling up to her throat. Nobody else seemed to be worried, but why should they be.

Chris walked out into the light of the brazier. 'Jane,' he said, 'they want you. They say they have a warrant for your arrest.'

'What's the warrant for?'

'They didn't say. All they said is that we've got ten minutes to hand you over before they break the whole place up. We're saying we don't know who they're talking about. Looks like we got a situation.'

Jane stood up. The blanket she had wrapped around her dropped to the ground. She grabbed her pack from the lounge, then scanned the section for routes of escape. A high picket fence surrounded the property, separating it from adjoining sections, while the cold, black, deep water of the Balloong River blocked any escape from the back. She seemed trapped. She turned to Chris.

'Thanks, Chris. Remember our promise. I'll meet you at camp.' She stepped forward and hugged him. 'Go out the front and buy me some time.'

Sky stared at her in shock.

Jane stepped forward and hugged her, squeezing tightly. 'Be careful, Sky. I love you. I'm going to try and go into hiding. Look after yourself, but I'm sure with me out of the picture you'll be safe.'

Sky whispered back, her breath smelling of vodka, and her voice thick with emotion. 'Here, take my spare key. Take the car, if you can get to it. You're a crazy bitch, but I love you too, hun.'

'You,' Jane pointed to the boys around the fire, 'give me a hand up over this fence. Hopefully the neighbours won't get too much of a shock.'

Chris walked through the lounge and out to the front porch, where something of a picket had formed and Herb the commie was yelling abuse.

'Move now mate, are ya deaf?' An officer demanded.

'Take me too, ya swine thieves,' Herb slurred. 'Go find some real criminals ya scumbags. Cops suck cock for money. Under the control of international forces! Get those animals off those horses!'

'Put that bottle down now, mate,' replied the Sergeant.

'Make me.' Herb spat in the Sergeant's face.

The officer's fist connected with the commie's cheek and he stumbled back, swearing. The police charged the half-drunk men and women through the bottleneck of the steps. Dragging them out of the way by their hair and violently pushing them away. Chris saw a girl he knew thrown to the ground then kicked hard in the ribs.

He stood in the doorway and shouted, 'Lock arms.'

Chris felt his friends' arms tighten on both his elbows, and he felt for a moment that glorious feeling of solidarity in the face of violence, and then the police pushed into the miniature picket line, shoulder barging him in the chin, splitting his lip. He fell to his knees, the taste of blood in his mouth.

Jane jumped down onto the neighbouring property. In contrast to the wild untrimmed grass on Chris's side of the fence, she found herself in a neatly kept flower garden, bordered by trimmed bonsai willows. A paved pathway ran down the side of the wooden house and light poured from its windows. A dog began to bark and the door of the house opened. An old woman brandished a walking stick, and shouted something in Greek.

'So sorry about the flowers,' Jane called, as she ran down the path, a rose bush tearing at her shirt as she headed toward the road.

Jane could hear the sound of violence and yelling from next door. The street flashed red and blue in the evening light. She could see a paddy wagon and Sky's car parked just down from it. If she made it across the street without being stopped – she felt a strong arm grab her roughly around the waist. She opened her mouth to scream but a large hand gagged her mouth in a rag that smelled sickly sweet. She looked up and saw the face of a man, grim and flat, a broken nose, a stubbly chin. Her hands grasped at her camera, dizziness overwhelmed her, and she fell into unconsciousness.

It was ten pm when the contractors pulled into Camp Balloong behind two other parked cars. Johnno cracked his knuckles. Oh, those greenies are gonna get it. They won't know what's hit them. Teach them to force honest folks to lose their jobs. He felt a quiver of excitement and adrenaline.

They opened the doors of the truck and as they exited they heard the high pitch scream of the air alarm in the cold night. Johnno ran over to the source of the noise, a hut made from tarps and sticks at the edge of the parking bay, Front Watch. He tore down the cloths at the entrance and stared inside. Lauren stared back at him. She was tall, long limbed and strong with long brown hair. She was dressed in a black singlet and cargo pants and held the red air alarm in her hand. She looked right into Johnno's face, afraid and tense. He could see her heart pounding and her hands shaking. He felt his pent up rage rise through him. He picked her up by her armpits, and hurled her against the wall of the hut. Her head crashed against one of the poles. She looked up blearily, and touched her head. It was bleeding.

'Greenie slut!' Johnno kicked over the table. The candles went out, throwing the hut into darkness.

Johnno walked out into the starlight. Pete and Hank, were taking to the greenie cars with a couple of crowbars. They had levered open the bonnets and were smashing the radiators with the sharp edges of their tools.

'Up the road, boys!'

The contractors, crowbars and torches in their hands, marched over the rope bridge, which crossed the defensive ditch dug by the campaigners.

The climb was longer and steeper than Johnno had anticipated, and after they'd climbed over the fallen swamp gum they arrived at the big yurt to find it dark and empty. A few hot coals glowed on a fire that had been hastily kicked and extinguished. Empty mattresses surrounded the fire. Books sat on a makeshift bookcase and dog collars and harnesses hung on the wall. But there was nothing of particular value that would sate Johnno's appetite for destruction. He saw an old and heavy satellite phone sitting on the bookshelf, grabbed it, threw it on the fire, and stomped it onto the coals before exiting.

Moving forward, the contractors flashed their torches over the kitchen, an open structure of tarps, large sealed drums, benches and a gas stove. A possum with a young one clinging to its back bared its fangs at Johnno, before scuttling into the shadows. He aimed a kick at the makeshift washing up bench. It fell with a satisfying clatter of cutlery, accompanied by the shattering of ceramic bowls and plates. He flashed his torch at the eaves of the forest.

'Come out of there ya bloody greenies! Ya yella-bellied, fag-balled pussies.' Johnno's voice reverberated through the trees.

'Come and get us, mate!'

Two torches flashed on, revealing two people standing just on the edge of the forest and within a few metres of the contractors. Johnno launched at them. Pete and Hank followed.

The little rats were fast, and he was losing ground to them as he ran, crashing through the thick, damp bush. One quick lunge now, thought Johnno, and I'll grab the cunt. Putting one booted foot in the ground he threw himself at his quarry. His foot fell through the soft ground and into a mouth of an old wombat hole, while the momentum of his charge pushed the full weight of his body forward fracturing his shinbone. Johnno cried out in pain and his torch flew from his hand. The lights of the runners went out. Pete and Hank caught up with Johnno. They flashed their torches over the scene while Johnno swore through gritted teeth.

'You right there, mate?'

'I broke my fucken leg.'

A black currawong cried its night time call from the trees above, and the gentle patter of rain began.

The activists had been enjoying, courtesy of Jeanette and Holly, one of the best meals they'd had in a long time – organic avocados, and nice cheeses on soft fire toasted rolls, fried marinated tofu and bottled white wine.

Jeanette had become slightly drunk. She was lounging back on cushions, wearing a pair of pink pyjamas and was laughing at a story Goldy was telling about waking up in the night with a possum on her face. It was then that the air alarm sounded.

Lui threw his wine into the fire, instantly sober and alert. Can't be cops, they always make a bust at dawn, smashing and sound of violence, must be vigilantes. Get everybody to safety.

'Mark, take our visitors to Rat Camp.'

'Come with me... my dears,' cackled Old Mad Mark, flashing a blackened toothless grin at Jeanette and Holly. 'This way. Fear no darkness. Old Mark knows the secret paths, he does.'

The two girls quickly grabbed their jackets, sleeping bags, camera and notebook and followed Mad Mark.

'Aaron and Karl,' said Lui, 'go check on Lauren at Front Watch. Go through the bush and stay off the road. Make sure she's ok. Do what you need to do, then rendezvous back at Rat Camp. Goldy, hide in the bushes and film what you can. Tom, you stay with me.'

Aaron and Karl had sneaked slowly and silently through the bush. When they arrived at the Front Watch hut they saw that the door had been partially kicked in. They entered and saw Lauren sitting upright on the bed, nursing her bleeding head with a towel.

'I'm fine!' She glared at her would be rescuers, who stared glumly back. 'Now get your minds off that pink, prancing tart, and let's make those fuckers pay! We start with their truck.' She pulled out of her pocket a switchblade. 'You'll find a bag of sand and a funnel in that box over there, grab it. There's a hatchet in the corner, grab that too.'

Lauren slashed the tires of contractor jeep with her switchblade then turned her attention to the fuel tank, smashing it open with the hatchet and pouring the sand inside.

'Now we can head to the Rat Camp.'

Rat Camp was a secret camp, deep in the forest. It consisted of a few tarp huts, three old dome tents, gathering dirt, and a single large tarp, hung between the trees to create a central space. It served two purposes, as a secret support base during a bust, and to contain the excess of people when the area around the yurt became too crowded. One of the dome tents was stocked with tinned food and medical equipment. The rain began to spatter off the tarp, and the crew began to argue.

'I know that it's a horrible thing to happen, but this'll be great material for my article,' said Jeanette.

'Is that what you journalists do,' said Lauren, her head now wrapped in a white bandage, 'just think of how you can profit from others' suffering?'

'Who cares about that now,' said Goldy. 'The contractors are lost in the bush out there, they could be looking for us, and besides we can't just leave them out there. Lui said that one of them sounded badly injured. It's raining and it's freezing. They'll catch hypothermia.'

'I don't see why we can't just leave them out there,' said Lauren. 'When you attack somebody's home, bent on grievous bodily harm, and you're so stupid as to wind up like those brainless thugs, you get what you deserve.'

'Goldy's right, Lauren, and you know that,' said Lui, digging his toenails into the soil. 'I'm not suggesting we take them into camp, maybe just take them some tarps and medical stuff if they need it, tell them they'll have to settle in for the night. Unfortunately we can't get rid of them because you sabotaged their vehicle.'

'Excuse me. I'm not the one that led those Neanderthals into the bush, creating the whole situation we're in. If you just hid and let them do their thing they would be gone by now. What did you think you were doing? Don't look at me like I'm stupid, acting all superior, oh I'm Lui and I'm sensible. Dick. Furthermore, if you feel like doing a shift on Front Watch, instead of drinking champagne with her,' Lauren pointed at Jeanette, 'then you might have a right to criticise my decisions. Besides, how do we know those aren't the thugs that dumped that rubbish, and that body in the coupe?' The tall girl glared around her.

'There's no need to be rude,' said Jeanette, 'hold on, did you say "body"?'

'That's right, sweetheart,' said Lauren, 'did Lui not tell you? It's not all hot coffee, pretty birdies and bright flowers in the life of an eco-activist.'

They heard loud shouts coming from somewhere off in the forest. Lui stood up, knocking the tarp and sending water spilling onto the people huddled below it. He switched on his torch.

'I'm going to try and talk to them.'

'Don't get too close, Lui, Those animals might be feeling horny,' Lauren wiped the water out of her face.

Lui approached the light of the contractor's torches. He announced his approach with his own torch and the sound of his shoes on the wet leaves. He stopped at a fair distance from the two hulking figures and shouted out to them.

'Your mate's injured?'

One of the contractors shone his torch at Lui's face, and he winced. 'Our mate Johnno has got a broken leg. We need to call a rescue helicopter, mate. He's in a bad way.'

'Turn your torch away.'

The contractor did, and Lui flashed his own torch over the scene. Johnno sat on a mound not moving, while on either side of him two other contractors stood, their torches pointed at the ground. They were holding crowbars. 'That's a serious injury. He's a big man. Can you carry him?'

'He's a big bastard, but we reckon we could lug him out of the bush if we had to.'

'Right, there's a satellite phone at the camp. I'll call the rescue chopper.'

The contractors were silent for a minute. 'There ain't no satellite phone anymore,' said Johnno, 'I crushed that puppy into the fire.'

'Well, you're fucked then,' said Lui, the anger at the loss of the phone coming through his voice.

'Ring 'em from a cell phone,' croaked Johnno.

'Not a hope in hell. There isn't cell phone coverage for at least a fifty K radius.'

'Then you'll have t' get me up to the truck, chuck me on the back, and drive fifty K's.'

'Not a chance, the girl whose head you cracked open, took the liberty of pouring sand in your fuel tank. Your vehicle's a write-off!'

'You greenie bastards. Come over here, ya poo-pusher, and I'll bite ya face off. That truck was worth ten of yas. If you weren't trying to put us all out of work we wouldn't have to come up here and teach ya a lesson! Wait till daylight and my boys here will take down the lot of ya.'

Lui felt a prickle of fear on the back of his neck. The men were dangerous, and he desperately needed a peaceful solution. 'Look, we're prepared to help you. It's dangerous and we're all stuck here. It's gonna be a cold night. I'll bring you blankets and tarps to keep dry. We've got medical supplies, bandages, painkillers. We can make a splint for your leg, get you some food, even a thermos of hot tea. But we've got to know that there's no danger. If you fight, you'll lose.'

The contractors were silent, and Lui thought for a moment that they were going to attack him, but the rain became heavier and the contractors had no choice but to agree.

Chapter 6: Saturday

Light streamed in through the glass wall of the cafe.

'I take it you've heard the news,' said Johnston.

Warwick ripped into his breakfast – sausages, potatoes, free range bacon and eggs smothered in hollandaise sauce on toasted ciabatta bread, Portobello mushrooms and organic tomatoes, lightly grilled with pesto seasoning. It was a lot to attack with his cutlery, and he liked to pile each flavour onto the fork. This was the way to save the environment: ethical consumption.

'Yeah, course I heard,' said Warwick through a mouthful of ciabatta soaked in egg yolk. There had been a terrorist attack on the Australian embassy in Jakarta. Suspected Indonesian jihadists had blown up a wing of the building with a car bomb, a dozen dead and injured.

Johnston slid a copy of The Australian over the wide glass table.

Warwick stared sceptically at the cover photograph – dust, rubble, an injured man on a stretcher. The whole thing was hardly surprising given the way Australia treated her northern neighbour. 'What's it to do with us, surely it's more an issue to do with Canberra or Queensland?'

'In response to the tragedy in Jakarta the feds are pushing through a bill, making it simpler to deal with domestic terrorism, getting rid of procedural impediments, the new laws are flexible and could be applied to your friends in Ecology First, who after all, are involved in industrial sabotage.' Johnston's eyes didn't leave Warwick's face. 'The new measures are an opportunity, an opportunity to make money. China and Japan want our woodchips and they'll get them. We now have a free hand to operate. Thanks to the raid you witnessed on Miss Thistle's house we discovered that she had connections with a militant terrorist organisation.'

Warwick choked on a potato halfway through a mouthful of coffee, sending spurts of brown liquid onto his plate. 'And I'm Osama Bin Laden. What a crock of shit. I didn't know I was working so you could frame some girl on a trumped up charge of bullshit, what have you done with her?'

'Keep your voice down.' Johnston looked at Warwick. 'You're getting fat. Jane's connections with terrorists are a matter of national security and the appropriate authorities are investigating it. We appreciate everything that you've done, Warwick. You've helped bring a terrorist to justice, and recovered evidence of murder. But things are changing. We feel that your work with us is over. Your services will no longer be required. A final pay-out will be transferred to your bank account. You are advised to stay away from members of Ecology First. I suggest you go on a holiday. I hear there's cheap flights to New Zealand.'

'You're firing me.' The cold Portobello mushroom no longer tasted so good.

Sky had returned home and was drinking a coffee at the kitchen table. She looked around the kitchen. It was still a mess from the raid the day before, cups smashed on the ground. She'd half hoped to come home and find that it had all been a bad dream, but it hadn't. God knows what had happened to Jane. Sky rubbed Roofus's ears.

'At least you're all good, eh dog?' she said to the animal. 'You don't care about all this, do ya?'

The dog yawned appreciatively.

Sky heard a sharp rap at the door, Roofus barked, and she felt a surge of fear and uncertainty. Shit, she said to herself, I need to calm down. I'm starting to get paranoid. It's probably just Jehovah Witnesses. Coffee in hand, she walked down the hallway. It was white and she noticed the relief on the archway, white thorny roses cut into white wood. Through the shards of frosted glass, where the window had been broken during the raid, she could see what appeared to be a large person on the other side of the door. The knock came again, and Roofus yelped running down the hall, past Sky. She pulled open the door, and two men dressed in black suits stood on the threshold.

'Sky Thistle?' one of them asked.

She nodded.

He pulled out a badge, 'State Police, you're wanted for questioning regarding the activities and whereabouts of Jane Thistle.'

Sky gulped some of her coffee.

Roofus barked.

'Come with us, Miss.'

Chris woke. He was on the hard bed in a police cell. It was cold and smelled of urine. The walls were covered in flaking plaster and one detainee had managed to scratch 'fuck the pigs' into the wall. He felt his lip. It was split, sore and puffy. He waited in the cell for what seemed like a long time. There was nothing to do, nothing to read. He tried counting the minutes, but lost count. Finally a local cop came and opened the door to the cell.

'You're off, mate. We've decided not to press charges.'

The cop was dressed in a nice pressed, blue shirt. And Chris had a sudden desire to spit blood all over it. A night in the cells was always a traumatic experience, harsh light, fingerprinting, and removal of all jewellery, treated like an animal.

'Yes, sir,' he said and kept his eyes to the ground.

The spring rain drizzled outside. He had nothing. His pockets were empty. He wondered if there'd be a soup kitchen at the protest, but he wasn't even sure how to get there. He sat down on the curb, wishing he had a cigarette, and watching cars speed by. Chris watched as a figure walked up the pavement toward him. Chris stared as if the person were a mirage.

'Rotten bloody Johnny, what are you doing round here? Shit place to hang out.'

'Looking for you, shit locks. I heard you were locked up. Got a cig?' said Johnny Vegas.

'I've got nothing.'

'It's all right, I found a few butts man. You want one?'

'Go on then.'

They carefully ripped up the cigarette butts and rerolled them into two small cigarettes, which they smoked.

'Let's get out of here, man,' said Johnny, when they had finished the skregs of the tobacco.

After a long trek they reached a bakery, and Johnny fished out some coins. He bought them a cream doughnut and coffee each. They sat down on the tin chairs outside the bakery to eat and watch the rain collect in puddles on the footpath. The coffee was too hot and the doughnut too chewy, but it tasted good. And Chris began to cheer up.

'Thanks, Johnny,' he said, 'why were you looking for me?'

'That's Johnny Vegas to you, man. Oh yeah,' said the American through a mouthful of cream, 'shit's gone crazy, man, your place wasn't the only one to get raided. The warehouse on Broomfield Street also got whacked. And get this man, you know how you told me to keep an eye out, well I saw one of Nails' mob in a nice cafe, down South Side, this morning. He was talking with a suit, looked real spiv and shit. Thought he might be ratting.'

'Really.' Chris licked the coffee foam off his split lip. 'What did he look like?'

'Oh you know, chubby guy, pale, short blond hair, medium height. He was having one hell of a breakfast, poached eggs, sausages, bacon, avocados, Portobello mushrooms, ciabatta, hollandaise sauce, a fruit shake...'

'Enough on the damn breakfast. Did you hear what they were saying?'

'Oh, you know, I didn't really hear much, man, but the spiv dude seemed pissed off and I heard them talking about that chick friend of yours, Jane, and the spiv dude said he was fired.'

'Very interesting, Johnny,' said Chris, as he ran the people he knew from Ecology First through his head. And he remembered talking to a guy that fitted Johnny's description at a meeting a few weeks ago. What was his name? 'But, Johnny, what the hell were you doing at a cafe at South Side this morning?'

'Ohh,' the American drew the sound out in the nasal manner of his people. 'One of my girlfriends lives over that way, her mom's like totally flush, takes real good care of me.'

'One of your girlfriends! Jesus, Johnny, stay away from our children, will ya.' Chris playfully punched the young punk.

The Saturday morning sun rose over the hills shedding its pale light over Camp Balloong to the sound of screeching parrots, and the patter of rain. The activists had relocated back to the yurt. They'd brought the contractors everything they needed to survive the night, and they'd given no trouble. But the activists were tense, and Lui, who stirred a large pot of thick communal porridge, kept looking over his shoulder in the direction of where the contractors were camped, half expecting to see them come raging out of the trees at any moment.

Jeanette, dressed in her pink pyjamas and a raincoat, tiptoed over the rough ground of the logging road to the kitchen and embraced Lui from behind. He dropped the spoon into the pot of porridge.

'Lui poo possum,' said Jeanette, 'Holly and I were thinking it was time to leave this morning. It's been great. Thanks for everything. I've got heaps of material for my article now, but the supplies we brought are getting low so we really must be on our way.'

Lui disentangled himself from Jeanette but not in time to avoid the wolf whistle from Lauren, who walked towards the kitchen carrying a green bag. Lauren's head wound had developed into a nasty black eye, but she seemed oddly cheerful.

'How're you going to leave?' asked Lui.

'With the car, of course.'

'But, Jeanette, your radiator was smashed by the contractors. You're stuck here with the rest of us until relief comes.'

'But we're running out of food.'

'Don't worry, honey,' called Lauren, moving closer and patting Jeanette on the back. 'There are plenty of things to eat in the bush. One time during a bust I had to live off leeches.'

'Are there leeches around here?'

'You bet there are, sweetheart. Allow me to let you in on a little secret. It's best to leave them on your arm for a good ten minutes until they are nice and fat. A tasty wee treat when grilled on the fire, though not so bad raw. When you bite into them they're kind of chewy but the juicy blood inside just explodes into your mouth, all sweet and salty. But don't make the mistake of swallowing them whole.' Lauren rolled her eyes meaningfully. 'Then they can latch on to the inside of your throat and then you've got a problem.'

'She's being ridiculous,' said Lui, taking the porridge off the heat, 'we don't eat leeches. We've got more food than we can eat. We've barrels of dried goods. We don't have any more fresh fruit and vege though and we're running low on water. Would you like to come to the stream and help me collect some?'

'Such a kill joy,' said Lauren.

Jeanette ignored her. 'Is it ok to drink that water?' she asked Lui, 'it looks a bit brown.'

'It's good for you' said Lauren. 'It's the blood of the earth. The Aborigines believed it was connected with period blood. The red streams were considered sacred and women bathed in them during menstruation.'

'Now I really don't believe you,' said Jeanette.

'It's true,' said Lui, taking the white plastic water container from the bench, 'but it's fine to drink. The colour comes from tea tree leaves. They're harmless tannins, probably good for you.'

'Even better with a few mosquito larvae for protein. Well, I'm off. Enjoy your trip to the red river.'

'Where are you going?' asked Lui.

'I'm off to see how my mate Johnno is getting on.'

'Are you crazy? They're pissed off and dangerous.'

'They've already hit me, and let's face it, they'd beat the crap out of you just as easily as me. I reckon deep down they're only bogans. I can deal with bogans. Besides somebody has got to check on them and it may as well be me.'

Lui looked down at Lauren's green bag and saw that it had rice and books in it. 'Just be careful.'

Lui and Jeanette left to fill the water containers and Lauren, a knot of fear in her stomach, picked her way through the forest in the direction of the contractors. When she spotted their camp she coughed to alert them to her presence and walked slowly, raised arms, to show she came in peace. Two tarps were hung from the trees to create rough shelters. On the ground a small fire smouldered next to a crusted pot, which had been used to cook the baked beans provided by the activists. One contractor sat on a hump of ground whittling a stick with a knife, while Johnno, her attacker, lay prone under a tarp slung between two myrtles. He looked pale and sick, his leg bound with a temporary splint. Lauren noticed that the contractors had managed to trample and slash back all the plants in their immediate vicinity. The cans of food they'd given them lay scattered around and they'd not, to her knowledge, bothered to build a toilet. She suspected that they had been shitting in the bush nearby. This was a minor environmental hazard. It attracted flies, and in the case of rain, water could wash the shit into the stream, contaminating the water.

Camp Balloong had developed a clean composting system. The occupant was seated on an elevated throne and the stools would plop several feet down into a steel drum. They were then covered with sawdust, or ash that had a strong alkaline content, which dried up and broke down the poo. When the drums were full they were left to stand for a while before the mulch was emptied into a designated spot nearby. The activists had debated over whether the compost should be used for making gardens that could supplement the camp's food supply. The opposing group had argued that the creation of a garden could potentially damage the local ecology by introducing alien plants; they, led by Nails, had come out on top.

The contractors watched silently as the lanky brunette drew near.

'Morning,' said Lauren.

The man looked up from his whittling. His face was lined and tanned, a labourer's face. His hair was short and brown, he wore work boots, blue work pants, and a bush shirt.

'How ya going,' he said.

'Apart from one hell of a headache, I'm good. Do you mob normally go around bashing girls in the head?'

'You bloody hippies fucked the grapplers,' said Johnno from under the tarp.

'I'm not a hippy, but I know a joke about one,' said Lauren.

The contractors were silent.

'Go on then,' said Johnno. 'Tell us your bloody joke.'

'How do you know if a hippy's been on your couch?'

'How's that?'

'He's still there.'

Johnno laughed, and then the other contractor joined in, and their laughter echoed through the forest until it became a coughing fit, and Johnno hawked and spat on the ground. 'Still there eh, still there.'

Lauren relaxed a little. It seemed that the contractors were not in the mood for more violence. 'Where's your mate gone?'

'Went for a walk.'

'And how you feeling, mate?' said Lauren 'That coughing didn't sound too good.'

'No I'm not feeling good at all,' said Johnno. 'I'm blowing snot like a Balinese hooker. It was wet last night and those damn mosquitoes buzzing round. Then there was that possum nearly getting his head stuck in the can. I don't know how you greenies can live out here for months at a time.'

'Yeah right, well, about those cans,' said Lauren, 'do you think that you could keep your camp a bit tidier?'

'Are ya having a go, love?' said the contractor who had been whittling. There was a hint of menace in his tone and Lauren wondered if she'd gone too far.

'I've brought you some supplies.' Lauren forced herself to smile. 'We're running low on canned goods, but we have an abundance of rice and lentils. We've even given you some salt. Rice provides for your carbohydrate and lentils for protein and minerals. If it's good enough for a billion Indians, it's good enough for you.'

'No meat,' said the contractor with the knife. The man's tone carried no emotion and Lauren wasn't sure whether it was a question, a statement or a threat. But she sensed a hint of chauvinistic arrogance in the man's tone and that made her angry.

'That's right, beef face, I'm sure enough cows have been slaughtered for your appetite to feed a small nation. It's time to turn off the carcass, and join the lentil revolution.'

The whittling contractor looked like he was about get up and hit her, but Johnno laughed again. 'She's got a bloody mouth on her, Hank. Probably bigger balls then you.'

'Do you carcass-munchers know how to cook?' asked Lauren.

'I know how to slap a steak on the barby,' replied Johnno and he winked at Hank. His tone was jovial.

'Well, good for you,' said Lauren, and she gave Johnno a hint of a smile before explaining how to cook the food.

'I don't suppose you could bring us down a couple of coldies, love?' asked the contractor with the knife.

Lauren didn't like the delivery of the last word that the contractor had left to hang. Love. She couldn't control her own anger rising in her again. 'Does this look like a fucken hotel to you? And don't ever call me love again. Now for the good of your precious souls I've brought you some reading material. First book, a great read for any first timers in the wilderness, and even recommended for a few veterans, How to Shit in the Bush.'

Lauren threw the book and it fluttered through the air to land at Hank's feet.

He looked down at its cover, showing a picture of a spade.

'Now,' she addressed Johnno with her best no-nonsense tone, 'should I see to your injury?'

He looked back at her. 'If ya could.'

As Lauren approached her attacker from the previous night she recalled the violence in the Front Watch hut, the big man smelling of drink picking her up by the armpits and throwing her against the wall. She took comfort from fingering her own switchblade in her pocket, knowing she was not completely defenceless. She felt vulnerable as she stepped under the tarp. Johnno's face was pale and he coughed up some phlegm. She touched her hand to his forehead and noted that he was feverish. She unbound his leg wound. It was red and swollen. She applied some arnica cream before rebinding the splint.

'Keep your body warm and your leg cool. We'll also bring you another blanket, and some hot water and lemon that might help with your fever.'

Warwick arrived at the steps of Parliament for the demonstration. He wasn't certain why he'd come. Since he'd been fired that morning he felt empty, like his life had suddenly lost its meaning. He'd spent a long time out in the bush with these feral people. It had surprised him, but the first thing he had felt, after his meeting with Johnston, was sadness. He would miss his friends. His role had given him a sense of belonging that he had never felt before, he even had a girlfriend up there – Goldy. She had been good to him. Through the cold winter nights he had bonded with these people. They may not be right, but they weren't wrong either. He felt a surge of guilt at narking in Jane and Nails. He'd never realised what would come from the intelligence he'd provided, had he?

Warwick looked around him. The central square was paved with large granite tiles. In its centre a statue of Captain Cook stared vacantly in the direction of the ocean, one hand on a sabre, the other holding a sextant. His head was splattered with the droppings of pigeons and seagulls. The square was lined with two rows of old oaks. They bloomed with spring growth, while their roots were slowly crumbling the pavement. They led up to the steps of the colonial government house, which was ringed in engaged columns, ending in flowering Corinthian capitals, a remnant of Rome, uprooted and flung to this end of the earth.

A grassy tear separated the steps of parliament from the square and here the protesters had assembled. And the demonstration was ringed with the banners of various interest groups. Warwick noted with pride the use of the placards he'd helped to create. Soup and bread was served from a marquee. Under the statue of Cook, Nails had set up her stall covered in pamphlets and the A2 sheets of the petition she was presenting. Next to the stall were a soap box and a microphone.

It was a considerable gathering, larger than other such events Warwick had attended. People were standing and chatting, some holding placards, others just sitting, showing their support simply by being there. A mob of scruffy young punks were drawing messages with multi-coloured chalk on the ground. A group of Polynesian migrants stood around smoking and talking. A musician began to play on a clarinet and lonely notes of haunting, folky jazz floated through the air. A crew of excited teenagers, their faces smeared with blue war paint and pictures of flowers danced through the drizzly day. A coterie of the usual suspects stood conspiratorially, nodding knowingly. A circle of university students in grey coats nursed second-rate takeaway coffees. A group of clowns stood forlornly beside a large blow-up white elephant. A man in a kilt was selling fizzy drink from a rickshaw. It felt like a carnival, and it cheered Warwick.

It was the lines of still riot police that made Warwick shiver, and gave the event a surreal appearance. It was horrendous overkill for such a peaceful gathering, far less violent than a boy's night out on the town. Yet here they were, dressed in black, helmets fronted with clear plastic visors. They carried long batons. They were silent. Behind them were rows of mounted police. This was unprecedented. Usually at such gatherings there would be a dozen local cops guarding the doors of parliament, or if things got rowdy a few mounties would turn up. But this, this was bizarre, a brazen show of force.

A gentle tap on the shoulder brought Warwick out of his revere. It was Chris. He was eating soup and bread hungrily and soup dripped from his beard.

'Hey bra,' he said and grinned, 'cops are out in force.'

'I'll say. It's bizarre.'

Chris was a pretty decent guy, thought Warwick, he was usually standing at the back of the meeting and saying sarcastic things about the speakers. He clearly believed in the cause but he wasn't a dick about it. It seemed to Warwick that Chris simply hated authority and that was why he was drawn to the movement, and yet cynical of it. One thing that he brought to Ecology First was his physical presence. He was large with thick dreadlocks and muscular arms. He looked like someone who could take a beating. He had a split puffy lip.

'You've been part of the campaign for a while now haven't ya?' said Chris.

'Yeah,' Warwick began spinning his well-rehearsed lie, 'to be honest I only turned up originally cos Goldy was really passionate about saving the forest, but now that I understand everything – I feel I've got to do something. I mean, where are we gonna be when it's all gone? I can't just stand by and do nothing.' Warwick had said this story so many times that in moments of weakness, like this, he even believed it. 'I just,' he stared at the dark line of riot police, 'I just feel totally helpless.'

'I know what you mean. I feel the same every day. But there's hope.' Chris pointed to riot police. 'That's not a show of force it's a show of fear.' He took out a twenty cent coin flicked it into the air and caught it. 'Where do you stand, Warwick?'

It was a funny question. 'With you, of course, with the campaign.'

'How do ya reckon the cops knew Jane was at my place? I was thinking it was odd, how they seemed to know.'

'Pretty weird, alright.'

'So you knew about it then?'

Warwick realised he'd been tricked.

'Do you often have cafe breakfasts at posh cafes on South Side? I've heard the quality of their hollandaise is premium and their fruit shakes are delicious. How does it feel being fired over such a breakfast?'

Warwick stared silently at the soapbox where a speaker was talking about the need for an independent inquiry into forestry. He felt sick. He'd been caught out and he felt fear, guilt, and shame all at once. He closed his eyes.

'You're a rat, aren't you, Warwick? You sold out your mates for lattes and poached eggs, ya piece of shit. You think they'll protect you.' Chris motioned toward the police line. 'They don't care about you. You're useless to them now your cover's blown. They'll throw ya away like a discarded condom they've just used to fuck us in the arse.'

Chris grasped the collar of the spy's shirt.

'Wait,' said Warwick. And in that moment, as Chris held him, he thought of Goldy – her cute squashed face and yellow curly hair – and realised that he loved her. 'I can be useful. I regret everything I did. I want to work for your mob, change sides. I know what's going on from their end. Please don't tell anybody. Give me a second chance.'

Chris relaxed his grip on Warwick's shirt.

'I've got information.'

'What information?'

'Well, I can tell you for a start that they've taken, what's-her-name, Jane's cousin, Sky, into custody this morning. The state police, that is. I can tell you that they are claiming that Jane is connected with a terrorist cell. I can tell you the date of the bust.'

Jane woke, her head reeling. Although dizzy and disorientated she became aware that she was in a tunnel of some kind, made from smooth concrete, and lying on a mattress that smelled of mould. She was still dressed in her clothes from the previous night, black thermals, top and bottom, light canvas shoes, a scarf, a hoody and a knee length skirt. She tried to stand, but felt sick and she crawled to the edge of the mattress and vomited, emptying her guts onto the cold curved floor. As the retching subsided images of the previous evening began to flood back to her: the party, the police arriving, her escape, her capture. From the end of the tunnel came a dim light and she could also hear a rhythmic scraping, which sounded like metal on stone. Jane crawled on all fours toward the light. Here the tunnel opened out into a larger space with more passages going off in different directions. The light of an old oil lamp silhouetted the bulky figure of a man. He was hunched over, and sharpening a long knife on a whetstone.

'You finally awake,' he said. 'Come here. Ya gotta drink water.'

Jane's head pounded, but her mouth was dry and she obeyed. As she entered the space she looked around her trying to commit it to memory. She could see another moulding mattress, next to a pile of bedding. In front of that was a gas cooker and some tins of food. Leaning against the wall was a large backpack, and, what looked to Jane, to be a Kalashnikov.

She walked over to stand across from her captor, and he stopped sliding the blade of the knife across the whetstone. He looked up at Jane and passed her a two-litre coke bottle filled with water. His face - it jolted her memory and she remembered him, looking down at her as he'd covered her mouth with the sweet smelling rag. She drank greedily, the water spilling over her face, before putting the bottle down. The man said nothing but returned to sharpening. Jane stood, silently listening to the scrape of steel on stone, wondering what she should do. She became aware of other sounds: water dripping, rats scrabbling.

'Where are we?' she asked.

'In the drains underneath Port Town.'

She felt around her neck and noticed her camera was missing. 'Where's my camera?'

The man reached into the pocket of a grimy brown coat and pulled out Jane's camera and passed it to her.

It felt comforting to have the camera back in her hands, and she resisted the urge to starting using it. Perhaps he's a hired thug, she thought, but somehow it didn't seem like it. He was too scruffy and the place looked like he'd been living there for some time.

'What do you want with me?' she asked.

'I saved your neck from the cops.' The man stopped sharpening and ran the blade across his thumb. 'I followed you from North Side. You were at that bloody fire. I've been on the trail of a girl, Anya. The old Greek told me you'd been asking after her.'

'Why are you looking for her?'

The man stared at Jane. His face was broad, and stubbly, his eyes and his repeatedly broken nose were small. He showed no emotion. 'She's my daughter.'

'I'm sorry,' said Jane.

'Sorry for what?'

'She's dead.'

The man's expression didn't change. 'How did she die?'

'She was murdered.'

'Do you know who killed her?'

'Not exactly,' Jane fingered her mobile, which was still in her jersey pocket, 'but I know where we might be able to find out. What did you poison me with?'

'Good old fashioned ether.'

'Who are you?' Jane fancied she saw a subtle smile playing at the edge of his mouth when she asked the question.

'A mean bugger.'

Chapter 7: Saturday Night

Senior police sergeant, Michael O'Connell, watched the protest swell. It had grown far larger than he'd expected, and the speakers, whose words he could not make out, had grown more fiery. The restless crowd responded with loud chants and boos. Sergeant O'Connell knew he had to act. He gave the order to kettle the demonstration.

Kettling was a tried and practised method of crowd control. Riot police would surround a densely packed protest, like this one in Central Square, on all sides. Protesters would be allowed out through the police lines, but not in. People gradually left from the discomfort of the situation, and the protest dispersed, like a kettle letting off steam. Or, like a man choking to death from hanging, as the police line could tighten like a noose, increasing the discomfort on the inside.

O'Connell watched as the new, well drilled riot squads moved into position. Visors down, shields forward, they surrounded the colourful mob in a ring of black. He'd be dammed if he let anything go wrong, and he had horses to make sure it didn't. The horses could protect the flanks of the police line if anybody dared to try and break the kettle from the outside. While other countries used tear gas, rubber bullets and water cannons for crowd control, the Australian police favoured more traditional measures: batons, shields, pepper spray, mounted police and paddy wagons. There would be no anarchy on the streets of Port Town.

Nails twiddled with the cord of the microphone. Her warehouse had been busted. The police had wanted to confiscate her computer, her address books, and search her house for evidence of collusion with some ridiculous terrorist group, but their warrants weren't signed by a judge, they hadn't counted on a lawyer, and Nails had threatened them with prosecution if they proceeded. They'd backed off but it had been close. The sergeant had clearly been torn between obeying his superior and the fear of the law. She'd done her bit, the rally had attracted a lot of people and they were sick of corruption. The riot police were moving to kettle the protest, they'd left it late enough, but still there was no sign of Herb's unions, or Mateen's immigrants. The gentle rain had eased and the late afternoon sun reflected off their cloth banners and eclectic placards. Her mob wasn't going anywhere in a hurry.

'Nails,' it was Chris, 'you gonna hang around in this ambush?'

'Of course,' she said. 'I didn't organise this rally to run away at the first sign of trouble. What are you grinning at?'

'I love trouble,' replied Chris. 'Look, I have some information, the state police are after Jane on trumped up terrorism charges, and they've taken her cousin into custody. Good news is, they don't have her. Also, I hear they're planning to bust Camp Balloong late next week. I promised I'd go up there so I'd be keen on a lift —'

Shouts and screams rang out from the edge of the protest where the police were pushing protesters back with shields and batons. 'That's very interesting, Chris, but I'll talk to you later. I think I'm needed on the frontline. People need to know they're not to be intimidated.'

Nails spoke into the microphone. 'It'd seem that the police want to intimidate us and take away our right to peaceful assembly. We need to show that we'll not let them. We'll not move until our concerns have been addressed. The police have no right to arrest or detain you. Bunch together and link arms to avoid arrest. They'll want to take you one at a time. Don't let them.'

A cheer ran through the crowd.

Chris's body still ached from his night in the cells, and the prospect of re-arrest didn't appeal.

'Come on,' he said to Warwick, and they moved to the point of the cordon where police were letting people out, and they slipped through the line without any hassle. Once on the other side, Chris stopped to bludge a cigarette from another protester. Things were developing in a curious way. From inside the police cordon, angry, rhythmic chants told him that the protesters were standing strong. Some, like himself, had left the kettle but many had not dispersed. They lingered hesitant, watching from the outside. Not only that, but more people were arriving, workers and immigrants. Already the crowd was several ranks deep, and Chris noticed they had placards and red union banners, mingled with hand painted wooden signs demanding justice. Something unexpected was happening.

'Chris.'

He spun around. It was Herb the commie. He had a black eye and was missing a tooth. He was dressed in a black hoody, and had a black bandanna tied cowboy style around his thick neck.

'Chris,' the commie said, 'we're going black bloc. You wanna come?'

Chris didn't answer straight away. He could hear angry shouts and cursing from somewhere inside the police picket. The mounted police waited on the wings, still as statues. One of the horses whickered. They'll try to disperse these spectators soon, thought Chris, as he pondered Herb's offer. The famous black bloc: a tactic favoured by radicals in southern Europe. A group dressed all in black would plant themselves in a peaceful protest and aim to turn it violent, deliberately inciting a heavy handed response from police.

Chris felt like telling the trouble making commie to go get fucked. But the memory of the cells was still fresh in his mind. The sneers of the cops as they processed him, and made him remove his belt and the rings from his hair, the stench of piss in his cell. His split lip still throbbed from the violence of the previous night, and where was Jane? And this, this was already brutal. He looked over at Warwick who seemed lost in thought, studying the lines of police. This was an opportunity to allow the rat to prove himself.

'Sure, me and Warwick'll come.'

Herb led Chris and Warwick to a white van parked in the nearby university car park. Inside the van were four others, three men and a woman. The woman was tying a bandana around her face. Two of the men were siphoning petrol from a can into bottles. The third man was playing with a heavy river stone. He tossed it up, and caught it, before putting it down and giving the newcomers a curt nod. He then reached behind him, pulled two bandanas from a rubbish sack and threw them to Chris.

'What we need,' said Herb, 'is somebody to start a fight with the cops.'
Nobody spoke for a while.
'I can do that,' said Warwick.

Sergeant O'Connell was beginning to feel uneasy. The spectators had grown to the point where they nearly outnumbered the kettled group in the square, which had hardly begun to disperse. He could hear them singing songs and see their banners waving. There'd been minor scuffles with the picket line, but on the whole the group inside the kettle had remained peaceful. O'Connell was acutely aware of how heavy handed the police response was. For the love of God, he thought, we shouldn't even be here. We should just have let them have their protest and go home. But the superintendent had seemed intent on making an example, and it was no good arguing now.

It was the group outside the kettle that bothered O'Connell. It had become apparent that they were not mere curious passers-by. Some of them looked like rough criminal types, others had banners or were dressed for a protest, and still the group kept growing. As long as they kept their distance from the kettle trouble could be avoided, but O'Connell doubted that would be the case. He gave an order to the reserve squad to ask them to disperse or be forcibly removed.

As the squad approached the spectators they fell silent, but showed no signs of leaving. He saw the officers conversing with the protestors. A man in a black hoody came forward from the line and grabbed an officer by his vest. The rest of the squad moved quickly to arrest him. Shouts of 'shame' rang throughout the square. Both groups quickly took up the chant, and they began to shout, 'shame, shame, shame.'

A tussle broke out as protestors charged the police, who responded with batons and shoves of their shields. Several protesters went down.

The spectators, enraged by the attempted arrest, surged forward and surrounded the squad who found themselves trapped inside an angry mob. Christ, O'Connell swore under his breath, it was time to send in the horses.

O'Connell breathed a sigh of relief as the disciplined line of horses broke into a trot. The riders held long batons and wore protective helmets. No mob could stand up to horses once they built up momentum. There would be a few injuries if people didn't get out of the way, but they had been warned, and assaulted his officers. Anybody stupid enough to stand in the way would get hit by a baton or trampled. It would soon be over.

The protestors were chanting, 'shame, shame, shame.' The kettled group was getting more desperate, more violent, but there was nothing they could do against the shields and batons of the riot squad.

Chris watched as the horses built up speed. They seemed to him to move in slow motion, the heads of the horses protected by Perspex helmets. The riders he saw were mainly women and they held their long batons close to ground. He leapt forward from the shouting crowd as they turned to face the police charge. He was hooded and his bandana covered his nose and mouth. Chris lit the oil soaked rag, which stopped the top of his Molotov, and holding it in his right hand, he hurled it awkwardly in front of the police charge. The bottle exploded in a shower of flame, blocking their advance. Chris felt the heat on his face and a mad rush of adrenaline surge through him.

The horses reared or swerved to avoid the incendiary. More Molotovs exploded on the stone, and a new chant erupted from the crowd: 'Take control of our national forces; get those animals off those horses.'

The excited mob on the outside surged forward to aid the kettled protest, which was getting more violent. Chris could see the rise and fall of batons, and hear the angry screams of injured people. The point of the police picket closest to the mob was unable to protect both their front and rear from the angry protesters. The line broke apart and the two groups of protesters surged together. The trapped police lashed out around them, hitting anyone who came close. The square quickly became a bloody melee.

Chris saw some students pull a cop to the ground. A pair of dishevelled clowns tried to drag an injured associate away from the violence. One cop lashed out with his baton catching a screaming girl on the back of her head. Johnny Vegas was steeling handcuffs from a policeman's belt. Behind him Chris heard a rock smash through a window – the shattering of glass, the sound of chaos. The sun was lower in the sky.

Jane's captor had carefully prepared for leaving. He had disassembled the Kalashnikov, wrapped it in blankets and stuffed it into his metal-framed backpack. The oil lamp, gas cooker and mattresses were stacked on the edge of the central space. His old, brown leather boots were laced to the top. He wore grey cotton trousers, fastened with a belt just above the hips; his sagging belly concealed the buckle. On top of his grey T shirt he wore a brown baggy coat. To Jane he looked like an ogre – tall, fat, tough, and ugly, with a scarred and battered face. He heaved the pack onto his back, flicked on his torch and stubbed out the lamp.

'Don't do anything clever,' he said. 'It'll make life difficult for the both of us.'

Jane nodded and fiddled with the phone in her pocket wondering how the plan would go.

They set off with Jane in front, and walked for a long time through the underground drain networks. Most of the drains were large enough that she barely had to stoop. They appeared to be old, and in some places cracked and crumbling. In one part they walked ankle deep through cold water, which soaked through Jane's canvas shoes. She tried not to imagine what filth the water carried down toward the harbour. Rats scuttled out of their way, their eyes pale violet in the reflection of the torches. She had no idea where they were. All she knew was that they were gently climbing. They walked in silence, as Jane's captor only spoke to say left, right or straight, and the sound of dripping echoed airily through the tunnels. Eventually they stopped by a steel ladder, and the man told Jane to –

'Get on up there and push the lid open.'

It was dark outside, while sirens and car alarms filled the night with the electric sound of battle. The wind ruffled Jane's hair. She could smell the sweet scent of heather, and she wondered what was happening in the city below. It was a beautiful clear night, and she couldn't resist photographing the waxing, yellow moon as it rose over the Pacific Ocean to illuminate Port Town in its fey light.

The big man grunted as he pulled his heavy pack out of the manhole.

They appeared to be in some kind of old industrial area halfway up the hill, which overlooked the centre of town. Parked across the road was a rickety white van. The man walked over to it and, fishing keys out of his pocket, opened the boot and threw his pack inside.

'Bad moon rising,' he remarked, as he paused to follow Jane's gaze. 'A yellow moon means trouble.' He pulled open the door to the passenger seat. 'Get in and give the door a good slam.'

First they drove through sleepy suburbs, where only stray cats and hedgehogs roamed, but it wasn't long before they hit the coast road, where the crash and boom of the wild ocean mixed with the rattle and hum of the engine, making Jane feel oddly relaxed.

'What's your name?' she asked her captor.

'Salt.'

'Salt? That's a strange a name. You've been in the army haven't ya?'

'Yeah,' he drew out the vowel sounds, with a gravely, occa accent, 'I was a mercenary, Afghanistan, Syria, Iraq. It was awful. Nothing like the smell of melting flesh in the Central Asian summer to wreck a man's mind.'

'But you're not in the army now?'

'Yeah, screw the buggers. The jihadis knew what they were doing, a stray bomb, a rogue rifleman. We started to see enemies everywhere, that's when things got nasty. I deserted and got across the border to Pakistan, then India. Eventually, I caught a flight to Sydney, but I didn't stick around. I went north, to Arnhem Land, found my roots, found culture. But I couldn't stay because violence is all I know.'

'I don't think you're that violent.'

Salt's gaze remained locked on the road. 'When I was young, my old man would chain me to the truck and beat me black and blue, 'cause he thought I looked like a black fella. He taught me how to take a beating. It's violence I know.'

'You're Aboriginal?'

'A long time ago a white pig tupped a black bitch. The white horses stole the litter.'

'So what happened, you're a long way from Arnhem Land, what are you doing way down here?'

'Got troppo. Tropical infections caused parts of me to swell up like pumpkins, but I'm from here originally. I'm home, and there's some people who better be watching their backs.'

'You're from here, but I thought —'

'That's enough talking.' They'd arrived at Man-O-War Bay.

Man-O-War Bay was a beach community, an outer suburb of Port Town. It had once been a small fishing community, a mere collection of old colonial houses and dinghies pulled up on the marram grass, clear of the surf. But Man-O-War Bay, with its commanding cliff top views, soft sandy beaches and close-to-city location had boomed, attracting big money. The fishing shacks were gone and so were the dinghies. In their place super yachts rolled on the gentle waves, and modern mansions made from glass and stone covered the ridges and cliff tops.

Salt stopped the van by the side of the road and pulled a crumpled road map from a pocket on the door. He leafed through it. 'What did you say the address was?'

Jane opened the message on her phone and read it out.

The club was a one storey rectangle built from large panes of glass and black-painted wood. The low ambient light that emanated from its windows illuminated a well groomed lawn. The front of the building appeared to be a reception and bar, with a tiled floor and gentle lighting. Several people stood, drinking and chatting behind a wide glass panel.

Jane and Salt crept past, staying close to shadows of the eucalypts and grass trees that bordered the lawn. The east side of the club appeared to be quite plain, a smooth wooden wall with no windows. They kept moving toward the back of the club. Here, two men were smoking beside a few parked cars.

Jane thought they would be seen, her heart pounded and she felt a creeping fear, but nobody noticed them and they kept moving toward the building's west side. Here it extended in a small rectangle, and in the light of the moon Jane could see a wooden door. They moved back to crouch among the foliage, and Jane shivered, feeling the cold.

'It's not what I was expecting,' she whispered.

Salt chuckled, 'Nah it's not the kind of seedy dive you find on North Side where old Tommo goes to spend the pennies he's saved up on the sheep station. Nah, this is a brothel for money grubbers with hundred dollar bills coming out their arses. You can dress it up as much as you like but it's still a brothel, and that's something I know about.'

'What do we do now?'

'Well, we gotta get in,' said the big man, 'see if you're right, that Anya worked here. I don't fancy going through the front door, every bouncer in the place would be on us like flies to pig shit.'

Jane was no stranger to clandestine missions. She'd broken into logging coupes on multiple occasions, sneaked past contractors and sabotaged equipment. Although fear ate at her stomach she wanted to get in too, so she made a suggestion.

'What about through the back?'

Salt shook his head. 'Too many unhelpful people. Nah, we go through there,' he pointed to the third entrance across from where they crouched, 'the security entrance. I'll bet my boots, and they're my only pair, that's where the important traffic comes in and out.'

Jane looked again at the entrance. The door was closed, light spilled from the long windows at the top of the building.

'There's a couple of security guards up there,' said Salt.

Jane stared at the source of the light. 'I can't see anybody.'

'Nah, you wouldn't, not in a place like this. They want to make it look like there's nothing going on inside.'

Jane began to realise how dangerous breaking into the club would be. It seemed almost suicidal. Salt's mad, she thought, and he'll bring us both down.

'What we need to do,' said the big man, 'is draw them out.'

'How do we do that?'

Salt grinned. 'With you, snot face. You'll be the bait.'

Jane felt terrified. She imagined being up in the building being interrogated by security. How long would she last, she wondered, not long. 'What do you want me to do?'

'Take this.' He pushed the torch into her hands. 'Shine the torch, wave your arms and shout, "help".'

'This isn't gonna work.'

'Just shut up and do it.'

Jane felt sick with fear, she flashed the torch at the building, and tried to yell but she couldn't. She opened her mouth but no sound came out. Perhaps it was the fear. But somebody must have noticed because the door opened and the dark silhouette of a bulky man exited. Then she shouted, 'help, help!' And she meant it.

The man did not react immediately but waited until a second man had joined him. He pointed toward Jane and said something. The second guard responded with a nod, and they set off toward her, walking quickly, the second guard tailing behind. They flashed their high beam torches at her face. And she felt like a possum caught in the headlights of a truck. When they got within several metres of her they stopped.

'This is private property. What're you doing here?'

'My car ran out of gas down the road.'

The two men seemed to ease up. Jane noticed that they carried guns on their belts, not the big, old heavy revolvers that the police used, but small, modern handguns. The tailing guard moved forward to get a better look at Jane, and at that moment, Salt, with surprising agility, leapt from where he had been hiding in the grass and tackled the tailing security guard, knocking the wind out of him. The leading guard spun around, and grabbed his gun, but he was too slow and Salt grabbed him by the waist in one arm while with the other he pushed an ether soaked rag into his face. The guard briefly struggled before he succumbed to the ether and fell unconscious on the ground. Before the winded man had time to recover his breath, he too was anaesthetised with ether.

Salt took a wad of cable ties from his pocket and bound the two officers by their wrists and ankles. 'They're green. They should have kept their distance. If they'd been in the war a roadside bomb would have killed them both.' Salt grinned at her. 'Ya did well. You want a gun?'

'No.'

'Suit yourself.' Salt stuffed one gun into his pocket and threw the other one into the bushes. He removed the ID cards from around the necks of the unconscious security guards, also pushing them into his pocket. 'Come on, let's move. Those buggers will be wondering what happened to their mates.'

No one stopped them as they ran across the lawn to the door. Salt flashed one of the ID cards over the screen on the lock, pushed, and the door opened. Inside was a hallway with a tile floor. Bonsai trees were arranged at equal intervals along it, while several wooden doors led off to either side.

'Might be in luck, those two were the only boys around.'

Salt slid the card over one of the doors and pushed it open, and Jane, wanting to stay as close to the safety of his bulk as possible, slipped in behind him. The room was warm and lit by low globe lamps. Opposite the door was a sleek double bed, and there was a bar set up on one side of the room. A naked, brown girl knelt on the floor, while a flabby naked white man, who looked to be in his fifties, stood behind her with an erection and his index finger buried in her arse. Another topless brown girl mixed a cocktail at the bar.

Jane felt a mixture of anger and disgust rise through her. This was the culture that had killed Anya. Part of her wanted to be sick, but she managed to take her camera from around her neck and photograph the man.

'What the fuck,' he said, and Jane watched as his erection shrunk.

Salt closed the door behind him till it clicked. 'I'm guessing,' he said, 'that these rooms are pretty sound proof. And these guns,' he pulled the hand gun from his pocket, 'are pretty silent, and I'm a mad bastard, so be very careful about what you do.'

The girl who had been on all fours crawled to the bed where she sat, her folded arms pressed against her young breasts. The girl who had been mixing a drink at the bar stood frozen, a glass of whiskey and ice grasped in her left hand, which shook slightly. The glass dropped, hitting the floor with a thud, spilling the brown liquid onto the thick white carpet. Salt's eyes flicked between the two girls while the gun he held remained trained at the man.

'I want to see the boss of this establishment,' Salt said, 'and you're gonna help me.'

The man stared at Jane, with what she felt to be hatred, disgust and contempt all at once. His hair was short, black and flecked with grey. His arms were long and thin while a gold watch hung on his wrist. His chest and belly were flaps of empty skin covered in grey curly hairs. 'How the fuck should I be able to help you?'

'You know what Chopper Read said about chopping off fingers?' said Salt. '"Use bolt cutters; they just pop right off."'

The man stared at the floor.

'I can't hear you, ya slime ball.' Salt tramped over to where the man knelt. He pushed the barrel against the man's neck. 'It's been too long since I killed a man.'

'What do you want me to do?' The man sounded sulky, resigned.

'We want information,' said Jane. She was filled with anger. She didn't like being in the room. It made her feel trapped, it was filled with the smell of ether, and Salt seemed to be enjoying himself too much. 'We want to know what happened to Anya Ivanova, an underage prostitute.'

'I don't have a fucken clue what you're talking about.'

'Horse shit,' said Salt. 'Take us to the Pimp. And I'll tell you again I'm a mad bastard with a death wish and if I think you're trying to fuck with us there'll be more than good whiskey staining your flash floors. Now get your glad rags on. Jane, grab me a couple of those full proof bottles of grog.'

Jane went over to the bar, grabbed a couple of bottles and stuffed them into the pack while the man put on his trousers and buttoned his shirt with shaking fingers. The two girls watched, still as lizards.

They exited the room and the man led them down the hall around a corner and up to a set of wooden double doors. The man looked around, pale, frightened. Salt flashed the security card over the electronic lock and pushed. The doors swung open. Salt, the muzzle of his gun pressed to his captive's temple, entered. And Jane, feeling like she was walking into a trap, followed. The doors swung shut behind her.

They walked into a large room with a wooden floor, and a long, glass bar opposite the door. Against the wall and adjacent to the bar, two elegant divans were placed at right angles to a rectangular glass coffee table. Bonsai willow trees grew from pots, placed at every corner and a large abstract painting hung on the far wall, a mess of different coloured ticks and dashes.

A woman lounged on one of the divans. She was dressed in a sleek black strapless dress. She had a tangled main of dark red curls that framed her pinched, pale face. Over which her thick red lips formed a sensual smudge. A bottle of whiskey sat on the table beside a half-filled glass. A laptop computer also rested on the table and the woman held a phone in her hand.

Salt kicked the man who had led them to the room in the back of the knees so that he fell forward. 'You mob need to think about getting better security. Drop your phone, love. I can see your fingers.'

'Well if it isn't Jack Salt,' said the woman, and she laughed, a high pitch hysterical laugh. She placed the phone on the table. 'I always welcome an old buddy. You could have come and asked for me at reception instead of breaking in and disrupting me in the middle of a game. But you never were one for tact, were you now, big boy? Very sweet of you to pop by all the same. Looking a bit worse for wear though eh, Salty? And what's this? You have a little hippy girlfriend.' The woman laughed again. 'How sweet.'

Salt seemed suddenly unsure of himself. Jane watched as the two exchanged a long look.

'Becks,' Salt eventually said, 'I should've known that you would be behind this somewhere, ya two-faced molly. You seem to have come a long way from your back-alley twenty-buck blow-jobs.'

The man who had led them there looked up at Salt from the floor.

'Don't worry, Hal,' Becks cooed, 'Salty doesn't mean it offensively. It's just his manner. Now, farm boy. Have a drink and a line, and tell Becky what you came for.'

'What happened to Anya, Becks, ya groomed her for it didn't ya, ya greedy bitch? Was Kat not pulling the doe anymore?'

'Oh, I see,' said Becks, 'Sweet little Anya – the absent surrogate father returns. Hal, be a dear and bring us a couple more glasses from the bar. Come on now, Salt, have a seat. You too, camera girl. And let's have a chat about darling Anya.'

'Stay where you damn well are, mate, or paint the floor red.' Salt said to Hal as he made to rise.

Becks sighed and took a sip of her drink. 'Anya practically begged me to take her on. If I hadn't of given her work she'd be on the street selling her arse for a fraction of her value for a two bit North Side pimp. I did the girl a favour. Have a seat.'

Salt pulled his rag from his pocket, doused it in fresh ether from a small glass bottle, grabbed Hal by the hair and anaesthetised him. He then padded across the room and took a seat on the divan. Jane slid in beside him. But she couldn't help feeling like a fish caught on a line and being slowly drawn to the boat to be gutted. She watched the red haired woman and wondered what her connection to Salt was.

Becks remained oddly calm, and spoke in a voice that sounded more flirty than frightened. 'Salt! What have you done with Hal?'

'He'll wake up in a few hours with a hell of a hangover.'

'He'd better. He's a high paying regular. Drink?' Becks pointed to the bottle on the table. 'It's double malt.'

'No.'

Becks turned inquiringly to Jane, watching her with a glassy stare. Jane was reminded of fox eyeing a plump rabbit.

'Thank you, I don't drink,' she said, and felt quite silly like she was casually turning down a drink at a party.

'No? Perhaps you would like a line of coke?'

'I'll be fine, thanks.'

Becks giggled. 'She's perfect, Salt. Where did you find her?'

'Keep your claws off her.'

'Somebody's jumpy, ok, ok. So you came to find out about Kat's little girl did you? And decided to leave a trail of destruction on your way in. Well, I'm afraid I can't help you, big boy.' Becks leaned forward, slid her hand almost seductively across the glass table, plucked a cigarette from a packet and lit it with a zippo. 'Anya quit a month ago, said she didn't need me anymore. I begged her to stay on, of course. Men will pay a lot for girls her age.' She offered a false smile. 'I suggest you go and pay her a visit instead of rampaging through my little community. If you leave now I might just forgive you.'

'Anya,' said Salt, 'is dead. Somebody killed her, and I want to know who.'

'Really?' Becks seemed more curious then sympathetic. 'I can't help you there either. I hate violence. That's why it's good to be working with the rich, less messy stand overs. Don't look at me like that, Salt. I didn't bloody kill her.'

'No, but you bloody well tied the noose. Who was the last client to see her?'

'Salt!' Becks giggled nervously and waved her cigarette at him, 'We have a strict code of anonymity here. The clients pay the money and we ask no questions.'

'Horse shit.' Salt punctuated this sentence with a shot from the gun. The bullet smashed through Becks's whiskey glass sending shards and yellow liquor over her face and dress. Salt stood and lifted the coffee table, flipping it onto to the floor – broken glass, liquor and laptop mingled on the wooden tiles.

Salt grabbed Becks by the hair and pushed the barrel of the gun against her temple. 'I'm not here to fuck around. Tell me what you know, unless you want to cash in your face insurance.'

Salt's voice lost the jocular calm that Jane associated with her captor. He had shouted the words and his voice shook with rage. Jane worried that he really would shoot the woman. And she wondered how long it would take before the rest of the club security arrived.

'Anya went behind my back,' Becks screamed the words back at Salt. 'The little bitch made a private deal with a client. I told you the fucken truth. I don't know his name, Anya did call work for some super-rich cunt. A driver picked her up and dropped her off. I just handled the cash.'

'What was the address?'

'Fuck you.'

'Tell me the address, Becks. You wouldn't let a little goldmine like her waltz off without knowing where she went. Spit it out, Becks, the address.'

'302 Dead Horse Road.'

'Let's get out of here,' said Jane. She stood up and headed toward the door.

Salt didn't move. He kept the gun pressed against her head. 'Give me one reason why I shouldn't pull this trigger.'

The woman didn't speak.

Jane walked back. She touched Salt's shoulder. 'Come on,' she said, 'let's go. Let her be. She's not worth it.'

Salt shook as he released his hold on Becks and slipped the gun into his pocket. Jane hurried toward the door. Salt followed.

They ran back the way they'd come along the tiled floors, past the bonsai trees, and no one stopped them as they ran out into the night, into the shadows cast by the yellow moon.

Dead Horse Road, narrow and winding, weaved its way through the rolling hills on the west side of the Balloong River, and the old white van rattled its way past patches of scrub and open pasture. The yellow moon sliced through the thin shreds of cloud and lit the contours of the hills and valleys with a colourless light. It was a land of sleeping sheep, whispering trees and watchful owls; the two companions didn't speak but gazed at the unfolding land as they drove.

'Here we are,' said Salt, '302.'

He parked the van outside a pair of grand iron gates and the two trespassers climbed out to stare at the high concrete wall that bordered the property. Salt gave Jane a boost and she was able to scramble over the wall, hang and drop onto the other side, jarring her feet as she landed.

The section beyond contained a vineyard with rows of grapes stretching up a hill, on the top of which was a large house. The driveway was made of white rock that shone in the night and cut a straight line between the gate and the mansion; it was lined on both sides by young olive trees. For the second time that night Jane felt the illicit thrill of breaking in, a peculiar pleasure that she experienced from being somewhere she shouldn't.

'Anything to fix a line to?' said Salt.

'Yes.'

The knotted rope hit the wall on Jane's side with a thud. She secured it with a bowline to the one of the posts that secured the rows of grapes. Salt soon joined her and together they followed the line of olives to the house on the hill top.

The building was a pseudo Mediterranean affair – three storeys built from grainy concrete ending in a flat terraced roof with a commanding view of the land receding back toward the sea. The lights were out and it seemed that nobody was home. They moved to the back of the building where there was single glass sliding door. Salt took off his coat, placed it against the door, picked a large rock from the landscaped garden and threw it against the pain of glass. The door shattered. Salt rolled inside, an alarm began to ring and the building began to flash red.

Jeremy Patterson was spending a balmy night in the back room of a Singapore restaurant. The banquet had been spectacular, with dish after dish cooked to perfection, dumplings, steamed bamboo shoots, roasted duck, roasted pork belly, sautéed shrimps, bluefin tuna, buttered clams, sweet cakes and shark fin soup. Patterson knew the Chinese way – impress with displays of wealth. Evade the negotiations, and then finally, after a round of serous drinking, a deal would be made. It would then be ironed out later behind the scenes.

It was almost the opposite, mused Patterson, to the frank, jocular and matey way that Australians did business. Where the Chinese required a structured protocol and tended not to speak directly to the issue, Australians had no protocol and got directly to the point. The only similarity was the booze.

The negotiations had reached an impasse. The Chinese wanted the woodchips cheaper and would accept fronting the capital for the necessary investment, or they would accept the higher price of the wood but provide no capital. Both of these positions impacted Patterson's bottom line. It was at this point of deadlock that his phone rang, and he was glad of an excuse to leave the table. Let them simmer over it, he thought, while I look busy.

The call was an automated one from his comprehensive security system. Somebody had broken into the house on Dead Horse Road. Patterson felt a creeping concern that had nothing to do with the Chinese.

Salt sat at the kitchen table seemingly unperturbed by the flashing lights and the screaming sound of the alarm. He was eating tiramisu ice cream from a tub they had found in the freezer and drinking wine from a bottle he had taken from a rack. The house was clearly some kind of holiday residence, but even still it seemed bizarre that they had found nothing to identify the owner, no letters, no books, no cards, no shopping lists. Everything seemed like it had been placed in the house for the sake of it and barely used, including the stocked fridge and wine rack.

The lower storey of the house had two kids' rooms, stocked with toys. The second storey was an open plan lounge and kitchen, containing more alcohol than food, a set of soft couches and a flat screen TV. The third storey had a master bedroom, a balcony and a spa pool. Everything was tidy, clean and devoid of any personal touch which might have offered a clue to the owner's identity. It seemed more like a hotel than a residence. The only thing of mild interest was a locked cupboard in the bedroom, containing a number of sex toys, vibrators, whips and a collection of pornography that featured 'barely legal' models. All they had learned was that the owner presumably had a family, had a thing for young women and liked his drink.

'The cops will be here soon.' Salt shouted over the sound of the alarm and pointed with his spoon at the flashing light. 'We'd better get going.'

Jane felt dejected. They had come a long way out here and learned very little. She was frustrated and Salt's sudden indifference annoyed her and the screeching of the alarm made it difficult to think, and it felt like her ear drums were about to explode. 'I'm going to have one more look at the bedroom,' she yelled.

Jane ran up the carpeted stairs to the bedroom. There was a king sized bed against the wall, an empty wardrobe, the locked cupboard, and two bedside tables. A glass sliding door opened onto the balcony. Jane sighed. There were no clues here. She was about to run back downstairs when something caught her eye. Perhaps it was nothing, but as the light flashed red she saw that the carpet on the floor had been ruffled beside one on the bedside tables. Like something had been dragged across it. The bedside tables were solid white cubes, and looking more closely, Jane saw that it was on a slight angle to the wall. It was probably, she reasoned, nothing but it aroused her curiosity, and she moved over to the bed and pulled the table away from the wall – it was heavier than she had anticipated.

Jane felt her heart skip a beat. On the wall behind where the table had been, a small safe had been built into the wall. It had a circular dial with numbers zero to nine running along the outside of it. She stared at it for several moments while the alarm still shrieked in her ears. This was interesting, but she had no way of opening the safe.

She was about to call Salt when a thought occurred to her: the series of numbers that had been written on the back of the photograph at Anya's house. Jane turned on her camera and scrolled back through the photographs till she found it, and there it was, captured on camera, a series of numbers scribbled with blue pen against the glossy white paper. Jane turned the dial to each number in sequence. She heard a click, pulled the door of the safe and it opened without resistance. She reached her hand into the black cavity. It appeared at first to be empty and then her hand settled upon it – a simple, A5 notebook. She drew it out. It had a black leather cover that clipped together to hold it closed.

'Show a leg, snot face,' Salt yelled from the foot of the stairs. 'We have to make like diarrhoea and run.'

Lui sat by the fire in the yurt, his thoughts lingering on the dead girl. Possums fought, currawongs sang, and Old Mad Mark muttered in a drunken sleep. The afternoon and evening had brought peace to Camp Balloong. The contractors had stuck to themselves, and Lauren seemed confident of their cooperation. They had eaten a communal dinner of lentil and barley soup. Most of the activists, tired from their long night and day, had fallen asleep early. But Lui couldn't sleep, so he sat by the fire thinking of the dead girl and listening to the sounds of the forest. The flap of the yurt opened and Holly, Jeanette's photographer, walked in. She looked around as if bored and sat down by the fire close to him. She was a perfect, tall blonde, who seemed often shy next to her flamboyant friend.

'Can't sleep either?' asked Lui. 'Would you like a cup of herbal tea?'

'Sure.'

The activist knelt forward, took the stainless steel teapot from the edge of the fire and poured the tea into a jar. 'You know why anarchists only drink herbal tea?'

'Why?' asked Holly, taking a tentative sip.

'Because proper-tea is theft.'

Holly smiled politely. 'Very funny. Got anymore?'

'What's the difference between an Australian and a piece of cheese?'

'What?'

'Leave a piece of cheese in the desert for two hundred years and it develops culture.'

Holly snickered, but without genuine mirth.

'Have you seen the moon?' asked Lui.

'Mmm, it's very yellow.'

'Maybe that's why we can't sleep.'

'I don't think it's the moon,' she replied. 'Well for me it's not. It's the forest. It scares me, and not in an icky way like it is for Jeanette. It's so dark in there and the trees sometimes look like they have faces, or I think that they're listening to me. Sometimes at night I think they don't like me, and they try and trip me up or turn me around, or I imagine there are other things in the forest. Evil things. I'm not like you. I like the city. I like people. It scares me up here.'

Lui looked at the glowing coals of the fire and pictured the face of the dead girl. 'It's not the forest I fear,' he said.

The van rumbled to a halt, at the end of a sandy drive. In the light of the moon, Jane could see that they were outside an old farmstead. No lights came from the farmhouse, and the open door looked like the maw of a lonely ghost, whose eyes were the windows, visibly broken in the yellow witch-light. Its skin was the fading whitewashed wood. Long grass spread over the ground, and silver barked ghost gums, loomed over the van. They'd escaped.

She had expected that police would catch them up and they'd be caught and arrested. But it hadn't happened. Salt had driven through a maze of country roads, nobody had stopped them, and Jane had in her pack a notebook, a notebook that was valuable enough to be kept in its own safe. She hadn't told Salt about her discovery. She wanted to know more about its contents before she mentioned it. And she wasn't sure if she trusted Salt. Jane wanted to know who killed the girl and why her body had ended up in the logging coupe. She believed that Anya's death was somehow connected to the forest and that drew her on, enticed her. But Jane had no interest in being an accomplice in a madman's vendetta and she had made up her mind to escape from Salt as soon as the possibility presented itself.

'Where are we?' she asked.

'The family farm.' Salt hopped out of the van and stretched.

'We're not going to sleep in there, are we?' Jane pointed to the farmhouse.

'Not unless you want to be eaten by the ghost of the old girl. You can sleep in the van if you like. I'm just gonna roll up in a tarp underneath one of them trees.'

Jane slithered out of the passenger seat and onto the damp grass. 'Do you believe in ghosts?' she asked.

Salt did not answer straight away. The wind shook the silvery leaves of the gums. 'I met a kalka, a medicine man, in Arnhem Land who could sing a person to death on a didge. Then there is the Gadachi Man. He is everywhere. He is nowhere. He wears a koala skin cloak, and boots made from emu feathers. His skin is as black as night, and his eyes are red like the coals of a fire, and you had better be careful for he will take your soul. Yeah, I seen too many ghosts to not believe in them.'

As Jane drifted to sleep in the back of the old white van the Gadachi Man entered her dreams. He squatted on the bough of a tree, gripping it with his feathered feet. He looked at her and his eyes glowed red. He lifted a bony hand to his lips and blew dust in her face.

And she dreamed. She dreamed she was in a bedchamber. It was a plain wooden room with a bed at one end. A thylacine rug lay on the floor, and the head of the dead beast stared at Jane. There was one window, mostly covered by curtains of red brocade, but Jane could see that behind them iron bars were set into the wall. Sitting on a low stool by the window was the woman with the facial tattoo. The woman she had seen in the vision at the psychic's. She was dressed in a white linen petticoat, and a low-cut whalebone corset. Her thick curly hair cascaded over her shoulders. She was smoking from a long wooden pipe, lighting it with the stub of a candle that sat on the floor beside her.

A key sounded in the lock and the man, Grey, whom she had seen in her previous vision entered. He closed and locked the door behind him, placing a large iron candle holder with six smoking whale oil candles on the floor. He sat on the bed and beckoned for the woman to approach. She slid from the stool on to her hands and knees and crawled over to the man. And as she turned toward him, Jane saw that her exposed shoulders were covered in weeping red welts. She kissed the thighs of the man and while she worked on him she sang and the sound was sad like the tide clawing at the beach.

Grey grasped her hair strongly in his fist, roughly pulling her head back so that her face looked up into his. 'You black bitch. I think you have cast a spell on me. All day I think of nothing but your hot, sinful flesh. Is it true what the sailors say, that you are a witch?'

Chapter 8: Sunday

It was in the early hours of the morning when the carnage finely stopped. The rioters had either been arrested or had fled, and Sergeant O'Connell surveyed the damage. Wellington Street was back under the rule of law and order, but it had violent. Once the looting had started more people, who O'Connell would have described as criminal types, had come into the city intent on looting the Wellington Street shops. Only large quantities of pepper spray and liberal use of Tasers had finally dislodged them. The paddy wagons had been filled to capacity. Twenty police and over a hundred protesters had been injured and the damage to property would be a hefty bill to insurers and local government.

A young aide appeared, bringing O'Connell a hot coffee, from which he took an appreciative sip. It was time to talk to the superintendent. Something needed to be done. If they did not want more anarchy in Port Town, they would have to give a little, ease up. O'Connell would do his best to make sure of that.

It was morning tea time at Camp Balloong, and the activists drank tea and ate stew. Lui was concentrating on eating. Jeanette and Holly were wrapped in matching woollen blankets and Jeanette was typing something on a small laptop. Tom the anarchist lounged on the cushions at the back of the yurt, and Lauren was talking to Goldy.

'Well that's why I prefer a moon cup. Everything else has the problem of waste, especially up here, and I've yet to find biodegradable pads.'

'I know,' said Goldy. 'I just don't find them comfortable. They're kind of weird, and big.'

'But you can collect your blood,' said Lauren. 'When I was back down on the farm I used to put it into a bucket, ferment it and use it for fertiliser.'

Goldy wrinkled her nose. 'That's a bit gross, isn't it?'

'Well, there's no need to be like a Boob Brain,' Lauren rolled her eyes meaningfully in Jeanette's direction. 'It's the richest part of our bodies, all that goodness, all that moon juice.'

'Lauren,' said Lui, 'we're trying to eat.'

'Do the natural processes of women disgust you, Lui? Are you trying to oppress me with your patriarchy, and stop me from discussing my body, my sacred womanly body? I will not be oppressed.'

Lauren was interrupted by the sound of a vehicle as it pulled in to the Camp Balloong parking bay, but no alarm came from Front Watch and the activists took their tea and stew with them as they filed outside to greet the newcomers. Lui watched as a rough looking guy with a split lip, and thick dreadlocks walked up the road. Behind him was a squat man, with a stubbly chin, a ruddy alcoholic face and a black eye. He was wearing a red T shirt, emblazoned with a soviet flag. Behind them walked Nails and Warwick.

'So we are the first.' The guy with the split lip declared as he glared at the welcoming party. He reached into his pocket and pulled out a near empty tobacco pouch, and grinned at Jeanette, 'who's the babe?'

'Babe?' repeated Lauren, 'Chris, does this look like a brothel to you? I object to your chauvinism. Jeanette's a woman too —'

'At least I don't collect my own period blood,' said Jeanette.

'— And the first of what?' Lauren continued to address Chris. 'The first retards to have a head butting competition?'

'We're the first of the refugees,' said Chris. 'There's a bit of an exodus from town. This is Herb. He's a shit stirring commie, and we're the vanguard of the reinforcements. I see you've got some tea on the brew?'

Chris tried to sidle past the welcoming committee and into the yurt.

Lui blocked his way. 'Good to see you, Chris. It's been a while, mate.'

Chris took his hand. 'Yeah, you too, Lui. Good to see you and Lauren are still keeping it real.'

'Pleased to see everybody's looking happy,' said Nails, as she arrived. 'Let's go inside – there's a lot to discuss.'

'So you've been in a riot, and now you're leading every cop between here and Uluru to bust us for sheltering fugitives?' Lui paced the yurt, while the others stood or sat, drinking tea and listening.

'Don't be ridiculous, Lui,' said Nails, from where she sat on an upside down crate near the bookshelf. 'Camp Balloong is here for this reason. We're here to save the bush. For that we need people, and we need them now. We have information that the government plans to begin clear felling in the Balloong Valley next week. That means all that precious work that we've done will come to fuck-all. All those trees and possums you love so much, Lui, they'll be nothing but piles of burning waste. We need every person we can get, and still we won't have enough. Thankfully people are pissed off, and after the protest, mobilised. A fair few are coming up.'

'Wish I'd been at the protest,' said Tom the anarchist, seated on a cushion at the back of the yurt. 'I love the smell of burning bacon.'

Lui was picking his teeth with a stick, still pacing. 'Next week you reckon, eh. Shit. Well I guess you're right. We'll need everybody we can get. But if you don't mind me asking, how do you know?'

The four newcomers were silent, the embers in the hearth crackled, light rain spattered off the yurt, Jeanette's fingers whirred rapidly across her keyboard. Holly sat next to her, fiddling with her camera.

'I told them,' said Warwick who was standing close to the entrance. 'I was working for forestry, spying on you. I was privy to some information. But —' he looked at the ground and drew in the dirt with his foot. 'I was wrong to betray you – I feel that I belong here.'

'What the fuck are you doing here then?' said Tom, and he stood up.

Lauren also stood.

'Hold it,' said Nails. 'Warwick has provided us with some interesting information. I'm convinced of his sincerity. I've assured him of his safety here. We need everybody we can get, and he is more useful than some.'

'He proved himself last night,' added Chris, quietly, he too stood close to the entrance.

At that moment the calm, and always-ready-to-see-the-good-side, Goldy seemed to explode with rage. She stepped forward from where she had been sitting at the back of the yurt. White lipped and shaking, she pointed her finger at Warwick and shouted. 'You arsehole! You wanker! I brought you here. I trusted you. I invited you into my tent. Did you just snuggle up with me, did you get close to me, did you fuck me just so you could sell us out?' Her voice shook and quavered as it reached a crescendo. 'You cowardly prick. How much did they pay you to fuck me? You cunt.'

Warwick held his head in his hands in shame.

Goldy left the yurt, pushing past Chris and Warwick, out into the daylight. She was followed by Holly and another girl, Ellen.

'I guess Warwick can't stay after all,' said Lauren. 'Camp Balloong is a safe place for women.'

Nails looked troubled.

'I've got an idea,' said Chris. 'What if Warwick stays confined to Rat

Camp. I'll stay there too.'

'Did you not hear me, Chris?' said Lauren.

'Maybe some kind of compromise is possible,' said Lui. 'I mean Warwick's here now after all. We'll talk to Goldy about it. If there's no solution, well I guess somebody will have to take him back to town.'

Nails nodded in approval, and it seemed to Lui that she was eager to move the meeting on. 'That sounds fair.'

'I think Warwick should leave right now, that's if he wants to keep his pretty face,' said Lauren. Tom hooted in approval, but the spy had already gone before she had finished speaking. He'd slunk off into the forest without a word. The activists were silent for a few moments, the circular space buzzing with the electricity of emotion.

'Where's Jane?' asked Lui.

Nails got up from her seat on the crate and walked over to the fire to refill her cup with steaming tea before returning. 'We don't know. The cops wanted her, and badly. But, according to Warwick, she managed to evade arrest and is hiding somewhere.'

'Jesus,' said Lui, 'shit's gone mental.'

'Mmm,' said Nails, 'But there's more, Jane was onto something. She managed to trace, with Chris's help,' Chris grinned, 'the trail of the dead girl to the Vitoria Club, some kind of high class brothel. As soon as Warwick told his boss what we were up to, or what Jane was on to, the state came down like a ton of bricks. The house in which the girl lived was burnt. Jane, Chris and I all had our houses raided. They tried to arrest Jane, and when I go to a peaceful protest the next day I'm met with a wall of riot police. Coincidence? Somebody wants us to shut up about something.'

'They also took Jane's cousin into custody,' said Chris.

Old Mad Mark began to cry – a spitting, wailing, gurgling noise. 'She's such a beautiful girl. So strong, so beautiful. What've they done with her? They'll kill her like the dead girl in the coupe. They'll take her soul.'

'Don't worry, old mate,' said Chris, leaving his position by the entrance and walking over to comfort the old man as he rocked back and forward.

'She'll be back. She promised.'

'Well seeing as we're all sharing good news,' said Lui, 'I may as well mention that we've been having issues of our own. Vigilantes attacked Camp the night before last, and long story short they're still here. They destroyed the satellite phone and gave Lauren a head injury though she reckons they're all right, but the rest of us – well they could attack at any time. So now that you're here we can drive into mobile range and get rid of them.'

'Why should we do that?' asked Nails.

'Well they're a drain on resources for a start,' said Lauren.

'And they're a threat to our security,' said Lui.

'More importantly,' said Jeanette, 'poor Johnno's got a fractured leg and he's sick.'

'Poor Johnno,' murmured Lauren, her voice saturated with sarcasm.

'Have you questioned them?' asked Nails.

'About what?' said Lui in an irritated tone.

'Well for a start ya could have found out if this good-old-boy Johnno knows anything about forestry's plans, but you could also have found out if they knew anything about what we saw in coupe D67. The guys who dumped that trash looked like contractors after all. Let's not give away our hostages so quickly.'

'Hostages?'

'I'm sorry, Lui. It's been a long night. I just want to question them first. That's all.'

'You'll have better luck conversing with a rock than good ol' Johnno,' said Lauren.

'Did you bring any food supplies?' Lui asked, abruptly changing the subject.

'Yeah,' said Chris, 'we hit a bin. All the good shit from the dumpster. We hit gold – boxes of fresh fruit and veg, sweet potatoes and potatoes. We also got large trays of feta and sundried tomatoes, a heap of French sticks, some buns —'

'You mean,' said Jeanette, 'that you got it out of a rubbish bin?'

Chris scowled. 'You don't have to eat it. But I promise you it's in perfect nick.'

'I think I'll stick to the lentils for a little bit,' said Jeanette.

'Did ya bring any goon?' croaked Old Mad Mark, in a miserable voice.

'You're in luck, old mate,' said Chris. 'Chateaux de Cardboard is now available at the Hotel de Long Grass.'

Salt had woken Jane early in the morning and, after they'd eaten white bread with peanut butter, he had shouldered his pack, locked the van, and led her past the ghost gums to the dilapidated farmstead. In the light of day Jane saw that it was just a rundown old farmhouse with faded white wash and broken windows. At the back of the house was a tap.

Salt turned on the tap, splashed the water over his face and snorted snot into the rusty basin. 'Ya want a quick wash?'

Jane looked sceptically at cold, swirling water. It was hardly her idea of a nice wash. But she felt so crusty and fancied she could even smell her own armpits, and her teeth felt like they were covered in a thick coating of fur. Salt was looking at her expectantly. 'Yeah all right then. Do you mind?'

'Oh shit, sorry,' said Salt, 'Must of lost my manners somewhere between here and Queensland.' He turned and walked off around the side of the house.

Jane took the cracked yellow bar of soap that sat on the edge of the basin and began to clean herself in the freezing cold water. She dried herself off on her hoody. She had just got her clothes back on and was rummaging in her bag when her fingers touched the leather cover of the diary. She gave a quick look around her; Salt was nowhere to be seen. She drew the diary out of the pack and opened it.

'Finished putting on your war paint?' Salt's voice from close by.

Jane hurriedly thrust the diary back into her pack. 'Yip, so this land is yours?' She waved her arm, indicating the farmstead.

'That's right, the old girl gave me the land, the house and a couple of horses. One of the big reasons I came back was to take care of the two of them. The stallion is a big old boy, but he's a bit lame and he's calmed a lot. We'll see if he's ready to come out of retirement. I also got a dappled mare, she's a bit more feisty, hard to stop her once she's running.'

'What's the plan?' asked Jane.

'They'll be after us, the cops, the club, the rest of them. We've gotta take the horses and go bush. Can ya ride?'

Jane hesitated. Should she follow Salt into the bush? Why did he want her with him. 'I've ridden before,' she said, 'well, when I was in a pony club back in primary school. So not really.'

Salt led them past another stand of eucalypts to the edge of a paddock with a stable at one end. The two horses trotted over to greet the two fugitives. Salt fed them some oats and stroked their heads. The mottled horse whinnied and trotted around. But the brown stallion seemed extremely placid and Jane stroked his snout.

Salt coaxed the horses to the stable, feeding, watering them, and checking their gums. They packed tarps, blankets, and some food into the saddlebags. The horses didn't fight the saddle or the bridle, and after several fails and laughter from Salt, Jane managed to clamber onto the back of the old brown stallion, and slide her feet into the stirrups. The horse whickered underneath her and she leant forward and rubbed his ears.

'I think I'll call you Old Brown,' she said.

They rode the horses out of the paddock with Jane clinging to the saddle with her thighs, just as she'd learned all those years ago. Despite nearly losing her grip a few times, Jane got used to the rhythm of the horse's trot as they rode in the direction of the bushy hills.

They rode through a ghostly blue-grey sea of stringy barks and thorny bushes. Here the land was dry, and the trees sparse. The ground was rough and hard, littered with spiny sticks and long strips of bark. Bull ants ran to and fro, their pincers high. Large blood sucking horse flies buzzed around the horses ears or landed on Jane's hands. She had to spur Old Brown on, and struggled to keep control of the reins, when he stopped to sniff at a wombat hole or the small blue flowers that dotted the landscape. They passed through areas that had been burned – evidence of seasonal fires, where new shoots of eucalypts shot up around the charred stumps.

As they gained altitude the landscape began to change, and the horses waded through slopes thick with button grass and tea tree. Eventually they came out onto the summit of a high hill and a fresh wind caught Jane's hair. She felt invigorated despite her aching thighs. The land was beautiful. She was riding. She was free. Salt dismounted and tethered his mare to a stunted blue gum, while Jane tumbled off the back of Old Brown.

'We'll rest here for a bit,' said Salt, as he stroked the mare's muzzle and fed her some oats from the saddle bag.

The two travellers rested their backs on clumps of button grass, while they drank water and chewed on jerky.

'Salt?'

'What?'

'Where are you taking us?'

'There's a hut in the hills about a day and a half's ride from here. We'll bunk up there until things cool. I owe you one for putting me on to the Vitoria Club.'

The two chewed in silence for a short while. Salt seemed distant. She wanted to talk to him but couldn't think of how to connect.

'Why did you join the army?' said Jane, after a while.

'I needed to get away, and violence was something I thought I knew.'

'Yeah, but didn't you have a family and stuff, I mean I'm sorry for asking, but what was your life like before the army?'

'None of your business is what it was.'

Jane flushed and anger rose through her. 'Why are you such a mean, untalkative brute? You kidnapped me, and I've helped you. Now you're taking me to woop woop. You won't even tell me a thing about you. I'm going.' She stood up and headed toward her brown horse. She wondered if she had gone too far and the old soldier would do something violent.

Salt stared at the distant hills and when Jane reached her horse he spoke, 'I grew up on the farm. I had a baby sister, sweet as ya like, and the old girl an' old boy loved her. They loved her you see, much more 'an me, being the brown bastard I am. I never held it against her, but when I grew up I had to leave. The old man virtually threw me out the door.

'I went to work in the city and 'cause I was a big boy I got a job as a bouncer for Wild Cats, a seedy club on North Side. That was when I met the Russian girl, Kat, Anya's mother. She was the most beautiful thing I'd ever seen. She had fair skin, fair hair, and eyes as blue as forget-me-nots. I was young and I loved her. I tried to tell her she shouldn't be a working girl, that I'd look after her, and I did, and then Kat had a baby girl. I was on top the world.

'But there was a change in ownership in the gangs of Port Town. My boss got whacked and I was out of work. Kat went back to work in a brothel, and I got so angry one night I lost my temper and I hit her. After that she left me and took wee Anya with her, broke my bloody heart, and I had no money, no nothing anymore so I joined the army, where I learned to kill. And all the time in the heat, in the war, in the desert, in the dust, in the mountains and among black fellas in the north, I remembered my baby girl. And when I heard that the old girl had died I came back south, back to Port Town and went to find Kat and little Anya but they were gone, disappeared like they'd never existed, and nobody cared. Now there's only one thing I want: vengeance.'

A chill wind blew across the hill, and Jane realised she was cold. 'It's a sad story,' she said, and in her mind's eye she could see Salt's daughter, dead, rotting, forgotten. They sat quietly on the hill while the minutes ticked by and then Salt pulled himself up from his sitting position.

'Ya any good at climbing?'

'I'm a professional.'

'Maybe you could climb up one of them blue gums, and tell us which way we should be headed, we wanna be taking the quickest route to the river.'

An expert climber from her days in tree sits, Jane scaled the stunted blue gum. Looking back the way they'd come, she could see the glittering grey expanse of the Pacific Ocean. To her right, thick swamps and wetlands glistened – an impenetrable expanse of mud and pampas. To her left, thick barriers of bushy tea tree and boxthorn blocked their way. In front of her the dry eucalypt forest continued, and she thought she could glimpse the muddy brown bend of a creek in the valley bellow, but how to get there? Jane stared at the rustling blue leaves until she could see what looked like a path, maybe a sheep trail, winding its way down the hill.

The air hummed with the sound of bees as the travellers wove their way through the scratchy bushes, and into the land of eucalyptus and grass trees. Eventually they reached the bottom of the gully, and the horses drank from the cold, murky creek. Jane's legs ached from riding, and they rested briefly on the riverbank, while she pulled seeds from grass stems, threw them onto the water, and watched them float downstream. She felt lonely and she missed her friends. She heard a sound in the grass, and photographed the large, grey, black headed tiger snake as it slithered into the water with a splash.

'How are we gonna cross the creek?' asked Jane.

David Johnston stood and stared out the window, looking at but not seeing the rows of grapevines. Behind him the state premier sat at a dining table munching on a shrimp salad and drinking Bordeaux wine.

Johnston was originally from Liverpool, England. His parents hadn't been particularly well off but they'd scraped together the money to send their only son to varsity to study finance. Johnston, however found that he didn't have the patience for study so he immigrated to Australia where he used his greatest asset, his charm and good looks, to marry his way into local money. His father in law gave him a management job in a transport company. But this position did not sate Johnston's thirst for power. He outsourced most of his managerial work and spent his salary and time giving gifts and sending ingratiating letters to people with power and influence. He gradually won himself a reputation as a glib, unscrupulous and well connected man.

He quit his job at the transport company and began his career as a lobbyist. He carefully grew and maintained his web of connections and with it came the kind of money that his parents had never dreamed of. His ambition had led him to neglect his marriage and his wife had recently divorced him. Johnston was a man who coveted information, which was why he took care to listen to the reports of seemingly insignificant informers such as Warwick. Johnston hated the poor and cherished wealth in the way that only a self-made man can. And his web now reached to the highest level of state government.

'That was a good old chopper ride, Dave. The Forest State is looking good.' The premier loved riding in a chopper, surveying his domain, as he saw it, from the sky. He pushed his plate across the table and sloshed some more wine into his glass. 'What do you want, Dave?' he said.

Johnston turned to face the premier. 'We got a problem.'

'You're a bit pale there, mate. Not drinking enough.' The premier poured some wine into another glass. 'Drink up, tell me your damn problem, and tell me that it's not gonna cost me anything.'

Johnston picked up a wine glass, stroked its bowl and took a good quaff. 'Last night a couple of criminals broke into the Vitoria Club. I believe you're familiar with the place.' He finished the glass with another quaff. 'They were on the trail of client, a mutual friend of ours, J.P. Becks gave them the address to J.P's house up the Balloong which they also broke into, and as I just saw from the security footage, they removed a notebook.'

'Cry me a river, Dave, you didn't give me a round in the chopper to tell me about petty crime. What's it to do with me?'

Johnston gave the premier a meaningful look. 'What do you think J.P. kept in a notebook locked in a bloody safe, in a secret house?'

The premier paused, his wine halfway to his lips. 'Well, fuck me,' he said. 'What are you doing about it? Can't you just bring them in and shut them up, without having to bother me with these headaches. And what on earth did he write shit like that down for anyway?'

Johnston liked the premier, he was a blustery old-school conservative who wasn't afraid to call a spade a spade, and they were qualities which endeared him to his electorate. But he had a love of money and good things, and Johnston knew that his bluster was simply a negotiating position. The lobbyist poured them both more wine. 'J.P. considered it safer then electronic records that could, after all, be hacked. The good news is we know who the intruders are. The man is an army deserter, pretty dangerous and the girl, Jane Thistle, is connected to the forestry blockade in the Balloong.'

'The bloody hippies?' the premier smiled as if thinking of his vocal opponents on the street was a pleasant diversion. 'Won't they ever learn to give up? You know there was riot in the city last night and I'm feeling a bit of heat. I need to throw the public a bone. I'm considering a bill to protect the damn trees. It'll shut the greenies up and make me look like a good guy.'

'You can forget about the poll ratings if that notebook gets into the wrong hands.'

The premier sighed. 'Tell me what you want, Dave, and make it quick. I've got an appointment downstairs with a Thai girl who's got legs up to here, and rack to die for. Whatever you need to make this go away, you got it.'

'A number of concerned parties have come to me about the incident and I've engaged a military contracting company. They're ready to begin searching for the fugitives.'

'You're hiring mercenaries?'

'The contractors understand the need for discretion as much as we do. They're on the scene to apprehend the terrorists. That's all.'

Johnston opened a leather briefcase he'd kept on the ground, drew out a document and slid it, along with a pen, across the table. 'That,' he said 'Is an authorisation for the military operation. The other interested parties will cover the bill for the contractors, but it needs your signature.'

The premier did not pick up the pen or even look at the paper, instead he poured himself some more wine. 'I'm not a legal expert, Dave, but last I heard burglary didn't come under the terrorism act.'

'The operation is pre-emptive. Salt deserted from a military contracting company. There is reason to believe that he is planning an attack. Jane Thistle's house was raided by police two days ago; they discovered that she had contacts to a radical organisation. The pair are dangerous. You'd be acting in the best interests of the state. And here's a sweetener.' Johnston slid his hand into his jacket pocket and pulled out a white envelope, which he slid across the table. 'First class holiday in Thailand for you and your family.'

The premier took the envelope cautiously, skimmed over the paper in front of him and signed it with a flourish at the bottom. 'There you go, Dave, but it sounds dodgy. If it wasn't my arse on the line I wouldn't have touched this authorisation with a barge pole. Anything else I can bloody do for ya?'

Johnston refilled the premier's glass. 'I believe you own some shares in Woodchips Ltd. The situation with the fugitives adds more urgency to the Balloong contract. Once a tree's cut down it may as well be sold. And the Chinese are now interested in the woodchips. We need to send a strong force to break the activist blockade, and push on with logging on schedule.'

The premier relaxed; this was the kind of topic he liked. 'There's another option, Dave.' He waved his glass at Johnston. 'I refuse to renew the tax subsidies to the so called essential forestry industry. Take the wind of out of the greenies' sails. Make me look like the good guy and do my bit for market liberalisation by balancing the budget. What do you think about that? Don't forget if you want to bust this camp, whatever it's called, it'll be us that'll be footing the bill for the cops.'

Johnston knew his cue. 'I think you've been smoking too much of the hippies' grass.'

The premier laughed. 'Another day, another dollar, eh Dave. Now I better be off. If I have any more of this wine I'll be too limp to enjoy that little bombshell downstairs. You're only as old as the woman you're feeling.' The premier manoeuvred himself out of his chair, and oozed his way out the door. Johnston was left staring at the empty bottle of red.

Warwick sat underneath the drooping tarp and watched as the water dripped off it to splash onto the wet ground. He had tried reading his book, Into The Woods: the Battle for Tasmania's Forests by Anna Krien, and it was a good book he supposed, but every time he picked it up to read a line he saw Goldy in his mind's eye – her round face, her wafts of curly hair, her small mouth, her warm smile – and the page simply turned into a blur of black and white, and he could do nothing but dwell on the excruciating pain in his heart. In his restless state he could almost feel Goldy's warmth beside him, her breasts pressed against his chest, her piece of rose quartz that she always wore wrapped in a twine basket, and hung around her neck.

'To give her confidence, and help their love,' Goldy had said.

The pain felt like a claw inside him, twisting, and it suddenly became so much that he wanted to vomit, but couldn't. Fuck her, he thought, fuck me, fuck them. Chris had brought him some wine and he gulped it, but it didn't help, and then the tears began to roll down his cheeks. He had to do something. He had to talk to her, make her realise that it had been genuine. He stood up and walked out into the rain. He played the imaginary conversation in his head; Goldy forgiving him, he telling her how sorry he was. He walked along the trail until he hit the logging road.

He thought about heading up to the yurt but lost his nerve and decided to head for Front Watch instead. When he got to the bridge he saw two big men jump out of the bushes onto the parking bay. They ran to Nails' car.

'Trouble,' Warwick shouted. And he ran across the bridge toward the car. He didn't know what he was going to do. His only thought was that if he somehow stopped them he'd ingratiate himself with Goldy. The door of the car must have been unlocked because the two men opened the doors and got inside. Warwick heard the engine revving as he ran. He was nearly there. Perhaps he'd throw himself on the windscreen. Lauren emerged from Front Watch and also ran to block the car, but it reversed, spitting gravel. It spun around and sped onto the main road before either Lauren or Warwick could stop it.

'The contractors,' said Lauren, 'they've gone. Nails shouldn't have left her keys in the car.' She turned to Warwick. 'What're you doing here?'

Warwick squinted across at her. She was tall and had strong arms. She wore a dirty white singlet, and even dirtier blue jeans. Her brown hair hung past her neck in a loose ponytail, and her face was disfigured by a bruise. Warwick's vision settled on her shoulder tattoo. A cartoonish goblin, who held a spotted toadstool in one hand and a pair of bolt cutters in the other, stared goggle-eyed back at Warwick.

'Come to snoop around, have you? Come to have a little bit of a spy, get back in the good books of your corporate wank buddies?'

'I wanted to talk to Goldy.'

'Oh is that, feeling like you want to push cock into something, like you haven't done enough damage already. Well she doesn't want to talk to you and don't give me that look like, "poor miserable little Warwick wants to talk to nice Goldy and tell her the truth about why he slept with her for money." Get out of my sight.'

Warwick fled into the trees.

Keeping to the less densely wooded valleys Jane and Salt rode on and as evening began to set in the bush became lusher. Temperate rainforest began to replace the eucalyptus. Myrtles, tree ferns and sassafras took over from grass trees and stringy barks. Jane began to feel the unsettling fear that people experience in the forest at twilight, and her body ached from riding.

'We should look for a place to camp,' she said.

They settled for a flattish spot beneath a big eucalypt that showed evidence of a burn, several years old. Jane remembered being told that the burning of eucalyptus cleared the energy of restless spirits, and she gathered sticks and long strips of bark for a fire, lighting it with matches. She liked the phosphorus smell as they flared, and she blew upon the sticks and bark, placed where the old fire had once charred the trunk of the eucalypt. Soon the flames illuminated the trees above and around, so that their claw like branches appeared to reach toward the light, and the two travellers were surrounded by slowly dancing spirits, swaying and shifting to the crackle of burning bark.

'Do you think that dreams can be real?' asked Jane.

Salt's face seemed different in the light of the fire, older, wrinkled, darker. 'The black fellas believe that the world was created by dreams, the dreams of animals. When the ancient ones walked across the bare land, they dreamed into being the hills, the forests and the rivers. When the dreamtime ended the world became more solid, but still bits of dreamtime echo through. Dreams to the black fellas are as real as rocks and water.'

Jane lay back, closed her eyes, and fell quickly asleep.

Jane stood in a forest of blue gums. A long line of men walked through the trees. They were dressed in light tunics. They wore breeches and leather boots. Each man carried a musket; some had swords and knives. Leather belts hung on their shoulders from which dangled cartridges and powder flasks.

The Palawa appeared from between the blue gums. They carried nothing but long, light spears. They whooped and danced, keeping a distance from the advancing men. One man leapt forward dancing like he was about to hurl his spear. A musket shot sounded and smoke floated through the blue gums, as the line erupted with shot.

When the smoke cleared the Palawa were still there, dancing, just out of the range of the muskets. And as the men knelt to pack the powder into the barrels of their guns, the Palawa sprang forward, screaming, to throw their spears, which sang through the air and sank into the throats and chests of the musketeers. The Palawa fled into the forest.

The dream changed and Jane saw that she was in a grand, high-ceilinged room. Sun streamed in through large gilt-framed windows, and a painting of a sailing ship, riding a wild storm hung on the wall. A middle aged man wearing a decorated military uniform – a red coat with gold tasselled shoulder pads, white breaches and ornate buttons, lounged on a divan. He had a glass of whiskey in his hand and was smoking a pipe. In front of the divan was a low table on which sat an ornate teapot. Grey paced the room. He was dressed in a black tailcoat with white pantaloons tucked into high riding boots. He had a silk cravat round his neck. His black-gloved hands held a china teacup and he was speaking with animation.

'The blacks are causing us nothing but problems. Their fires are a constant threat to our farms. And they have no qualms about stealing livestock or squatting on land. They are discouraging settlement. If a solution is not found the colony will fail.'

'What can be done?' asked the man in military attire. 'The black line is failing, we're losing men. It's near bankrupting the colony, it's raising eyebrows with the colonial office, and the church doesn't like it. This is capital whiskey by the way, Grey. Genuine scotch is it?'

'I import only the best. What we need, Lieutenant Governor,' Grey approached the man on the divan and lowered his voice, 'is to use professionals. Put a price on the heads of the blacks, five pounds for an adult, two for a child. After that, I promise you, we won't have a black problem.'

'The church won't like it, and it must be said neither do I.'

'Damn the church. The future of the colony is at stake. You fought in the battle of Vitoria beside my father did you not, Sir?' Grey poured another glass of scotch for Lieutenant Governor.

Chapter 9: Monday

Lionel exited the black hummer, and surveyed the terrain – a rough, rocky landscape, dry, dotted with tussock and grass trees. The ocean wind blew the boxthorn into wedge shaped clumps, silvery ghost gums shielded the farmstead from the wind and further inland great tracks of stringy bark woodland covered the hills in an airy blue haze.

They had found nothing of particular interest in the van – empty tins of food, some bedding, an old newspaper, a two dollar coin and a photograph of a young fair haired girl. Somewhere out in that tract of wilderness were a couple of rebel terrorists, some anarchist girl and a son-of-a-bitch deserter.

Lionel had no patience with people who threatened the stability of Australia. Down here people didn't seem to realise that the world was at war. Terrorists like those that had blown up the embassy in Jakarta were in their midst, and it was people like him who kept Australia safe. He had fought in Syria and Afghanistan – the bombs, the guns, the hatred. He had seen friends torn apart by suicide bombers and sliced open by

Kalashnikovs. Damned if he would see that happen here. He would find the fugitives and bring them to justice. He took out his Glock, and felt its weight, its balance – nothing wrong with American manufacturing.

'They took horses and headed into the hills. Their trail's clear,' his junior officer reported.

Shit. The company was over stretched and missions like his own were under resourced. 'Make some calls. We need to commandeer a chopper.'

Lauren and Jeanette sat in the Front Watch hut waiting. Front Watch was a poorly named post, for they did not so much watch as listen. It consisted of a banner, which spanned the road, an information hut, and a slightly hidden hut of tarps and cloths, placed back in the bush by the pullover zone.

During a moment of boredom Lauren had calculated that the mean amount of cars per hour for a twenty-four hour period was about zero point seven, most of them on their way to the highland lakes. The two young women sat in silence – Jeanette working on her small laptop, Lauren carving a lizard into one of the polls with her pocket knife. She had been working on the carving for some time, it had been cut deeply and smoothly into the wood.

'That thing hasn't stopped working yet?' Lauren pointed at the laptop.

'Not yet,' said Jeanette, 'I've got spare batteries and I can turn on the car engine just to charge it, but obviously I don't like doing that. With the smashed radiator I keep thinking it's going to explode or something.'

'Do you think you could live without a computer?'

Jeanette closed the lid of her notebook. 'Why don't you like me?'

'I don't not like you.' Lauren stopped carving and looked down at Jeanette.

The journalist stood up, turning her back to Lauren. 'That's not true. Ever since I've arrived you've had it in for me. You're always making jokes and treating me like I'm stupid, especially when the men are around. Not that I care what they think. It gets to me, you know. I wanted to go, remember, and I wanted to go yesterday as well, now that there were working cars around, but Holly talked me out of it. She seems to think there's some reason to stick around. It's funny too because she hates it here, and I actually think it's interesting. But either way, I'm stuck here now and you're not making it any easier.'

Lauren put down the knife she was using to carve and walked over to the young journalist, putting her arm around her. 'I'm sorry,' she said. 'I didn't think you'd take all that crap I said to heart. I can just be a bit of a social retard sometimes. Maybe I've spent too long in the bush. It's ok, there's no drop bears and we don't eat leeches.'

Jeanette gave a slight smile, pulled a silky blue handkerchief out of the pocket of her jeans and blew her nose. 'Thanks, it means a lot to me.'

'Do you hear that?' said Lauren. 'A vehicle coming. Who do you reckon it is?'

Jeanette listened, 'a truck?'

'Na, too low, I reckon it's a van.'

'A government vehicle?'

'Na, too rattly. It's a bomb. Unless it's a redneck-bogan, I'm guessing it's a friendly party.'

As the van pulled up Lauren and Jeanette were standing in the pull over zone to meet it. The van, painted with smudgy murals of mountains and waterfalls, spat a shower of stones as it stopped in the parking zone. Two men and a woman all slithered out from the front seats. The girl was wearing blue, yoga pants, and a flowing blouse. She had long multi-coloured hair entwined with wire butterflies. She danced to the nearest tree.

'Wow,' she said in a tone that suggested genuine amazement. 'It's so beautiful. I can feel its soul.' She laughed. It was an odd laugh, almost hysterical. 'Look at the trees.' She stretched out her arms and stared upwards at the sky, spinning around on the spot.

'Yip,' said Lauren, 'you'll find those in the bush.'

One of the men had long hair that he pushed away from his eyes. He wore a colourful Indian shirt, and fisherman pants. He was taking things out of the van – a hacky sack, juggling balls, a fire staff, devil sticks and a ukulele.

'Wow, look, rocks,' he remarked after placing the uke on the ground. 'Feel them.' He bent over and began running his hands through the gravel.

The third person, a weasely guy, was smoking a large roach. He was dressed in a baggy op-shop suit, and his pupils were heavily dilated.

'Moth,' said Lauren. 'What are you doing here?'

'Wow, wow man, wow,' replied Moth. 'You got to chill that buzz right down, man. That is one tense buzz you got there. We got trippers here, man. You got to be gentle with their trip. They're feeling the love.'

'Drugs are forbidden in camp,' said Lauren.

The man in the Indian shirt had picked up one of the rocks and was studying it with great interest. The girl was standing in the moss.

'I'm standing on an ocean of energy,' she said, still staring at the sky.

'Saying that shit was not good for their trips, dude,' said Moth. 'Don't fuck with people's minds like that. This is Jaxon,' he pointed to the man in the Indian shirt, 'and she's Rainbow. She found her new name in meditation. You can't suppress our freedom of expression. LSD is not a drug, it's a vehicle for spiritual development and as for this,' Moth stamped out the roach, 'this is a medicine, man, prohibition is the real crime perpetrated by big tobacco. I know you mob smoke and drink. Your no drug policy is hypocrisy, sister.'

'It's about community credibility,' said Lauren. 'If the police find drugs here they can dismiss us as common crims.'

The confrontation had begun to bring curious parties down from the yurt. 'What kind of supplies do you have?' asked Lui, who had just crossed the bridge.

'Oh, we got heaps of shit, man. We got an ounce of skunky shit, we got some caps of MDMA, we got some ketamine, and we got a whole sheet of the good stuff, dude.'

'I meant do you have any food?'

'Hey, we know the festival buzz. We brought like heaps of instant noodles.'

Nails had arrived. 'This is not a festival. It's an ongoing political occupation. There's a reason why drugs are not allowed in camp. We have a rigorous PR campaign. If we break the law in one respect it discredits us in the other, and sabotages our ability to effect environmental outcomes.'

'Oh come on, I know you guys smoke pot. What if we just camp in the bushes? We got our own tents and stuff. Town is getting a bit hot at the moment for the small time supplier – the new laws and stuff. I thought I should get out for a bit and these lovely dudes came all the way from Byron Bay.' Moth indicated Jaxon and Rainbow. 'They've been begging me to take them out here.'

Lauren watched the girl with multi-coloured hair as she sat on a mound of damp moss in the half lotus position holding in her hand a flower with a look of intense concentration on her face. Lauren laughed. 'It's fine with me.'

Chris had sidled up. 'Did you say you had an ounce, Moth?'

Nails glared at him.

As the sun continued to rise over camp Balloong more people began to arrive, including Johnny Vegas and a couple of teenage punks, driven to camp by a concerned mother. While Lui was showing people around, doing his best to appear professional and safety conscious, Nails and Lauren moved off to question Johnno.

The contractor camp had not seen much improvement since Lauren had last visited. None of the rubbish had been tidied and the cans were strewn through the forest, giving the impression that they'd been scattered by possums. Johnno was still there. He no longer lay in the tarp structure but sat on a mound. As the activists approached he hawked and spat out a glob of green phlegm.

'So you are Johnno,' said Nails.

'Who the fuck are you?'

'A lawyer, and you're in trouble. How do you fancy being prosecuted for assault and vandalism?'

'How do you fancy shoving a carrot up your greeny arse?'

'How's your leg, Johnno?' asked Lauren.

'Not bloody good.'

'Couldn't make it out with your mates?' asked Nails.

'You got any water?'

Lauren pulled a water bottle out of her pack and came forward to pass it to the contractor.

He took a long swig. 'Yeah, them dipshits pissed off, left me here to goddamn rot. I'm starving. Ya got any real tucker?'

Lauren hopped forward to pass Johnno a French stick. 'Made it especially for you, mate. Feta, sundried tomatoes and salami.'

The contractor bit into the roll.

'How's your fever, Johnno?'

'Better,' but he didn't look it.

'Johnno,' said Nails, 'We're ready to help you, take you up to the yurt. It'll be warm and dry, you'll have good food and we'll make sure you get proper medical care, but I must say, professionally speaking, I'm very concerned about some of the things I've seen in the logging coupes in the upper Balloong.'

'Bloody hell,' said Johnno, 'ya talk like a lawyer too? What do ya want to know, love?'

'What can you tell me about the dumping of industrial waste in coupe D67? We know you were there, Johnno,' she bluffed. 'We took photographs.' Nails stood still, her arms folded, a black sentinel among the green, brown and grey wilderness.

The contractor paused before speaking, his eyes were fixed on the ground and his shoulders were slumped. 'I don't know what you're talking about.'

'You're a bad liar, Johnno. We know you were there, stop dicking us around. I don't want to prosecute you for illegal dumping, well, not unless you open up to us.' Nail's stared straight at the contractor, to where he sat, looking miserable on his damp mound.

He squinted back, then turned his head to spit again. 'Yeah, I dumped the trash, it was a shit house job too. Took longer than we expected, all the shit, from that old woodchipping plant. We got told to get rid of the shit. Took us all day piling tin and asbestos onto the truck.' Johnno pulled up the sleeves of his bush shirt. There were several fresh scars. 'Cut meself a bit doing it, too. Pay wasn't bloody worth it.'

Nails' gaze stayed locked on the contractor who looked away while massaging his big hands. 'Why did you dump it in a coupe instead of taking it to a refuse centre?'

The contractor shrugged. 'We wanted to get the job done. The refuse centre was miles away, already closed.'

A large iridescent beetle dragged itself across the moss. 'Who're you trying to protect, Johnno? Who told you they wanted the rubbish dumped quietly where people wouldn't see it, in a coupe you had scheduled for a burn off?'

Johnno looked up and actually smiled. 'Jesus,' he addressed Lauren, 'and I thought you were the proper ball buster. Yeah, you're right. Dave Johnston gave us the job. I assumed he didn't want to have to pay the tip.'

'Dave Johnston, the lobbyist?'

'That's the slimy cunt.' Johnno cracked his knuckles.

'But he's not your normal boss, is he?'

The contractor took another swig of water. The afternoon sun filtered through the canopy. 'He's good mates with the boss, comes out to visit us on the job with him sometimes. We all know him.'

'What would you say, Johnno, if I told you that within one of the drums in that trash that you dumped was the dead body of an underage prostitute,

Anya Ivanova?'

'I'd say ya had a screw loose woman. I've been honest with you about me job and then ya turn around and call me a goddamn murderer.' Johnno spoke in a low growl, and Lauren thought she heard a hint of a threat in his tone. He squinted back at Nails from out of his ruddy drink damaged face. 'I'll tell ya something for free. I'm not afraid to drop a cunt like a sack o' shit, but I'm no murdering pervert. Yeah, sure I dumped a bit of trash in a logging coupe, but what judge is gonna give a dribble o' cow piss over that?'

'I never said you were a murderer, Johnno.'

'Well, that's something.' The contractor took a bite from his roll. 'Got any more bloody questions?'

'No I think that pretty much answers it.' Nails stepped forward to the mound to offer her hand. She seemed tiny compared to the contractor's bulk. 'I'm Nalia Hunter.'

Johnno paused, and Lauren thought that he'd suddenly strike Nails, but he accepted her hand. 'John Thompson.'

'Lauren, would you be able to help John Thompson to the yurt, and I'll clean up this mess.'

Lauren took Johnno by the arm. He leaned on her, and gritted his teeth as he limped through the forest. He smelled of stale sweat and damp clothing.

'Nice tat,' he whispered.

It was late afternoon when Salt and Jane arrived at the hut in the highlands. They'd ridden all day along forest trails. They'd seen birds and lizards, but no mammals. Several times they'd heard a chopper, flying low over the canopy.

'The boys are looking for us,' Salt had said.

And they'd dismounted and hid underneath trees or bushes to avoid being seen from the air. Jane had felt sure they would be seen, but they'd arrived at the hut without trouble, though her whole body felt raw from riding.

The hut stood in a cleared area surrounded by low bushy tea tree, and eucalypts. The clearing was relatively flat, rocky and covered in patches of grass. The hut was a rectangle built of large stones and had a triangular roof built of tea tree. At one end of the rectangle was a stone chimney.

'This hut,' said Salt, 'was built by the old gold miners. They used it as a way station, bringing supplies up to the gold fields.'

'Who uses it now?' Jane felt so sore she wasn't sure if she was capable of getting off her horse, which was calmly cropping the grass.

The big man slid off the dappled mare. 'The odd ranger.'

Jane tripped in the stirrups as she dismounted Old Brown, grazing her hands as she caught herself on the ground. They tethered the horses to a tree at the edge of the clearing, and entered the hut, dumping their packs on the dry earth floor. The only furniture was some wooden crates, slowing being eaten by woodworm. In these there were a couple of packets of candles, some matches and some old newspapers. They explored the surrounding terrain and discovered a wooden long drop, and a small stream from which they collected water for themselves and the horses. Jane gathered firewood and lit a fire, while Salt sat on a crate, seemingly absorbed in his own thoughts.

'I'm going hunting,' he said eventually. And he hitched up his pants, tightened his belt, hung his coat on the rock wall, and left.

Jane waited until the sound of his boots had faded, then lit the candles, settled on a crate and took the notebook out of her pack. She unclipped the leather clasp and opened it. The first few pages were blank. Then, written in an angular, confident and legible script were the words, 'Outgoing payments'. The entry was dated the first of July in the previous year, to the 30th of June that year, covering the full length of the last financial year.

Jane turned the page. At the top left hand corner was a date. Two lines down from this was written, 'payment type: education, value: $10,000.'

The same confident script continued down the page. 'Payment to: Jonathon White, confirmation of payment: confirmed. Reason for payment: support of private members bill, to streamline environmental approval. Notes: White more than happy to oblige, payment facilitated by Dave Johnston.' Under this was drawn a straight red line, indicating all details of the payment had been entered.

Jane continued to flick through the notebook; each page documented the same kind of thing, one payment to a page. Many were for pretty minor sums to people she didn't know and others didn't give any reason for the payment. But the entry she found most interesting was a gift of a million-dollar home to the premier in exchange for the awarding of government contracts to certain businesses, including the renewal of forestry contracts in the Balloong.

Jane was still immersed in the notebook when she heard the tramp of boots. Salt had returned. Jane hurriedly closed the notebook and slid it into her pack. She experienced a moment of panic as she tried to look occupied and turned to face the empty fireplace.

Salt threw open the door. He had an animal slung over his shoulder. 'Feral goat, there's a few of them in these hills, eat everything.'

Jane held the light while Salt skinned and butchered the goat, with his long bone-handled knife. Jane felt nervous as she clutched the torch; the time had come to tell him what she'd discovered. 'Salt?'

'Uh.'

'I've got something to tell you.'

'Well spit it out.'

'When we broke into that house on Dead Horse Road, well I found something, a notebook.'

Salt pulled the offal out of the goat's belly. 'Go on.'

'Do you know what a slush fund is?'

'Something rich bastards use to keep their pennies secret.'

'The guy who owns the notebook, whose house we broke into, I think he's like a slush fund manager or something because that notebook, it's a catalogue of kickbacks. We've got them. It's all there, who they paid and what for. It's all written down and dated.'

'I guess that's great for you. You get to stick it to the pollies, and when that sack of shit hits the fan, heads will roll. But what good is it to me? It doesn't tell us who the bastard was that killed my daughter.'

Salt didn't look up but began to saw through the goat's haunch, and Jane watched him, hunched over, smelling of death.

'There was one clue, one name that kept cropping up, Dave Johnston. He seems to be some kind of go-between who facilitated a lot of the payments. Find him and maybe you've got your answer.'

The big man started on the other haunch. 'Well, that's something. I guess it's time for us to go our separate ways. I track this guy Johnston and you take that notebook and bring the buggers to justice.'

Jane shivered. It was cold outside.

Salt crouched on the ground, covered in blood, concentrating on his work.

They cooked the goat by roasting it on the fire, and ate it with boiled rice. Jane and Salt were both so hungry that by the time it was cooked they didn't notice that it was burnt in some places while virtually raw in others. It was only once they'd eaten their fill and were drinking hot tea tree tea that the big man seemed more relaxed. Jane broached the subject that had been nagging at the back of her mind for days.

'Salt?'

'Ah ha?'

'You know how I was asking you last night about dreams, and whether dreams can be true?'

'There's nothing wrong with my memory.'

'I know this is gonna sound crazy, but I think I can find out what happened to Anya, your daughter, through dreams, well, visions.'

The light of the fire illuminated the scars on Salt's face, and his eyes were hidden beneath thick bones. 'Go on.'

Jane told Salt about her dreams. She told him what she saw when she first went to the psychic with Sky, and the dreams she'd had since then. She told him how her visions were odd, vivid and recurring.

'What could this story from history possibly have to do with the death of my daughter?' Salt eventually asked.

'I don't know,' Jane admitted. 'I just feel there's a message in these dreams, and if I can only decode it, I'll know what happened to Anya.'

Salt picked his teeth with a fragment of goat bone. 'A few years ago, I'd have told ya to go tell ya fairy tales to someone who gives a shit. But all that time I spent in Arnhem Land – it turned me into a superstitious bastard and when ghosts are trying to tell ya something ya best listen up, so I'm prepared to believe ya, and ya know what? You're in a bit of luck 'cause I know just the person to help. She lives in the hills, along the old mining trail, or she used to, and uses paths that others don't know. She lives in a cave and eats feral goats and bush tucker. She's a half cast, like me, but she knows a thing or two about the dreaming. Yes, we'll see if Old Ra still lives in these hills.'

Evening was beginning to fall around camp Balloong and Nails picked her way through the tree ferns to where Lui sat on a rock staring off into the deepening shade. She crouched on the ground beside him and observed the slender shapes of the myrtles, while an animal, perhaps a devil, snuffled in the dark.

Lui broke the silence, 'Something on your mind?'

Nails didn't answer at first but like Lui gazed at the myrtles. 'It just doesn't make any sense, mate.'

'What doesn't make any sense?'

'The story good old Johnno fed us. I'm sure he's telling the truth, but think about what it implies. Somebody is a psychotic killer. He kills an underage Russian prostitute and dumps the body at the old woodchipping plant. He then tells his lobbyist to tell Johnno to hide it in a logging coupe along with all that other junk. Why? It just sounds ridiculous and any court would chuck it out. Why would you dispose of a body like that? This guy Johnston seems totally entwined in everything – Warwick's point of contact, Johnno's contact. He's the link that connects the strands. But I can't see further than that.'

A cold southerly gust blew through the trees, bringing with it the memory of winter, frost in the forest and snow on the highlands. The tops of the swamp gums swayed and sighed. Lui was silent for moment. 'Evil is faceless, amorphous. The destruction of the forest is evil, but who is the villain? Is it the contractors like Johnno who are paid squat, and don't know better, just trying to get by? Is it the shareholders who own shares in Woodchips Ltd, who just bet on numbers? Is it the executives who are bound by corporate law to maximise profit? Is it the consumers who buy the toilet paper? Is it the politicians who award the contracts? No, it is the faceless machine. It doesn't matter who gave the order, or who held the knife. It was the system that killed Anya, and the system will never, can never, be held to account.'

The light had disappeared from the woods. 'You think too much about it, Lui. Greed is evil. Greed is tangible. Individuals are greedy. And individuals can be brought to justice. We have the body. We have evidence. And we'll have justice. If just for satisfaction.'

'And what then, will the gallows, cure the world of greed? We don't have the body. The day you left to go to town, Tom and I went back to the coupe to find it. I was gonna call the cops. But when we got there it was gone.'

'What do you mean the body was gone?' said Nails standing up, and pushing a clump of moss with her foot. 'We were all there. We all saw it. Jane's got shots of it on her camera for Christ's sake.'

'Well it wasn't there, so somebody must've gone back for it. The rubbish sack was still there torn and blowing in the wind, but there was no trace of the body. You don't even have the photos. They're with Jane, and God knows where she is now.'

'That's really weird. What time was it that you were there?'

'About two.'

'So roughly the same time that Warwick had his conversation with Johnston. He wouldn't have had time to organise the body's removal. I don't understand.'

'Neither do I.' Lui got up and switched on his light, illuminating the myrtles in pale white. 'Let's get warm. It's a cold night.'

David Johnston sat in a comfortable armchair in a Vitoria Club room. He watched, in the dim light, as the Thai girl lay on her back and gracefully removed her pink frilly knickers with her high-heeled feet, and spread her smooth brown legs. She moved her long-nailed fingers slowly over the gently sloping mounds of her breasts and down to the shaven cleft between her legs, where she spread her lips to reveal the pink flesh of her sex. Another topless Asian girl, dressed in white underwear, walked praying-mantis like, over to Johnston to refill his whiskey. She leaned over to pour, dangling her pale breasts, punctuated by hard red nipples, in front of him. She filled his nostrils with the scent of her perfume and he allowed his hands to brush bare skin as he slipped his tip into the band of her skirt. Another girl knelt coyly in front of another man, Jeremy Patterson, and lit his cigarette. He blew the smoke in the direction of the dancer's exposed privates.

Johnston felt somewhat in awe in Patterson. The man was an enigma, a ghost in the business world. He wasn't a CEO and he didn't own a business. He had shares all over the place but rarely attended board meetings. On paper the man hardly existed and yet his subtle influence reached far and wide. Money flowed through him like a river and Johnston could only guess at his net worth. Accounts, tax havens, and currency markets were Patterson's business. He didn't just handle his own money but other people's, which he carefully and anonymously channelled into the hands of politicians, think tanks, and public officials on behalf of his secret clients.

That was where Johnston came in. The two men had been introduced at a private dinner party where they were seated together. Patterson had taken an interest in the ambitious Englishman and had asked him to do a favour by arranging a deal with one Johnston's political contacts. The deal went smoothly. And Johnston found himself taking on greater role in facilitating Patterson's political agenda.

Johnston viewed the man as kind of visionary. Patterson was no free marketeer. Despite his personal aversion to paying tax, Patterson was a firm believer both in subsidies and increased government spending, so long as the subsidies lowered the costs of raw materials and the government expenditure went into pockets of contracting companies in which he owned shares. 'Friedman,' Patterson once confided to Johnston, 'was wrong; the state is an important instrument of wealth creation.'

But Patterson, Johnston had recently discovered, had a weakness. He lusted for young women. It was something he had been sad to discover, for it lowered his opinion of the man he had held as a role model. And it was alien to his own disposition; to Johnston pleasures of the flesh were secondary to the real thrill which was the accumulation of power.

'So everything's cool with our political friends?' Patterson spoke softly.

'Yeah, they're cool. Karl is a sucker for chopper rides, women and profit. We're keeping our contracts. But he's worried about the raid. If that notebook makes it out, he'll go down.'

'I share his concern,' said Patterson, after he'd paused to admire the dancer, who had begun to slowly rotate a finger inside her pink flesh. 'I take it you're doing everything to ensure that it never makes it into, what did that German philosopher call it? The public sphere.'

'The military contractors are onto it,' said Johnston trying not to be distracted by the scantily clad woman massaging his leg. 'It will be destroyed.'

'That's good,' said the man, 'because if it isn't, then the politicians won't be the only ones to go down.' The man lowered his voice to a whisper so that Johnston had to lean in to listen. 'And there was another thing I wanted to ask you about, Dave. A matter of personal concern. I trust that there will be no evidence, of a different sort surfacing in the near future. I'm worried about what's happening up in the Balloong, and I want you to go up there yourself to ensure that nothing goes wrong.'

Johnston didn't answer but took a sip of his drink.

Chapter 10: Tuesday

Lionel struck while the land was still veiled in darkness. They'd located the hut. It hadn't looked like much, just a stone building surrounded by tea tree, but the light and smoke that streamed from it had been easily visible from the air. The dense bush made it impossible to land the chopper, and wanting to catch the occupants unaware, he had opted to parachute. The wind carried them a kilometre to the west where they landed in a thick swamp of introduced pampas and button grass. Muddy and sodden, the military contractors marched through the dark, slippery, dew-sodden forest to position themselves for the attack.

Orange light issued through the cracks in the rickety wooden door and the slit like windows cut into the stone. Covered by the two other officers, Lionel, Glock in hand, ran to the door, kicked it open and flung himself against the stone wall. One of the officers opened fire, spitting bullets from his assault rifle into the hut.

'Hold your fire,' shouted Lionel and he turned to shine his torch inside. The candles burned low, and the embers of the fire still glowed. A tea tree stake had been driven into the floor, and a grisly goat's head had been impaled on its top. A crossbar had been bound to the stake, and the goat's skin hung on it. The room stank of meat.

'Looks like we got some Satanist terrorists.' Lionel shot the goat's head a couple of times and watched as the brain seeped out from the bullet holes. The fugitives weren't here. Lionel and his men searched the grounds. They found fresh horse droppings, a pile of offal and a fresh trail leading north. Dawn began to seep through the trees. The mercenary captain gazed up at the hills wreathed with mist.

He'd only just missed them, and he reckoned he had a pretty good idea of where they were going. Lionel would've liked to locate them with the chopper and shoot them down from the air. But their trail went through the densely wooded valley, he knew that the deserter was clever, and they wouldn't be able to spot them through the forest canopy.

'What're we doing sir?' the voice of the junior officer pulled him out of his thoughts.

'We cut them off.'

Jane and Salt used their torches as little as possible and moved slowly, feeling out each step, while around them Jane could heard the scrabbling of possums and the rustle of wallabies. After some time they heard a commotion on the hill by the hut. She heard shots, followed by a man shouting.

Salt stopped at the noise, they led the horses off the trail, and hid behind a low leafy bank. He was silent, his face smeared with mud while his hands gripped his assault rifle.

'They're trying to kill us.' Jane's body ached. She was exhausted, and wet to the bone. She realised that their predicament was hopeless. The army was hunting them; they'd be caught and killed in the bush. The notebook would disappear, and she'd pay the price for Salt's vendetta.

'They're going to kill us,' she said again, and gulped as her voice broke.

'Shut your mouth,' said Salt through gritted teeth.

Jane started to cry, she couldn't help it. She bit down on her sleeve so Salt wouldn't hear her and let the tears wet her face. Sometimes she just needed a bit of human comfort, and that was something that her companion never seemed to offer.

Somewhere a bird began to sing, then more, and slowly the light of dawn began to filter down into the forest.

The early morning sun shone through the mist, which rose in wafts from the dark-green rainforest. Jane could hear the high notes of golden whistlers, small yellow breasted birds, and the chattering of rosellas, the red and green native parrots. They followed the trail until it came to the base of high limestone cliffs that rose above the forest and blocked out the sun. They stopped for lunch by a deep green pool, fed by a thin waterfall that trickled down the cliff. They ate cold roast goat and leftover rice, eating with their fingers, stuffing the food into their mouths. Jane splashed the water from the pool over her arms and face. The water was freezing but refreshing, and they refilled their water bottles.

'The old woman lived somewhere around here,' said Salt. 'We'll soon see if she's home.'

Jane remembered their conversation the night before, and realised that he was taking her seriously. She wondered who the woman was and if she'd still be there.

They followed a trail along the cliffs, riding the horses at a walk until they came to a celery topped pine. Here Salt dismounted and tethered the mare to the tree. Jane did the same, she was becoming more practiced at getting on and off Old Brown. The roots were entwined with the base of the limestone cliff and Salt put his foot onto the roots and pushed past the thick branches. Jane followed, and was surprised to find a narrow path, which wound its way up the cliff. They moved slowly, hugging the rock face as they ascended. After they reached a considerable height, the path widened into a terrace where basket ferns clung to the peaty soil. The terrace tapered into a cave and Salt had to bend down to enter, but Jane just ducked as she followed him in.

Inside, the limestone cave opened up to become spacious and dry. They turned a corner into a large chamber, and there, waiting for them was Old Ra.

She was dressed in a baggy yellow T shirt that hung down to her knees and looked like it had once been bought from a souvenir shop. She sat on a wooden stool and poked the coals of a fire on which an iron kettle boiled. The firelight revealed the contours of a face that was dark and wrinkled and her bony, spider-like arms protruded from her narrow shoulders. The fire sent shadows dancing across the walls of the cave, a space that she appeared to keep clean and comfortable. It had a wash station with two plastic buckets of water, a wooden stool, and a couple of towels folded on top of it. Next to this was a pair of black gumboots. Behind this was a kitchen with shelves made from branches of tea tree. Jars filled with preserves were stacked on more shelves and above them smoked meat and herbs hung from a wooden frame. At the back of the cave Jane could make out a bed elevated from the ground by a wooden frame, and she fancied she could make out a stack of books and candles. The woman stared at the newcomers, with undisguised interest, but showed no surprise at their arrival.

'Salt,' her voice was raspy, like the sound of possum claws on a tin roof, 'It's been a long time since you came to visit me, not since you were a boy running from your father's belt. What're doing back? It's not for the love of old Aunty Ra, I'm sure.'

'I brought ya some food,' Salt came forward and placed a haunch of goat on a flat rock beside the fire, 'and this girl.'

The woman opened her mouth to reveal a few blackened teeth. 'A cold piece of feral goat? I hope it's tender? Did you bring any salt, any sugar?

That's what I need most, and you should have remembered.

'I watched ya come, but you're not the only ones using the old miner's road. Death follows you, Salt, and you bring Death with you here. I dreamed of the miner's hut last night. Blood flowed from the windows, and the stones were made of bones.' Ra sat upright and prodded the fire with the poker. 'Who're you, girl?'

'My name's Jane.' Jane stepped forward and held out her hand but the woman didn't take it.

'And what do you want from a very old woman?'

'We're trying to find out what happened to, to a girl, a girl who was murdered.' Jane wondered how to explain things, she pictured how things had been that night when they found Anya, the stench, the peeling skin, the sound of Lui vomiting. 'We found her, found her in a logging coupe, in a Roundup drum, it was awful. I went to a psychic and... well I started having these dreams, well not really dreams.'

Ra looked up at Jane through yellow eyes, and she suddenly felt very weak, naked, even transparent. 'Come here, girl.'

Jane approached the fire, and stood close enough that she felt the heat on her legs and face.

'Closer.'

Ra stretched out her arms and uncurled her sinewy fingers, with which she lightly scraped the contours of Jane's face, while she stared into her eyes, unblinking. 'Yes part of you is entwined in the dreaming.'

Ra removed her hands from Jane's face. 'Salt,' she turned to the big man who stood, arms folded. 'Get out. This is women's dreaming.'

Salt turned to leave, and Jane felt like crying out to him not to leave her, not to leave her with this strange woman. But she found that she was frozen, and couldn't move, not even her lips.

'But before you go,' said Ra to Salt, 'leave me your knife, the bone handled one that you love to sharpen.'

Salt pulled the knife from his belt, and threw it on the ground in front of Ra. After the tramp of his boots had faded the only sound was the crackle of the fire.

'You want answers, you want dreams.' The kettle began to whistle, and Ra removed it from the fire. 'I can give you the dreams you seek and maybe you'll find what you're looking for, maybe not, but it is culture that you must give something to me.'

Jane didn't know what to say. She had nothing except her clothes and her camera.

'Give me a lock of your hair, and I'll guide you through the dreaming.'

Jane realised that she could move again, and she looked away. She felt a chill despite the fire's heat. She wanted to refuse to get up and walk out, but she thought of the dead girl, what she'd seen in the Vitoria Club, and the great forests of the Balloong reduced to desolate logging coupes, and she knew she could not go back.

Jane nodded.

'Brave girl,' said Ra, and she took Salt's knife, knelt close to Jane, grasped one of her dreadlocks, and sawed through it with the knife till it came off in her hand. She rose and moved to place the lock at the back of the cave, close to the bed, and returned with a bundle of objects wrapped in an old blanket. She unravelled the blanket and lay it on the ground.

'Lie down, girl.'

Jane stretched out on the blanket by the fire and watched the thin line of smoke rise from the fire and ascend through a circular smoke hole in the cave's roof.

Ra ground wattle bark, small brown mushrooms and a handful of sassafras leaves into a ceramic bowl and with the butt of a wooden spoon she mashed it till it was a fine paste. She scraped the paste out of the bowl with her fingers and deposited it into a cup, over which she poured hot water from the kettle.

'Undress.'

Jane hesitated.

'Well go on,' said Ra, 'I can't cook you up and eat you with your clothes on. Usually I prefer virgins, but you'll do fine.'

Jane blushed.

Ra laughed. 'I need to paint your body in preparation for the dreaming. So stop looking at me like the little girl who's lost her way in the woods.'

Jane, feeling slightly abashed, sat up and peeled off her travel worn clothes that clung to her with stale sweet. She then lay, her arms by her side, her palms upward, and her ankles apart. Ra made a paste with a white rock and dabbed Jane with dots. She gave her the bowl of liquid and told her to drink. She sat up and sipped it. It was bitter and foul, and made her want to gag, but she drank it and felt her weariness pull her back onto the blanket. Ra threw a bundle of eucalypt leaves on the fire and they flared before beginning to smoke. Jane coughed and her eyes watered. The cave began to spin, and the visions took hold.

Jane walked through a land of eucalypts. Their bare, mottled, silvery-blue trunks exceeded seemingly forever. Her vision moved, flying through the trees till she came to a river. Perched on a branch beside the river was a white cockatoo. The cockatoo threw its head back and made a shrieking, laughing sound, like a kookaburra, but faster and more human-like. The cockatoo stretched its wings and flew from the branch. Her vision changed, and she knew she was seeing through the eyes of the bird, and she watched the land fly beneath her – great, dry, stony deserts and silvery-blue forests. She flew to the coast and the wild wind whipped the seething ocean so that the salt spray blew onto the rocky land. And a white sailed ship skimmed like a stone across the frothing swells.

Jane flew over houses made from wood and stone, over docks where sailing ships were moored and men shouted as they brought in cargo, where red coated soldiers herded white men and women off ships in chains. She flew inland and saw brown wheat fields, and great ranches dotted with sheep, grazing like woolly maggots, receding toward the mountains. She flew down toward the earth and came to the wide and murky Balloong River, and carried by currents of cool air she glided upstream.

Jane watched as a convoy of empty barges pulled by longboats made their way north, the rowers fighting against the torrent of the deep emerald river. Thick rainforest over shadowed the banks, and the sound of birds was deafening. The bloated corpses of four Palawa floated, bobbing down the river and their bodies banged against the banks of oars. The men fell silent and crossed themselves. Eventually they came to a trading post, a bit of flat land where the forest had been cleared. Tents had been set up and log cabins constructed. Swamp gums had been felled, cut and stacked while fires smoked on the hillside. The men moored their ships, pulled in their oars and came ashore.

Jane saw no women in the settlement and the men looked rough. Their faces were ugly and bearded. Their clothes were dirty, torn and made from possum fur. Jane watched as a team of bullocks chained to a huge log dragged it through the mud of the main street toward the water's edge, driven on by the lash of a whip. The walls of the cabins and the branches of the few remaining trees were decorated with the skins of hundreds of animals – possums, thylacines, wombats and wallabies – and their skulls were stacked beside the houses.

Three men talked as they sat around a camp fire. They wore wide brimmed hats and possum fur coats. One man had an eye patch, another long greasy hair, and the third, three fingers missing from his left hand. They were passing around a bottle of white liquor.

'Who's the toff?' said the man with greasy hair.

The man with the eye patch coughed and spat, after taking a swig from the bottle. 'He's a businessman come up from Port Town to oversee the timber business.'

'Is that what you heard is it, Bill? I heard he's come to try his hand at hunting,' said the third man with missing fingers.

'Well he can damn well shoot grouse down by the coast, can't he?'

'It ain't birds he's here to shoot, least not the type ye want to eat.'

Bill shuddered, 'Blimey that ain't no work for a gentleman.'

The men were silent for a while, and the sound of the forest at night carried through the settlement.

'Who's the black whore he brought with him?' asked the man with greasy hair.

'She's his mistress. I've heard Sir Grey likes his cunny black,' said Bill.

'And I've heard he likes it black and blue,' said the man with missing fingers.

The men laughed.

'I also heard she's a witch, that she performs black magic for his lordship.'

'Witch or no witch I'd give cunny rollicking,' said greasy hair.

The men laughed again.

The vision changed and Jane found herself beside another camp fire outside a large canvas tent, set up under the eaves of the forest. Grey sat on a stool beside the fire, his legs crossed, a long rifle in his hands. Three others sat around the fire, a man with a bent nose, a narrow gap between his eyes and a fur hat on his head; a priest with a round face and a black robe; and the Maori woman, her hands chained behind her back, the tattoos on her face shining in the firelight.

'What you got there, if you don't mind me asking?' said the man with the fur hat pointing at Grey's rifle.

'A rifle.'

'Well, ain't that fancy.' The man with the fur hat grinned, revealing a set of crooked teeth and protruding gums. 'I still use an old smoothbore, and there ain't nothing wrong with it, so long as I can keep me powder dry, no small feat in this wet hell.'

'It has superb range and accuracy.'

'Oh, so it does, so it does, but that ain't much vantage in the thick bush now is it, and it takes a long time to pack the powder down it, don't it? And by the time it takes ya to fiddle with your fancy fowling piece, ya could have a black spear stuck through your belly.' The fur hatted man chuckled. 'The blacks are cunning. They won't stand around to be shot at like English pheasants, oh dear me no, they sooner come, sly like, and slit ye throat in ye sleep.'

While the two men continued to talk about weapons, the priest rose from his sitting position and came to crouch beside the woman with the tattooed face. 'Have you accepted the Lord Jesus Christ as your king and savour?' he spoke quietly.

The woman turned to stare at the priest, and whispered something in her own language.

'Answer me, you wretched woman.' Spit flew from the priest's lips. 'Are you baptised? Have you cast behind you your most wicked and unsanctioned beliefs? Or do you persist in honouring those repugnant, heathen institutions of your race?'

The woman looked away from the black robed man and began to sing softly to herself.

The priest's voice became animated with righteous fervour. 'How art thou fallen from heaven, O Lucifer, son of the morning. How art thou cut down to the ground, which didst weaken the nations. For thou hast said in thine heart, I will ascend into heaven, I will exalt my throne above the stars of God. I will sit also upon the mount of congregation, in the sides of the north. I will ascend above the heights of the clouds. I will be like the most high. Yet thou shalt be brought down to hell, to the sides of the pit.'

The words of the priest echoed in Jane's mind and she felt the vision fade and reform.

A family of Palawa sat beneath a gum tree, while the light of a full moon sifted through the branches. They sat, laughing and chatting around a small fire on which slabs of wallaby meat were cooking on hot rocks. An old man was telling a story and kept pointing at the moon. A larger fire burned nearby and others sang, beat sticks, clapped and danced. Faster and faster they danced around the fire, spinning and clapping, their bodies painted with white rock.

The vision changed and where the corroboree had been the ground was covered in bodies illuminated by the flames – babies slit open with bayonets, the guttural sound of English being spoken, the crack of a musket, the scream of a dying woman. The ground was slick with blood.

'How many ya think we got?'

'I count forty-eight left feet, and one alive, that should get about a pound a piece.'

The vision changed again and Jane found herself in a rainforest, from which the trunks of the swamp gums rose. She walked past a sassafras tree, and hanging from it were corpses – half rotten, naked corpses of Palawa, their eyes pecked out so that they stared at her through empty sockets.

She walked on until she came to an outcrop covered with moss and fern. The sound of musket fire rang in the forest and from among the trees ran a group of Palawa – old men and women, others carrying babies, and skinny children. They ran to the foot of the outcrop and they began to pull away the moss and turf, and there, Jane saw, was the entrance to a cave. The Palawa began to clamber down into the rock until the whole group but one was hidden from view.

The one that remained was a young woman. She was beautiful. She did not enter the cave but carefully replaced the moss and rocks around the hiding place, ruffling the ferns and chanting in low notes. Soon the cave was invisible from the outside. And just as she finished they came. Jane saw the net that caught her. She thrashed and screamed, and the men laughed while out of the trees strode Grey, rifle in hand. He looked at the woman thrashing in the net, and he did not laugh.

The images of what happened flicked quickly before Jane's eyes. She saw the woman bound to a horse and heard the men sing as they marched. She saw her bound, gagged and dragged by two men into a tent. She watched while Grey beat the woman till she screamed and bled, and eventually her eyes seemed to go dead and she didn't scream while she was raped. A rhythmic sound filled the air; it was like the humming of locusts, and the whir of bullroarers. The sound rose to a deafening crescendo, the world spun around her, and the vision darkened.

Lui poured the full kettle into a plastic bucket in preparation for his bush shower. Towel over his shoulder, and soap in one hand he carried the bucket of steaming water toward a fallen trunk of a swamp gum.

He had spent most of the day climbing. Some of the tree sits had started to rot and had to be repaired or strengthened. Using prusik knots he'd scaled the swamp gums that contained the sits, occasionally bringing wood, rope and nails where repairs were necessary. The exercises had been exhilarating and had drawn a crowd of spectators from the visitors. Lui smiled as he recalled the way Jeanette had looked at him and interviewed him on his technique, while Holly shot pictures. He knew that the blockade had a shortage of experienced climbers and he'd worked through the afternoon training new people. A couple of them were starting to get the knack of it, but they'd need more confidence to stand up to a police bust and Lui doubted whether they'd be ready in time.

Johnno had not given any trouble, for which Lui was relieved. He'd been sceptical of Nails' decision to move him to the yurt. The biggest problem now was that he rarely shut up. The carnival atmosphere and excitement, which imbued the camp preparing for a bust, was infectious. Its effect on the contractor, who now occupied the central space, was notable. He was constantly spinning the most inappropriate yarns, enjoying being the centre of attention. Worse, certain people, notably Chris, seemed to take pleasure in egging him on.

Lui finished his bush shower and dried himself off. He'd just pulled on his woollen thermals when he heard the crunch of boots on the forest floor and looked up. Nails was approaching.

'What are you doing here?' asked Lui.

'Looking for you.' Nails ran her fingers through her shaven hair. 'We have to discuss strategy, and there's work to do. More people are coming into camp, and they need to be shown around. You're looking nice and clean by the way.'

'Thanks.'

'The cops will come for us in a couple of days. There are more than thirty of us now and we're growing, but only a few are experienced campaigners. I don't fancy our chances against a full dawn raid.'

Lui pulled some sassafras leaves from a branch and began to chew them. Nails was right. It took a lot of nerve to stand up to a dawn raid, and their motley occupation seemed doomed. 'Have you got some kind of idea, Nails? Something you've been keeping to yourself?'

She smiled, a tight, barely perceptible smile, 'Yeah, I reckon we need some extra leverage. We've got to use the murder card. We've got four witnesses including Johnno. The cops will have to listen to our statement. It might throw them off, even if the body has mysteriously disappeared.'

Lui pushed some ferns out of his way and climbed onto the fallen trunk of the swamp gum. He watched as a black slug-like leech began to attach itself to his exposed ankle. He flicked it off before it could dig into his flesh. 'There's no evidence,' he said. 'Jane has the evidence, and for all we know she's been snatched up by the cops.'

'Are you all right?' asked Nails, as she clambered up onto the log beside him. 'You seem distant.'

'I know what will happen,' said Lui. 'If we cable the trees they'll cut them. If we lock on, eventually they'll cut us out, and if they really can't take us from our sits they'll cut around us. The Balloong will be chipped and burned. You know, that's the thing about environmental campaigns, you never win. Even if you get the forest protected it's only a matter of time before somebody tries to cut it down again, but if you lose, you lose for good.'

Nails touched Lui's hand. 'There ain't no climber like you, Lui. Don't you forget it. And a win is a win even if it's not forever.'

Lui took comfort from the light touch. He turned to Nails. 'Maybe I'm going a bit crazy. I'm sorry. I guess I might be distracting myself from what's about to happen. I've lived here for ages. I almost can't believe it's going to be gone.' For a moment he forgot about Johnno, the murder, Jeanette and everything else and he gazed at the forest and imagined it being turned into burning debris and he felt a lump in his throat.

Sergeant O'Connell flicked through the report. 'Are you sure this is a good use of police resources?' he asked the superintendent stationed across the large polished wooden desk. 'We've got major security problems in the city, and you want us out in woop woop.'

The natural light, which flooded in from the glass windows of the seventh floor office suite, gave the superintendent's face a grey tone. His brow was furrowed, and the wrinkles round his eyes gave him a tired, strained appearance. 'It's not your position to question,' he said. 'We have reason to believe that the instigators of the riot are hiding in Camp Balloong. In any case they're blocking essential infrastructure and need to be removed. You made a cock up of the riot, and you're lucky to keep your job. But you've got experience in crowd control. That's why I'm promoting you and putting you in charge. You owe me some gratitude. Make it quiet. Make it clean. Get the people out of there so that the boys can go to work.'

O'Connell broke eye contact to look out at a vista that the few glass skyscrapers of Port Town offered. The air conditioning made it cold and the superintendent tapped the wooden desk. 'Amoora,' he said, 'Indonesian hardwood. As you'll have seen in the report, the removal will be done as a joint private - police venture. A private security company contracted by Woodchips Ltd will offer support to the police and protect the government contractors so that the police can focus on the job at hand – removing the protesters. If the bust is successful it could point the way toward a model, where private security plays a greater role. You will be polite to the acting head of the security company, David Johnston. Any more questions?'

O'Connell had been looking at the only thing which adorned the desk, a printed photo of a younger man next to a woman holding a bouquet. The photo seemed very contrived, shot in black and white, dressed up. How many police and private security does it take to bust the famously non-violent, Save the Balloong Movement? he wanted to ask, but instead he said, 'Sounds fairly straight forward. Do the greenies have any surprises?'

'They're probably gonna be desperate,' replied the superintendent. 'I wouldn't rule anything out. Be careful, but you're the expert.'

Jane woke. She was in Ra's cave, her body was covered in a blanket and her head rested on a cushion. The fire burned low, the cave was lit by several paraffin candles, melted into the top of old wine bottles, and Salt paced back and forward by the entrance. Jane sat up, pulling the blanket over her shoulders.

'You see, Salt,' said Ra who stood in the kitchen, ladling some steaming liquid from a large pot into a bowl. 'There's no need to be impatient. The girl is awake.' Ra walked over to Jane and placed the bowl of hot goat stew on the ground in front of her. 'Did you find what you were looking for?'

'I don't know, I keep seeing this story from the past, from colonial times, it's vivid, clear, haunting, but, but,' Jane paused to spoon some of the stew into her mouth. 'I don't know what it's trying to tell me. I can't see what it has to do with me, Anya, Salt or anybody.'

Ra rocked back and forward on the balls of her feet. 'Perhaps,' she said, 'perhaps you are asking the wrong question. I do not ask what the dreaming can do for me. I ask what it is I can do for the dreaming.'

Jane pondered this between more spoons of soup, but she wasn't exactly sure what the old woman meant.

'Here,' said Ra, 'I have something for you.' She took from a pouch three long white cockatoo feathers and threaded them through Jane's locks. 'Cockatoo, he will help guide you. Follow the old mining road north to Croydon and cross the Balloong river at its beginning. That will take you to the upper Balloong valley. Your friends are there. They need your help and you need theirs. Salt,' the woman turned to the man who still paced at the entrance. 'Take care and watch her closely. Bring her up the Balloong, and there you may find answers in unexpected places.'

The occupants of Rat Camp huddled under the dirty blue tarp, and smoke from the small fire filled Chris's eyes, causing them to water, but he didn't move because he had a sneaking suspicion that the smoke would follow him. The group around the fire chewed on dumpstered bread. More people had come to join the occupation throughout the course of the afternoon – five students, and a couple from Queensland.

'So you guys know what we're gonna do during the bust?' Chris glanced across at the young punks, one girl, her hair normally in bright red spikes, had fallen limply round her ears. But her voice carried a tone of excitement as she replied.

'We hide in the bush, not get caught, take food and water to the people locked on and in the tree sits, and film the bust if we can.'

'Very good,' said Chris slowly as he waved the smoke out of his face.

'We should spike the trees,' said Jo the commie.

'What's tree spiking?' asked the girl, through a mouthful of bread.

'It's when you hammer metal into the tree,' said Chris. 'Nails, bottle tops, any piece of metal will do.' Then if the wood goes through a woodchipper it wrecks the machine.'

'Why don't we do that, man?' asked Johnny Vegas.

'Tree spiking can be lethal,' said Chris. 'If a chainsaw hits a spike it can break the chain which can lash back and injure or even kill the contractor. One thing I've thought about doing is putting up a sign saying, warning these trees are spiked, easier than doing the actual spiking. Then there's also cabling. That's when you get good climbers, like Lui, to attach cables between the tops of the trees. It's obvious to the contractors, but it stops them from working because they can't control the direction it falls or the other trees it will bring with it. It can halt operations for a long time. The banners we have roped between the trees can act as cables, but I think we're gonna put a few more up.'

'You were in the last bust, weren't you?' asked Johnny Vegas.

'Yip, I was part of the lock-on crew. It was my job to lock-on to the road. The cops beat the shit out of me, and in the end they slid those bolt cutters along my arms and cut me out.' Chris demonstrated.

Warwick stared at the fire, lost in his own thoughts. He raised his head to meet Chris's gaze. He was pale, his face was leaner then it had been a few days ago, and the bags under his eyes showed. 'We should give them hell,' he said.

Chapter 11: Wednesday

Jane woke, gasping for breath; she must have fallen asleep on Old Brown's back. She was in the rainforest, her head resting on a clump of moss, her body covered in a thick woollen blanket. In front of her sat Salt, polishing the muzzle of his assault rifle.

'Finally awake, eh? Morning, sleeping beauty.' Salt stood and handed Jane a coke bottle filled with water. 'Drink, you must be thirsty, and eat.' He thrust an ice cream container filled with potatoes to her, and she pushed the cold mushy vegetables into her mouth and swigged the water.

'How long have I been asleep?' she asked.

'A few hours.'

'Where are we?'

'We're still on the old gold mining road. We should reach Croydon this afternoon, then we'll cross the river, and head on to The Sisters.' The Sisters were the two mountains whose slopes created the bowl, which was the Balloong Valley.

'I don't see a road.'

'Look carefully.'

Jane observed the forest around her and she saw that there was a flattened space in front of them, in which the trees were younger growth, and half buried underneath the moss were long rotting wooden sleepers. Further along, a swamp gum had fallen and its trunk blocked their path.

'I've got a feeling we're walking into a trap,' said Salt, and he blew his nose on a handkerchief. 'There's a couple of boys following us. They can't keep up with the horses, but I saw a chopper heading north, and I reckon there'll be a couple more of them waiting for us up the way.' He stood and slung the rifle over his shoulder. 'Ya ready to ride?'

Jane nodded.

'Throw me that blanket.'

Jane stood up, pulled the blanket from her shoulders, threw it to Salt and shivered. It'd been almost a week since she had changed her clothes. The warm stockings and thermal top kept her warm, but her canvas shoes were wet and caked with mud and that combined with wet cotton socks sapped her heat. She knew cold was a killer in the temperate rainforest.

Salt half cut, half ripped a hole in the blanket and threw it back to her.

'Thanks for the poncho.'

The two travellers followed the ruined mining road for several hours. At one point they crossed a sluggish brown creek, where only the rusting iron railings of an old bridge remained. It comforted Jane to see the way that nature had reclaimed the road, she knew its rotting timbers told a story of a different time, and she imagined the pioneers cutting themselves a path through the wilderland. They were men with dreams, dreams of gold, of instant wealth, dreams of returning home one day across the ocean blue, back to cold bleak England, their bags and chests stuffed with the loot of the South Pacific's own El Dorado. Most had left penniless, become bandits or eked out a living where they could, for Australia's El Dorado had been an elusive dream.

It was late afternoon when the travellers arrived in the old mining town. The land around had been burned and the trees reverted to shrubs, eucalypts and grass. A strip of shops and houses lined the street, which was made of stone, and eucalypt saplings pushed their way through the cracks. The bank was a pile of crumbling brick, and the rest of the town, made from wood, was dilapidated and overgrown. A mouldering church lay at the end of the street. Its wooden cross had broken from the roof and was still visible, rotting in the yard. Australian ravens made nests in the charred rafters.

The residents of Croydon had come from around the world, drawn by the lure of gold. But as with so many other colonial gold rushes, it was the lure of the gold rather than the gold itself which brought development. Banks lent huge sums to developers and small business, which followed the gold rushes. The flow of yellow metal kept the town alive for a few decades, but it never delivered the rivers of promised wealth. Croydon had been built on a speculative bubble and when it burst, sending shock waves through the colony, the men, their gold lust unsated, wandered destitute back to Port Town to work in the packing sheds for the oligarchs. There they were paid a pittance, which they spent on cheap grog and bet on games of cards. Croydon was a town of broken glass and restless ghosts, and so the travellers did not stay, but hurried on to where the trail curved toward the river.

It was here that the ambush had been laid for them, and Jane could understand why. Since leaving Ra's cave the mining trail had run along a gully with limestone cliffs on either side while the sluggish creek ran through the middle, before it joined the Balloong at its headwaters. As the trail left Croydon following the creek to the river the limestone cliffs of the gully narrowed into a tight bottleneck, roughly fifty metres wide. The trail hugged the creek to the left, which in turn hugged the cliff, leaving a short slope between the trail and the other cliffs to their right. The gully was filled with mature tree ferns though the odd swamp gum grew from the wet ground. They moved cautiously in single file, leading the two horses. Salt wore his baggy coat, and held his gun in both hands. Jane carried her backpack in which was the notebook.

The gunfire erupted from the trees just as they passed the broad trunk of a swamp gum. The dappled mare must have been hit because it screamed and bolted. Old Brown reared, panicked and galloped after the mare. Salt grabbed Jane and threw her to the ground.

'Get behind the bloody tree,' he shouted.

Her heart pounding with adrenaline, Jane crawled behind the tall and buttressed roots of the swamp gum. There was another burst of fire, and the deafening snapping of the Kalashnikov caused her ears to ring, and when she peeked out from behind the high roots, she saw that the air was filled with thick black smoke. Salt came and crouched beside her, his back to the swamp gum's trunk.

'Where'd the smoke come from?'

A grin crossed the old soldier's face. 'A homemade smoke bomb. Chemistry was my specialisation.'

'What's gonna happen to the horses?'

Salt's grin fell away to be replaced by a stony expression, a look Jane had come to associate with her companion. 'They hit me mare. I don't know what'll happen to the poor beasts.'

'What're we gonna do?'

'We're in a hell of a tight spot, that's for sure. We're pinned behind this big tree. Those boys are entrenched up by the cliff and they'll have their pieces trained on us. If we show them so much as a pinky they'll blow it off.'

'Could we sneak back the way we came?'

Salt shook his head. 'The rest of them will be coming up from the south, if we headed back now we'd risk walking into the teeth of their guns, and it means we've got limited time. All them boys ahead need to do is keep us pinned down here before the rest of them show up and find us huddling like a couple of stoned rabbits.' He grinned again as if the idea of being hunted down and killed gave him some kind of pleasure.

'So what're we gonna do?' Jane felt terrified. She was just a girl, a photography student and people were trying to kill her. 'Can we surrender?'

Salt laughed. 'You really want to put yourself at their mercy? No, we'll do the one thing they haven't thought of. There,' he pointed to the limestone cliff, which loomed over them through the tree ferns, keeping the gully in shade. 'There's an abandoned mineshaft. We'll get in there.'

'Do ya know where it leads?'

'Nah,' Salt spat onto the ground, 'but they'll be brave bastards if they wanna follow us in.'

Jane imagined being trapped in a dark wet cave, trapped and unable to leave while trained killers waited ready to shoot them dead once they emerged. It sounded like the worst idea anybody could come up with, but she didn't express her feelings. Instead, she asked, 'How do we get to the mineshaft without being shot?'

It was a short run to the dark spot on the cliff where Salt had pointed, but the distance was surely long enough for them to both be blown apart by the gunners, and while Salt may have had a death wish she did not.

'That's the tricky part,' said Salt, 'I only got two smoke bombs left and that ain't enough to screen us both.' He dug in the pockets of his coat and pulled out the handgun he had taken from the security guard when they'd raided the Vitoria Club. He unlocked the safety on the side of the gun, and handed it to Jane. 'You take this, it'll be perfect for ya, light, no recoil. Hold it in both hands.' He demonstrated. 'That's how you keep your aim straight.'

Jane looked at Salt from her mud splattered face, her dreadlocks had begun to join together at the top and she realised she must look like a feral creature. 'If you're suggesting,' she said, with as much firmness as she could muster, 'that I should shoot people... well I'm not going to.'

Salt waved away her objection. 'Nah nah, I don't expect you to hit anything, but just by firing in the right direction you might just give me a minute of God's good grace.'

Jane took the gun. Salt was right, it was light, but she noticed her hands were shaking.

'Good, now I'm going to let off the smoke bomb. We're going to run first to that clump of tree ferns. I'll cover you while you run to the mineshaft. When you get there you cover me and I'll follow. You ready?'

'No.'

Salt pulled a metal canister from his pocket, opened it and smoke began to pour out. He threw the canister on the ground in the direction they were going to run. Smoke filled the air. 'Run,' he shouted, and they ran. Jane leapt over the tall buttressing roots of the swamp gum. Gunfire sounded around her, but she kept running. She threw herself down behind the clump of tree ferns. Salt was just behind her. The smoke was starting to clear.

'Keep going,' shouted Salt.

Again the sound of the Kalashnikov shattered the air and her ears rang, and she ran. The fire of the Kalashnikov kept coming and she could see the mouth of the mineshaft in front of her. She stumbled over the roots of a tree fern, and smashed its brown fronds out of her way, sprinting over the mossy ground. Salt kept firing, and finally, it seemed, she was there. She leapt into the entrance of the cave and felt elated because she was alive. The Kalashnikov fire had ceased and she could hear the shots of the more quiet assault rifles of the enemy. She knew what she had to do. She held the gun out as Salt had shown her, and crouching behind a pile of rocks at the mouth of the mineshaft, she opened fire in the direction of the enemy. Another smoke bomb went off. A bullet struck the stones and fragments of rock and dust hit her face. The gun's clip was empty, and Jane dropped it, shaking. She realised that Salt was beside her.

'Ya did well,' he said, 'ya did well.'

Jane looked up at the cave mouth. It'd clearly been made by men, it was enough for two people to walk side by side and high enough that a tall man wouldn't have to duck. It ended in an almost perfect arch, but it was clearly very old; it was covered in tufts of moss and bushes grew out of the rock around it. But Jane didn't have time to think too long about it because Salt pulled her by the arm and they ran into the blackness, as the gunfire sounded behind them.

Lionel looked at the boot print lodged in the moss, the empty burned out smoke bomb canister, and the broken tree fern fronds.

'What the fuck went wrong?'

'They had smoke grenades, sir, and a bloody cannon,' the bedraggled, camouflaged junior officer replied.

'What you're telling me, is that neither of you can hit the broad side of a goddamn barn. Is that what you're telling me?'

The officer looked like he wanted to argue, opened his mouth then shut it again. 'Yes sir.'

Lionel felt like shooting the man in the face but restrained himself. These men were green. If they'd been special ops in Syria they'd have been pissing themselves and begging for a flight home. Lionel calmed down, by thinking of dead bodies in the desert, he was full of rage, and rage, he knew well, was a killer. When people were angry they acted rashly. They made mistakes.

'Did you consider going after them?'

'Into that bloody hole?' The officer's voice cracked, as he contemplated the possibility that Lionel might order him in. 'I'm sorry, sir, but I don't much like the idea of being blown to pieces in the dark. The big guy was a damn good shot.'

Lionel had to admit that going into the cave would more than likely throw the lives of the men away without any positive result, and he had precious few men, even if they were green. 'Do you know where the cave leads?'

'No sir, there's no intel on it. It could be the only way in, they're probably trapped in there.'

The officer could be right, but Lionel was vaguely aware that the limestone caves in the region were extensive and that it was likely that mine connected with natural caves created by ancient underground waterways, which could in theory allow the fugitives to turn up anywhere, if they didn't get trapped or lost.

'Sir.'

'Go on.'

'There's a forestry blockade close by. If they get out I think that's where they'll be headed.'

'Tell me more.'

The officer fished his tablet out of his pocket, standard issue for the contracting company. 'This,' the officer pointed to a ramshackle collection of building on the satellite image, 'is Croydon. And this is Camp Balloong.'

Lionel looked at the image. He could just make out the line of the abandoned mining trail as it cut through Croydon. To the west of Croydon was the Balloong River and further west was a road, not overgrown and rotting, but proper tarmac. The area between the west bank of the river and the highway was a maze of smaller logging roads, which gradually became sparser as the main route climbed into the highlands. Here a stub of a road cut into a patch of dense green on the satellite image, and Lionel could see a number of structures.

'It's a forestry blockade —' began the officer.

'I know what it is,' Lionel snapped, annoyed that he hadn't thought of such an obvious thing. The camp had, after all, been mentioned in the security brief for the girl, what was her name, Jane Thistle.

He was about to give the order to post two of the young mercenaries to surveil Camp Balloong from the surrounding hills, when he heard a rustling in the undergrowth. Lionel watched as a wombat emerged from the ferns. It was about a metre long with a glossy brown coat, small black eyes, and a snub dry nose. The wombat observed the mercenary captain with trepidation. He felt the urge to kill; it was almost reflexive. He pulled his Glock from its holster, and aimed it at the animal's head. Lionel and the wombat stared at each other for several minutes before it wrinkled its nose and retreated back into the undergrowth. Lionel returned the gun to its holster. He gave the order to surveil Camp Balloong, and for two officers to watch the mineshaft.

Jane didn't like caves. She didn't mind heights and could scale a tree, but there was something about being underneath the earth, enveloped by darkness that made her feel uneasy, even nauseous. The dripping water disturbed her and she couldn't stop thinking about the kind of creepy crawly insects that lurked unseen around her. As they'd entered the cave they'd disturbed a colony of tiny bats that flapped around them. Jane had screamed and wanted to run out, but Salt had held her, and slowly she'd relaxed. The mineshaft went down at a straight angle, along which ran an old mining-car track. There were passages cut into the side but when they shone their torches down them they saw that they were dead ends. As they followed the central passage it narrowed, the ceiling got lower, and the stone more roughly cut. Ahead of her, Salt was having to stoop, and it was getting colder. Jane had an unpleasant feeling that they were going to reach a dead end, and an even more unpleasant feeling that venomous spiders may be dropping from the ceiling and landing on her neck.

'Can you feel that?' asked Salt.

'Feel what?' Jane slapped at the back of her neck.

'The breeze.'

'Nah ah.'

'Here, you go to the front and tell me if you can feel it.'

Jane flattened herself against the wall, while Salt retreated to let her go ahead, his belly brushing against her as he passed. Jane went forward and she felt the breeze, a cold damp air that seemed to rush up from the depths and caress her face with clammy fingers.

'That breeze'll be coming from somewhere,' said Salt.

They went deeper and deeper. The rail track ended, and the passage descended steeply and sharply and it became so narrow that Jane was sure that Salt would get stuck. She remembered watching that film, 48

Hours, shivered, and cast it from her mind. Just when Jane thought they could go no further, she slithered through a gap in the rock, fell a distance of a couple of feet and landed in cold shallow water. She screamed with fright and the sound echoed back to her. She flashed her torch around and saw that she was in a large cavern. Water dripped from the ceiling off long jagged stalactites, while the floor was filled with the cold lapping water, even in the harsh light of her torch she saw that the cavern had the beautiful yellow colour of limestone.

Jane heard a muffled shout behind her and turned to see Salt's legs stuck between the passage and the chamber she was now in. It may have looked comical, but Jane felt an empathetic terror. Imagine being caught, jammed in the rock. There was nothing she could do. Her heart, which had been lifted by the magical feeling of the cavern, sunk as she realised it could be her tomb.

'Stand back,' she could just make out Salt's muffled shout as the sound reverberated in the stone chamber, and she ran, splashing through the water. The crack of gunfire boomed in the cavern, there was the sound of falling rocks, a splash and a curse. Salt had made it.

'My God,' he said as he flashed his torch around, 'this is a palace.'

They walked through the cavern, following it up, skirting an underground lake and stumbling over stalagmites, their curses echoing. They passed other passages going off to the side but these seemed to go down and were filled with water so the pair pressed on, and gradually the passage became drier and the walls smoother.

Salt was the first to notice the paintings. 'We're on sacred ground,' he whispered. Jane looked at the walls. They were a swirl of colour – ochre, black and white, dabs, dots and lines. People with large bums and square shoulders hunted enormous wombats and giant kangaroos. Narrow breasted women danced over rows of different coloured dots. Handprints the size of Jane's, the fingers framed by white and ochre. Jane thought of the people in her vision, how they'd hid in a cave and how it had been covered by the young woman.

Salt spoke in a soft growl. 'If the black fellas came in here then they knew a way out.'

Lauren sat on a fallen trunk and observed the hills around the valley through the camp binoculars, while Moth, seated on the moss nearby, lazily self-medicated in the sun. The base of the hills were covered in rainforest and swamp gums. Scrub and tea tree took over as the altitude climbed. At the top were the bare crowns of yellow button grass, from which a person could observe and be observed. A plane, high in the blue sky, sped overhead leaving a long white contrail in its wake.

'Look, a chemtrail.' Moth pointed at the sky.

'A what?' said Lauren.

'A chemtrail, they're drugs loaded into planes and discharged in the sky. You can see one right there. The drugs keep us all apathetic and controlled so that we don't question the system.'

Lauren laughed, 'and I suppose these crimes are perpetrated by our lizard blooded overlords.'

'They're called the Anunnaki,' Moth's tone took on a sullen, defensive edge, 'and they're real. All the powerful people in the world are descended from them, the Rockefellers, the —'

But Lauren wasn't listening; something had caught her eye. It'd been the flash of something shiny reflecting the sun. Zooming in on the hill, she was sure she could see a black shape that could have been a human head nestled among the button grass. She tried to adjust the binoculars to get a clearer view, but it was too distant for her to be sure.

'Hey, Moth,' she called out to the grey-hooded drug dealer. 'Can you come up here for a minute?'

Moth got to his feet and slowly clambered up onto the log. 'What is it?'

'Have a look at this.' Lauren passed him the binoculars. 'Can you see somebody up on the hill? Just there by that stringy bark, down and to the left.'

Moth scanned the hill. 'Yeah,' he said, 'I reckon I do. What do ya reckon it is?'

'Don't know, but it's making me paranoid.'

'Welcome to my world. You wanna puff?' Moth took a short, sharp drag of the joint, and held it out meaningfully toward Lauren. She peered at it, and hesitated before taking it.

'We've gotta investigate,' she said. 'It could be the cops or company security. Could you run a message up to the central camp, see if Nails or Lui are around.'

'Sure thing.' Moth slid off the log and dropped to the ground. Lauren looked around at the forest; it seemed unusually bright and colourful.

Chris, his body aching from rough camping – he didn't use a ground sheet or a pillow, and slept in his damp clothes – trundled down the logging road toward Front Watch. He was looking for Moth. Thank God the drug dealer had brought all that choof, and was generous with it. A sprinkling of the sweet skunk in his cigarette took the edge off the rough life. He spotted Moth making his way up the logging road, and waved to him, waiting as he approached.

'Where ya off t'?'

'I was just heading up to central camp.' Moth tapped his nose. 'Suspicious activity on the hill top.'

'Yeah right, suspicious activity, eh. What kind of suspicious activity?'

'Looks like there's someone watching us from the hill. Lauren reckons we should send a party up to investigate.'

Chris scratched his bristly beard. 'I could do that. I could take a couple of the mob from Rat Camp, and head up. What hill was it?'

Moth pointed north to the closest of The Sisters.

'Bit of a hike,' said Chris. 'Might be an over-nighter. Ya wanna come?'

'Nah fuck that. I'll just stick around here and chill, d' ya need some choof choof bra?'

Chris grinned. 'You're a mind reader, Moth. I don't s'pose ya got a pinch o' brown stuff as well, do ya?' The two men squatted on the ground and Moth rolled a spliff with peach flavoured papers.

'Hey, Chris,' said Moth when the joint was rolled, 'have you heard of the Anunnaki?'

It was warm in the yurt, and the group was onto its second round of tea. Johnno reclined on the cushions at the edge of the space, resting his injured leg, whilst he slurped on his milky tea. The greenies weren't all bad. Some of them even had a sense a humour, and they knew how to make themselves comfortable in the bush. His so-called mates, Pete and Hank, they'd regret deserting him, they would. They were gonna get it, the pansies. They'd better be careful if they ever ran into Johnno again. They wouldn't be feeling so smug with their noses rubbed in their own shit.

Nails, who was drinking herbal tea, sat on a cushion directly opposite the entrance. She flicked through a soft covered book – Naomi Klein, Shock Doctrine. On the other side of the yurt from Johnno sat Jeanette and Holly, perched on cushions and wrapped in their matching blankets.

'I'm not afraid to say I'm a Pantera fan,' said Johnno. 'Cowboys from Hell, now that's an album. It's some real hard core shit. Good for the soul.'

'I'm not really a fan of metal,' said Jeanette. 'I like soft, soulful music. I'm a big fan of Bjork actually, John Butler of course —'

'Pussy shit,' said Johnno, 'give me some good hard core rock any day.'

Nails lowered her book. 'Bikini Kill, Blood Sausage, The Butchies, Pussy Riot, Jack off Jill, Huggy Bear – '

'What the hell was all of that?'

'Riot Girl, an anarcha-feminist movement in punk music beginning in the early nineties. I have a very specific music taste, Johnno, I was even part of a band back in Melbourne, Cut Throat Kitty.'

'Sweet Jesus,' said Johnno, 'there's a feminazi band called Blood Sausage.'

'I think they sound lovely,' said Jeanette, 'fabulous. I've heard of Pussy Riot of course, but I've never actually listened to them. I would love to hear them.'

'Cut Throat Kitty,' Johnno drew the sound out in a low occa growl. 'Pretty good name for a band, Cut Throat Kitty.'

'Dubstep,' said Moth as he entered the yurt, 'that's Music. Shit, dudes, we've totally gotta have a bush doof up here, play some sick tunes, bring a sick sound system, blast that shit, get tripping balls, fucken sick.'

'I'm not really a fan of doof doof,' said Jeanette.

'Me neither,' said Nails. 'It gives me a headache.'

'I knew a farting, bloody dog that sounded more musical then that shit,' said Johnno. 'Old Jim was his name, Jimbo. He was a staffy, he was. Got put down after he clamped on t' delivery boy's balls.' The contractor chuckled.

'Have you got a wife?' Jeanette asked Johnno.

'Had one, she's a bloody harpy. I got a son as well. Not allowed to see him though. Women, eh? Women control this damn country now. Us blokes don't have any rights and still have to pay for damn child support. What about you lot?' Johnno turned to Nails. 'In t' the whole free love thing aren't yas, out here in this tipi going at it like rabbits. I bet you're into some kinky dominatrix shit.'

Nails stared sceptically at the contractor. 'It's not a tipi, it's a yurt, and I'm gay, Johnno.'

'I got some news, dudes. Is Lui around?' said Lui.

'He's teaching some of the new mob how to climb,' said Nails. 'You wanna cup of tea, Moth?'

'Is it magical tea?'

'No, its normal gumboot tea.'

'Would you like me to spice it up with something, maybe a few shrooms?'

'No.'

Moth sat down by the fire. 'Lauren spotted somebody watching us from the hill. Chris has gone to investigate.'

'Somebody watching us from the hilltop, eh? That's a bit weird.' Nails clicked her tongue. 'Well, if Chris has gone to investigate I suppose we can only wait and see what he says.'

Lauren, Goldy, Rainbow and Jaxon sat on the wooden benches in the Front Watch tent, their own tea bubbling away, while paraffin candles lit the inside of the canvas structure. It smelled of damp earth. Jaxon twanged on the ukulele.

'What's your date of birth?' Rainbow asked Lauren who was continuing to chisel at her carving.

'Seventh of April nineteen-ninety-two.'

'That means,' said Rainbow after doing a lot of adding, 'That your life path number is five in numerology.'

'And what does that mean?'

'It means you love adventure but have trouble settling down or committing to a relationship.'

'Sounds about right,' said Lauren gloomily.

'So how did you two meet?' Goldy asked Rainbow.

'We met in Byron,' said Rainbow, her multi-coloured hair framing her narrow face. 'At the Arts Factory. Jaxon's tent got wet so I invited him to come sleep in mine. We got real high and listened to the sound of bush turkeys all night.'

Lauren rolled her eyes. 'How romantic.'

'My other boyfriend was really upset. He burned a photograph of me. And wrote a poem saying he wanted to kill himself. I guess I shouldn't have had sex with him in the first place. I just find it so difficult to say no to boys when they're being charming, especially if they play me a song.' Rainbow smiled at Jaxon who was continuing to fiddle with the uke. 'Once they play me a song they're basically in my pants.'

'Men are bastards,' said Lauren. 'I thought I was in love with a guy once, turned out he was cheating on me. He was sleeping with some little thing from South Side, so I went over to his place, smashed up his car and broke his nose, true story.'

Jaxon stopped playing the uke.

'You're so tough,' said Goldy. 'It's great. If I was like you then guys wouldn't mess with me. God, at least your ex wasn't sleeping with you, making up a whole identity and living a lie just so he could spy on you and your friends. Ya know he could seem so nice, he used to go on about how he loved the environment so much. I feel totally used. I can't believe he's still around. Chris stuck up for him and even Nails.'

'Yeah that's definitely a relationship story for the books,' said Lauren, 'but don't worry, hun. I heard from Chris that he's been acting really weird, moaning and pining over you like a spoiled child who's lost his favourite toy. Maybe soon you'll be receiving some suicidal poetry yourself.'

Lui and Tom the anarchist had prusiked, a climbing technique using ropes and harnesses, to the top of one of the swamp gums while below Old Mad Mark and some other spectators handed up branches and rope to help the two construct a new tree sit. The rough triangular platform of lashed branches, perched fifty metres above the ground made the sit more comfortable, but it was the climbing knots connected to the harness that made Lui feel safe. Nevertheless, one needed a strong stomach to be a climber and the people below appeared as mere specks while the rainforest canopy spread out beneath them.

'Woohoo,' shouted Tom as he ascended to the level of the platform. 'Love to see the pigs try to get us down from up here.'

'Mmmm,' Lui's feet, which dangled over the edge of the platform, tingled with a queasy sensation brought on by the height. 'We're not gonna make it easy for them, that's for sure.' The two activists stared out at the vista below. 'Have you heard that there are tribes in Indonesia which climb huge trees and even build tree houses, which they live in, without any rope or anything, just rattan vines.'

'Nah, didn't know,' replied the anarchist. 'Hey so, I reckon that journalist chick is pretty keen on ya, hey.'

'Who, Jeanette?' said Lui, and he nearly slid off the platform. 'What gave you that idea?' A sudden surge of nervousness overtook him and combined with the immense height to make him sick.

'Well haven't ya noticed how she's always givin' ya the eye? And coming up and hugging ya. I see the way ya look at her with her pink pyjamas on and her —' Tom rolled his eyes in an imitation of Lauren.

'I'm pretty sure that's just how she is.'

'Lui, you're blushing.'

'I'm not blushing. It's cold up here.'

'Lui's in love,' cooed Tom, and he began to sing. 'She'll be coming round the mountain when she comes, yeeha, she'll be wearing pink pyjamas when she comes, yeeha.'

'Shut up.'

'Ohhh somebody getting defensive. Lui and Jeanette up a tree K I S S I N G.'

'You'd better shut up,' said Lui, 'otherwise right now it will be Lui and Tom up a tree K I L L I N G.'

Tom laughed and whooped, 'Finally found your sense of humour, eh, ya dry old kraut. But seriously now, Lui, I think she likes you. You should say something to her.'

'Like what? Hey, Jeanette, I know this gonna sound weird and you're a beautiful journalist whose stranded in the bush and I'm a bitter hermit who doesn't leave the forest —'

'Oh come on. Give yourself a bit more credit. Just ask if she wants to go for a walk with you, and see if she wants to kiss you.'

'Yeah right. Like that's gonna work.'

Chris and Johnny Vegas had, with regular cigarette and spliff breaks, hiked through the rainforest throughout the afternoon. The pair were in high spirits, and Johnny, clearly excited to be on a mission, chattered away to Chris, telling him everything he needed to know about the different subgenres of punk rock. Night was setting in when they reached the high ground of the West Sister, breaking into an open plateau of grey rock and button grass. After walking along the ridge for a short while Johnny Vegas stopped and began to rummage in his pack.

'What are you doing?' whispered Chris.

'Getting my torch.'

'We can't use any light.'

'Dude, I can't see a fucken thing.'

'Don't talk so loud.'

They walked in silence, treading in shallow pools and stumbling over clumps of button grass and rock. Chris paused to look ahead of him, then moved carefully over to a large boulder, crouched behind it, and the young punk followed.

'Do you see that?' Chris was pointing to a flat space a little way down the slope next to a small gum tree, and from where a faint blue light emanated.

'I see it dude.'

'Do all Americans talk so damn loud all the time?'

'Oh shit, yeah sorry dude, but we do. It's our culture.'

'Johnny, how good are you at sneaking?'

'Dude, I'm like a cross between a cat, a spider and owl.'

'Sounds promising, how would you like to go down as close to the source of that light as you can, see who it is, get back to me and report without being noticed?'

Chris watched as Johnny, running from rock to rock, approached the light and disappeared from Chris's vision. The minutes went by and Chris resisted the urge to smoke. The waning moon rose higher in the starry sky and still there was no sign of Johnny Vegas. The blue light appeared to flicker, then it went out and he began to worry about what had happened to the young punk. Just as he was beginning to panic, the American arrived, emerging from behind the rock.

'Johnny, you're ok. You scared me. What took you so long?'

'I thought he had spotted me, so I froze and waited.' The American talked in an excited whisper.

'Who?'

'The sniper, dude. I sneaked up as quiet as a spider and hid in a patch of that long yellow grass stuff. There was like this army guy there, man. Crazy shit, dude. He was eating salami, and he had a little camouflaged tent thing, and then I saw that he had a sniper rifle, dude. Leaning against the tree. It looked just like on the movies. Then I thought it was time to get back, and I was crawling away when I put my hand on a stick and it broke. And the dude heard it. And started flashing his torch around, and swear to God I saw my life flashing before my eyes, man, and I just lay there and didn't move. Then the light went off and I thought it was safe to come back.'

'Johnny, you're a bloody legend.' Chris handed him a pre rolled cigarette and they smoked, crouching behind the boulder.

Chapter 12: Thursday

As the pale morning light shone through the canopy, Jane and Salt, weary and footsore, arrived in the Balloong Valley. Jane's legs ached from walking, and she felt as if her wet and muddy shoes would fall to pieces any second, while she was sure her feet inside were white, wrinkled and probably growing gardens of fungus between her toes. Salt seemed a little better and he tramped through the forest, silent and moody. They'd emerged from the cave via a hidden bushy entrance on the banks of the river as night had been falling. They'd followed the river upstream until they came to a place where a fallen log created a natural bridge. It'd been wet, slippery and dangerous, but they'd made it. A meal of a few muesli bars from Salt's voluminous pockets had given them some sustenance, and they'd chewed sassafras leaves to keep them going as they walked through the night. Jane knew the land on this side of the river and after a few false leads they had found the activist trail that ran from the Balloong River to the camp.

The pace of their walking slowed as they approached their destination, entering the rainforest on the eastern edge of the bowl. Jane felt a tremor of excitement. She was coming home.

'I wonder how your mob's gonna take me,' said Salt as he stamped along the path, showing what Jane took to be a rare nervousness.

'They'll welcome you, I'm sure. You've helped me a lot. I'll vouch for ya.'

'Your mob don't like guns much, do they?'

'Nah, they don't.' Jane's thoughts wandered as they walked and she began to fantasise about the warm yurt, the laughter of her friends, a hot cup of coffee, and some warm food, maybe a hot bush shower, a borrowed change of clothes, and toasting her feet by the fire. She punched Salt playfully on the arm. 'Don't worry. I won't tell them that you're the bad bastard that kidnapped me.'

Lui was boiling water for the dishes in the kitchen area, a tarp and stick construction built behind the yurt. Moth was smoking a joint in the sun nearby. Jaxon was practising juggling, and Rainbow was hula hooping. Jeanette emerged from the nearby bushes where her and Holly's tent was set up. She wore her pink pyjama bottoms and a white singlet, which revealed the gentle curves of her cleavage, while the space between the bottom of her singlet and the band of her pyjamas showed a pale crescent of skin. To Lui's distress he noted that her nipples were visible in the chill of the morning. She skipped over to the veteran activist and unselfconsciously kissed him lightly on the neck. Lui's body stiffened with embarrassment. He tried to smile at her but instead stared at her bosom, and he quickly looked away.

'Lui, kitten,' said Jeanette, 'are you ok, you seem a bit tense.'

'I'm —' Lui tried to say something, anything, but nothing would come out of his mouth, and he stared dumbly at Jeanette's hips. Focus on the task at hand, he thought as he backed away from the elegant brunette. He banged into one of the makeshift wooden tables, which fell over sending the cups and bowls he was going to wash onto the ground, and he retreated under the table to collect them.

'Ya right there, bra?' asked Moth who was still puffing on his joint.

'Poor possum,' said Jeanette, 'water's boiled, would you like me to make you a cup of tea. I hope you didn't bang yourself too badly on the table.'

'Yes please.' He realised he must look pathetic, under the table on all fours. He raised his eyes to see Jeanette's delicate feet arch onto tiptoes to pour the coffee. He heard the crunch of boots on gravel, crawled out from under the table and turned to face the newcomer.

He saw that two people had emerged from the bush. One was Jane. She wore a big, brown, mud splattered poncho. Her hair, which had been dreaded as long as Lui had known her, was more matted at the top and white feathers were entwined in it. She had changed. There was something different about her face, her demeanour. She seemed harder, older, and she still had her camera hanging from around her neck. Standing next to her was a man. He was tall, heavyset, had a battered face, and a Kalashnikov slung over his shoulder. The roach fell from Moth's fingers, Jaxon's juggling balls dropped, and Rainbow's hula hoop clattered to the ground.

Jane grinned and spread her arms. 'Lui,' she called out.

Jane watched as Lui crawled out from underneath the table to stare at her. It was comforting to see his small, suntanned face and short brown hair. A weasely man dressed in a second hand suit had been smoking a joint while two carnival people had been performing. A girl with pink pyjamas was pouring tea in the kitchen. All were staring at herself and Salt. She spread her arms to invite Lui to hug her but he seemed confused.

'I'm Jane,' she said to the people around the kitchen, 'and this is Salt. He's helped me a lot.'

Lui walked forward and awkwardly hugged Jane, patting her on the back. 'It's so good to see you, Jane. I can't believe you're here. We were really worried about you.' He took a step back and shook Salt's hand. The big man grinned, and Lui averted his eyes. Perhaps, thought Jane, he was intimidated.

'Firearms are forbidden in Camp Balloong.' Lui spoke to Jane. 'You know that. Christ, we worry about our composite bow and you bring artillery.'

'Please, Lui, these are crazy circumstances. We're tired. We've come a long way. Aren't ya gonna offer us a cup of tea, let us rest, and then we'll discuss what to do, including what to do with the guns.'

Lui looked like he was about to argue and then his shoulders slumped. He peered up at Salt. 'Come on,' he said, 'make yourself comfortable. We'll talk soon. God knows what Nails will say.'

Jane took off her shoes and socks and let her toes toast on the crackling fire. The hot cup of coffee in her hands and the vege curry on her lap felt like a fragment of heaven. Old Mad Mark had greeted her with a whoop of delight, embraced her in his bony grip, and breathed his alcoholic breath onto her face, before exclaiming, 'Jane is back. This calls for a celebration.' After which he had fetched a near empty goon sack from the edge of the yurt and filled a jar. Johnno eyed the newcomers, especially Salt, suspiciously. Lui, Jeanette, Rainbow, Jaxon and Moth had filed into the circular space after the travellers, curious to hear their story and they waited patiently while the two of them ate.

'Well, come on then,' said Lui. 'We're all wanting to know the story. For the love of God don't keep us waiting. You arrive with an armed escort out of the bush without warning while we thought the cops had snapped you up. I'm sure you've got one hell of a yarn to tell us. Go on.'

Jane pushed the empty bowl of curry away from her. She looked happy. 'Go get Lauren and Nails they ought to hear the story too.'

'Fair play.' Lui got to his feet. 'I'll go fetch them.'

'Lui told me you're a photographer,' Jeanette said to Jane. 'That's so cool. You should meet my friend Holly. She's a photographer too. I wonder where she is actually. I love your hair too by the way, how did you get it like that?'

Jane smiled. 'Thanks, yeah I went camping for a long time and didn't have a hair brush. What about yourself?'

'I'm a journalist,' said Jeanette, 'freelance. I'm doing a story on this blockade. Get the word out. I reckon you guys could do with some positive press coverage.'

'Sure could.' Jane took a gulp coffee; it was odd that Jeanette seemed oblivious to the armed soldier sitting on the cushions one person away, when everybody else seemed scared of him.

A short while later the flaps of the yurt opened and in strode Nails flanked by Lauren and Lui. Holly trailed in behind.

'Lui tells me that that you've brought an illegal assault rifle into camp.' Nails didn't look the slightest bit intimidated, but her expression betrayed by the tightness of her thin lips was one of icy rage.

Lui shrugged and lifted his hands as if to say: I told ya Nails would be pissed.

Nails pointed at Salt. 'Get out. Get the fuck out with your gun and don't come back. This is not a war zone.'

Jane felt her own anger rising. She'd been through rough times with Salt and he hadn't always been kind, but he'd saved them more than once, they were in the middle of woop woop and being hunted and Jane wasn't about to see him thrown out, with or without a gun. She stood up.

'Salt's with me and you'd better hear us out because this place could very soon be a war zone.'

She picked up her pack, unzipped it, pulled out the notebook and threw it onto the floor. 'You know what this is, Nails? It's what we've always dreamed of. It's a hand written record of illegal kickbacks to politicians. It shows the securing of government contracts, and favourable policy initiatives, including the forestry contracts for the logging of the Balloong.

You're a lawyer, Nails. With this notebook we could ruin them and save the Balloong for good.'

Nails was taken aback, Jeanette had her computer out and was writing something. Holly took a photo and Jane continued.

'Do you think they were going to let us get away with this? God no. They've been hunting us for days through the bush, shooting to kill, and if it wasn't for Salt we'd have been two more bodies and the notebook would never have got out. But we've won, haven't we? The notebook is here now. It's public. They can't kill us all.'

'How,' asked Nails, the anger in her voice replaced with her sharp curiosity, 'did you get your hands on that?'

'We whipped them out from right under their snotty noses,' said Salt.

Nails, who seemed to have temporarily forgotten about the gun, came forward to inspect the notebook. She flicked through it and scanned the pages and she smiled. Nails was not somebody usually given to smiling, but Jane saw what was possibly the warmest grin she'd ever seen grace the lawyer's face. She turned to Johnno who'd been lying silently by the fire and unexpectedly blew the contractor a kiss. 'I'm sorry, mate. You might be out of a job.'

'Screw the job,' he replied.

'I hate to put a dampener on things' said Holly, 'but it's not so straight forward. From what I understand about dealing with leaks you got to have a paper that's prepared to run with the story, and then there's legal issues regarding the way in which the notebook was procured.'

'But we could help with that,' said Jeanette who had stopped tapping on her keyboard and was looking excited. 'I have a few contacts that might be prepared to help. Once one paper breaks the story the others will follow suit. We might be able to get some kind of confidentiality on the source of the leak.'

'Hmm,' said Nails, 'well one thing is certain, we're far from out of the woods yet, excuse the pun. We need to digitalise this ASAP. While it remains only in hard copy, it could of course still be destroyed.'

At that moment Chris pushed his way into the yurt. He wore army pants and mud splattered green thermals. He looked tired, and a pair of binoculars hung around his neck. He winked at Johnno, blew a kiss to Rainbow and saluted Nails, then he saw Jane and his face broke into a wide grin.

'Jane, ya feral little scraggler! I wondered what became of ya. See I kept my promise, and I'm here, living in the god forsaken wilderness.'

Jane leapt up, met Chris in the middle of the yurt and gave him a tight hug. 'And I told you I'd see you here.'

Chris took the opportunity to kiss Jane on the cheek, before she pushed him away and he slumped down by the fire next to the cast iron kettle, which he shook.

'Nice, still a bit of water.' He placed the kettle onto the coals.

'You've been on a mission?' said Jane.

'Well yeah I have, I've been up one of the Sisters, me and Johnny Vegas. Lauren spotted somebody up there, so we sneaked up the hill. We didn't want to be seen so we approached from the steep eastern face, camped on a rocky crag last night, no fire of course, 'cause we were on the sly. It was damn cold. Anybody got any tobacco? Nah, well I'll guess I'll just have t' fidget then. So anyway we got close to the top, and hid behind a rock. We watched the hill face, where old mate had been spotted. And ya know what we found? There's a sniper up there. Nah, true story, that's right, dressed in camo with one of those black bulletproof vests, a little wigwam and a sniper rifle. So I has a little chat with Johnny about whether we should try and make contact with Old Mate Sniper, and he reckons no way, and not that I was afraid,' he winked at Jane, 'but I wasn't too keen either. So I think, shit, let's get back to camp and have a general discussion.'

Salt threw his tea into the fire and his hand closed around the gun, leaning against the wall. 'I'd better be going. Thanks for the tucker.' He stood up and his presence, as well as physical size seemed to fill the yurt. He walked around the edge avoiding the people on cushions, pushed open the flaps, and, before he walked off, he turned to look at Jane. 'You've been great. I'm in your debt.'

As their eyes met Jane felt a mixture of emotions. She felt a surge of joy at Salt's recognition of her. It was the sort of affirmation she'd wanted, recognition of the hardship she'd endured. But she also felt a sudden sadness. She had grown to like the old soldier and she had felt strong having him by her side. She had a strange feeling that she might not see him again and couldn't think of what to say as he turned his face away. The sound of boots on gravel faded.

'Was that a real AK?' asked Chris.

'Yeah.'

He looked disappointed. 'Now old mate's gone, ya didn't introduce me, and I've always wanted to hold an AK. When will I next get that chance?'

'Looks like the war zone's come to us faster than we thought,' said Lui. Jane surveyed the group. Old Mad Mark slurped on his goon. Johnno was silent lying on the edge, furthest from the fire. Jeanette, Lui and the others sat close to the door. Nails squatted on the floor reading the notebook.

'What about the dead girl?' Old Mad Mark's voice crackled like burning eucalypt bark. 'Did ya find out what happened to her?'

Jane didn't answer at first, and her mind wandered back to the night in the logging coupe, the rotting body, the smell, and the face of the woman in her vision. 'I'm getting close, Mark. I'm getting close.'

'I reckon you'd better tell us the whole story,' said Lui, who'd made himself comfortable on a cushion.

Jane thought of Salt, his grizzled face, his worn boots, and his vendetta. 'Salt,' she began, 'is Anya's, the murdered girl's, father.' She told the story beginning with the fire she'd witnessed at the old house on North Side, explaining how Salt had followed her, and captured her. She told the story quickly without embellishment, moving through the facts. She described the raid they'd launched on the Vitoria Club. She described their journey to Camp Balloong, and how they were nearly caught by the mercenaries, but she left out the visit to Ra's cave, and the visions she'd had in the forest.

Johnno chuckled. 'Damn good yarn that one, damn good yarn.'

Jane looked around at her stunned audience. 'Well, what about you mob? What's been happening around here?'

Lui and Nails, while being interjected by Johnno and Lauren, explained the events that had happened at camp, the disappearance of the body and the riot in the city. After they'd finished Lauren left to go back to Front Watch with Nails, Lui went to check on the climbers, Moth and Jaxon left to smoke a spliff in the bush somewhere and Holly and Jeanette offered to do the dishes and took the plates and cutlery back to the kitchen. Chris, Jane, Johnno, Old Mad Mark and Rainbow remained in the yurt. Mark threw some wood on the fire, while Jane filled the kettle with more water from a plastic container, and put it on the fire to boil.

Chris poured himself a tea. 'Why's everybody so quiet? Mark, stop pretending to sleep and play us a song.' Mark opened one eye and began a Latin strum.

'Chris?' asked Jane.

'Aha.'

'There's been something that I've been wanting to ask you. How did you know that Anya was involved with the Vitoria Club?'

Chris tapped his nose indicating a clandestine source. 'Nah jokes, it was actually one of Johnny Vegas's girlfriends. She knew Anya, same age.'

'Who's Johnny Vegas?'

'Johnny Vegas, living punk rock legend. He's here. Come to Rat Camp and you can meet him. I think he might have brought his girlfriend.'

The girl, her name was Amber, was playing cards in the tent she shared with the other young punks. No longer smothered in makeup her narrow adolescent face had blotches of acne. She wore two safety pins in her left ear as earrings, and her hair dyed half pink hung to her neck. She wore stockings and a black hoody. She was willing to talk, and walked with Jane and Chris to a clearing filled with golden rosemary. The three of them sat down on a sleeping bag among the flowers, the young punk seemed oddly out of place, as if she had been teleported from a grimy street corner to be transported to the wilderness in spring. Chris had somehow managed to get his hands on some tobacco and offered a cigarette to the girl who gratefully accepted.

'So you were friends with Anya?' Jane plucked off a sprig of the yellow flowers and began to slowly pull off their petals.

'Yeah, I guess,' Amber took a drag of her smoke. 'She was a bit of a weird bitch, but yeah we hung out a bit. I even went to her place once. It was pretty weird how she lived by herself there.'

'What do you mean she was weird?'

The girl took another drag on her smoke. 'Well, you know, she was real moody. Could be pretty nice sometimes but suddenly she could go all psycho, like just suddenly swearing at you, telling you fuck yourself slut, that kind of thing. No wonder she didn't have any proper friends. I guess it would be pretty hard if your mum died though and, you know, she didn't even know her dad.'

Jane threw away the ravaged flower. 'Do you know that she's dead?'

'What? Fuck! No.' Amber was clearly surprised but she did not seem particularly upset. 'I hadn't seen her in ages, but I guessed she'd just, you know, was doing something else.'

Jane flicked through the photos on her camera to bring up the shots of Anya's body, the decomposing flesh clear in the light of the flash. 'Do you recognise this body? Is it her?'

Amber took a quick short puff of her smoke, and took the camera off Jane as if it was some kind of disgusting corpse itself. 'Oh my god, that is gross! Yeah guess it could be her, but oh my god what happened?' Amber's eyes were locked on the picture with morbid fascination. 'What happened to her?'

'We're trying to find out. When was the last time you saw her?'

'Well I guess it was about three weeks ago. She had quite a bit of dosh, we were hanging out and she said she had to go. I asked her where and she said the Vitoria Club. I walked with her to the bus stop and then a flash car pulled up, a guy in a nice suit gets out and opens the door for Anya and she gets in. That was the last time I saw her.' Amber stubbed out her cigarette. 'Got another smoke?'

Chris began rolling another.

'What do you think about the Vitoria Club?' asked Jane.

'Well it's obviously a whore house isn't it? I mean, where else could she have got that money and the dodgy shit going on?'

'Did she ever talk to you about it?'

'Well yeah, one time we were smoking choof down by the old arcade over on North Side, and she looked like she was in a bad way, had bruises on her.' Amber indicated the left side of her face. 'She didn't tell me much but said it happened at work. Said she was going to get revenge. That she had a contact who was going to help her and all the people who had used her – well she was going to bring them all down.'

Jane played with the feather in her hair. 'When did this happen?'

'About three weeks ago.'

'So about a week before she disappeared?'

'Well yeah, I guess.' Amber took a drag of her second cigarette, and clouds blotted out the spring sun.

When Nails took a break from Front Watch in the late afternoon, and returned back to the yurt most of the people were napping. Johnno lay snoring in his corner and Old Mad Mark lay slumped over his glass of goon. There was no sign of Jane but Rainbow was awake and reading a book, something to do with tarot cards. Nails squatted down beside her.

'What are you reading?'

Rainbow pointed to the floor, where a silk cloth was spread out. Three tarot cards were laid upon it. 'The Devil, The Hanged Man and The Moon.'

Nails looked at the ground. The card of The Hanged Man caught her eye. Hanging from a tree with golden hair and a halo around his head, he seemed to stare at Nails with an expression of calm on his face, while his legs were crossed in a peculiar way.

'What does The Hanged Man mean?'

'He represents the pagan god, Odin. He was hung upside down on the world tree, had his eye torn out by a raven, stabbed with a spear and symbolically drowned. For that sacrifice he received the secret knowledge of the runes, the all-sight. The Hanged Man stands for sacrifice; a sacrifice is needed for the greater good.'

Nails stared at the Hanged Man and the Hanged Man stared back, his face a picture of serenity. 'Interesting,' she replied. 'I wanted to speak with Jane. Do you know where she is?'

'No,' said Rainbow, 'but Jane didn't tell us everything, I saw it in her face, she's been having visions. She's being guided from the spirit world.' She spoke in a distant voice. 'Do you believe in ghosts and visions?'

'No.' Nails stood up and left the yurt. Everybody's losing the plot, she thought, as she headed to the kitchen where several people were cooking and chatting. Time to put on some food. She had just begun to fry some onions when Jane approached. Her friend had changed. She looked lean, tough, and maybe there was something to what Rainbow said, because there was something about Jane's presence, which made Nails think of dreams.

'Nails,' Jane said, 'I want to ask you about something.'

Lui was chopping wood, a task he considered a kind of therapy, when Jeanette approached him. Her long, brown hair was mussed and she was wearing a long sleeved, tight, blue blouse and a long white skirt. Lui put down the axe, and the feeling of embarrassment he had felt that morning flooded back to him, and he looked away.

Jeanette sat on the stack of wood he had been cutting and fixed her doe eyes on Lui. 'Lui?'

Lui forced himself to look at the journalist. 'Yes?'

'I'm feeling really dirty.'

Colour flooded to Lui's face and he felt himself going bright pink.

Jeanette laughed but not cruelly. 'What are you blushing for, Lui? You should see yourself. Your face looks like a beetroot. And I don't know what you think I meant when I said dirty, but you obviously got it wrong.'

Lui felt paralysed with embarrassment, and wished he could magically disappear, somewhere, anywhere.

'What I meant was, Lui, that I really need a bath. I don't think I've ever smelled so bad in my life. Deodorant can only do so much. My hair is so greasy I could use it to oil a bike chain, the stench coming from my armpits is enough to kill a small animal, and my skin is covered in so much dirt I feel I could grow flowers in my belly button.'

'Have a bush shower,' stammered Lui, trying not to think of flowers growing out of Jeanette's belly button. 'You just boil some water in the big pot and then —'

'Lui, can you help me?'

Lui walked with Jeanette to the kitchen. He filled the big pot with water and put it to boil on the gas element, while Jeanette left to get soap and a towel. She returned, bringing with her a big white sarong, adorned with butterflies made from gold sequins. Lui poured the boiling water into buckets diluting it with some cold to make a warm mixture. Lui, carrying the buckets, followed Jeanette into the forest. They found what she deemed to be a suitable place in a grove of myrtles and she arranged the sarong as kind of curtain around her, pinning it to the branches with bobby pins.

'Shall I go now?' asked Lui.

'Please don't. I'm scared somebody might come.'

Lui fidgeted on the outside of the curtain as he watched Jeanette's garment's drop onto the moss covered ground, and he couldn't stop his eyes from fixing on the red lacy knickers placed on her white skirt.

'I'm ready,' she called from behind the curtain.

Lui lifted the bucket and pushed it under the curtain where Jeanette could take it.

'Lui, can you just pour it over me?'

'But, Jeanette —'

'Don't be silly, Lui. I'm not going to bite you. I know you like looking at me, and, well, I kinda like it. Now stop acting like a bumbling fool that's never seen a woman before, and pour this water over me before it, or I, get cold.'

Mateen's camp was, like his appearance, very well kept. In a patch of moss he had pitched a blue old style triangular tent. He had a foldout camping table, and matching camping chairs. His food was placed outside in sealed Tupperware containers next to a single-element gas cooker. These were neatly placed next to a single stainless steel cup, plate and bowl, a folded towel and a two-litre bottle of water. Next to these was a zip-lock bag in which there was toothpaste and a toothbrush. Mateen had fixed a line between two low rainforest trees, and a pair of hand washed clothes hung on it. His dress shoes were polished, and the polish and brush sat neatly next to a box containing small portions of different cleaning products.

When Jane and Nails came to visit, the Nigerian, who had been reading, looked up.

'Mateen,' Nails waved, 'we thought we'd come and see how everything's going with you. This is a friend of mine, Jane Thistle.'

Mateen put down his book, stood up and greeted his guests, shaking both their hands. He had only two chairs, which he insisted his guests use, while he sat on the ground. He had only two cups, the top of his thermos and his tin cup. He filled these with black tea and insisted that his guests have them.'

'Is everything good with you?' asked Nails.

'Yes, I have not yet been attacked by drop bears.' Mateen smiled, revealing his white polished teeth, and his awareness of the joke.

'You know we're expecting the police tomorrow?'

'Yes, I've heard,' he paused, 'I – you'll forgive me if I just watch. I don't want to get arrested.'

'That's perfectly ok,' said Nails. 'Bearing witness is important in and of itself.'

'In a way I'm glad,' said Mateen, 'not, of course, because of what's going to happen, but that it will soon be over. I need to get back to Port Town, I hate to think of what's happening while I'm gone.'

'Yeah,' said Jane, 'I wanted to ask you something about that.'

'Oh?' Mateen seemed happy to talk.

'I'm interested in a fourteen-year-old girl, first generation, Russian, disappeared a few weeks ago, Anya Ivanova.'

Mateen contemplated for a while, as if going through a catalogue of all the young Russian girls he knew. 'Yes,' he said, 'I know Anya. Well not in any close way. It was through my role as an advocate that she came to my attention. She's fourteen and living on her own you see, no legal guardian after her mother died.'

Mateen crossed himself. It was an odd gesture and reminded Jane of something, but she couldn't think of what.

'An associate of mine in the Salvation Army knew about her and asked me to check on Anya. I didn't make any promises, but I did stop by once. She seemed cheerful enough, and there was an old Greek who took care of the building and he seemed kind enough to her. I gave the girl my card though, if she needed support. And I got a call from her recently, she said she wanted to talk about something, and we arranged for her to visit me at my office. She never turned up. I just assumed – well North Side kids are tough, and I had a lot on my plate.'

'Sure,' said Jane, 'do you have any idea what she wanted to talk to you about?'

'I couldn't say. She didn't want to talk about it over the phone.'

Lionel watched from the hilltop as the sun sank to the west, reflecting a red glow onto the underbelly of the cirrus clouds. He had arrived in the Balloong Valley. The forest around the camp was full of civilians, and any action had to be done under the radar. He had reinforced his surveillance of the camp and had stationed a pair of officers on each of the sisters. Tomorrow he would go to the valley in person, and when he discovered the whereabouts of the fugitives he would strike swiftly. He took a silencer from his pack, screwed it onto his Glock, and watched as a wedge tailed eagle glided high above the valley.

'Sir?' A junior officer approached him dressed in camo with a flak jacket, and a camera in hand. Lionel took his eyes off the eagle to face the officer.

'Yes?'

'Sir, is this the guy we're after?' The officer held out the camera for Lionel to look at the screen, and scrolled through a series of stills, showing Jack Salt, his Kalashnikov in hand, entering a patch of open swamp slashing back some grasses and setting up a camp.

'That's him. Take Bruce, and approach the swamp from the north. Make sure you don't get seen. Get into a position where you can get a shot at the bastard. If he moves shoot him.' He turned his back on the view and went to the bivouac to prepare a cold meal.

Salt camped that night in the wetland, wrapped in a tarp in the long grass beside the oily tannin stained pools, and when the first black currawong called, and the new season frogs were still singing he heard a rustling in the grass and saw what he had been waiting for. The tiger snake froze as it became aware of Salt and it lay still as a stick. Its long grey body streaked with black, blending with the ground. Its head was small and angular, and large scales armoured it around the pits of its nostrils, and the hoods around its circular eyes. Salt prayed to the spirit of the snake.

Before the dimming sky was engulfed by twilight Jane took her pack and headed into the bush. At first she hurried through the tent city, a mess of ropes, tarps, tents, sleeping bags, camp stoves, rubbish bags, water containers and people. She followed the well-used track that headed to the highlands. People regularly walked the track and it was made with strong wooden platforms, elevating it from the swampy valley. Jane hurried on taking care not to slip. Despite her exhaustion she had resisted the urge to fall asleep in the yurt and an inexplicable feeling was pulling her into the forest, drawing her like a moth to a candle, closer to the grove of swamp gums, closer to the Green Cathedral.

At one point the track crossed a fallen log, and somebody had gone to the effort of carving steps into it. When the track left the swamp and began to climb, Jane stepped off the path, pushed through a stand of tree ferns, and walked into the Green Cathedral, her footsteps leaving slight depressions in the moss.

She came to the trunk of Old Gnarly. Moss and bark covered the base of the trunk and the roots rose up in high ridges, extending from the trunk like webbed organic buttresses. The tree was covered in knots bigger than Jane's head, which gave Old Gnarly its name. High above her the bark peeled off to reveal the sleek grey of the bare trunk. She placed her hands on the giant roots and felt a serene calm, accompanied by a sense of deep time. For the first time in weeks she felt at peace.

She unrolled her sleeping bag and a fly, making a bed cradled between the roots of Old Gnarly, using her hoody rolled into a ball as a pillow. As she lay and watched the tree above her, night came swiftly to the forest. There was no moon, no fire, just blackness.

'Dude, can you tell us a ghost story?' asked Johnny Vegas as they sat around the glowing embers of the Rat Camp fire, passing around a spliff.

'Yeah,' said Amber who sat cross legged, looking at Chris, 'are there any ghosts around here?'

'There is,' replied Chris. 'There's the ghost of Rosy Sutton.'

'Who's Rosy Sutton?'

'Rosy Sutton was the wife of Jack Sutton, who everybody called Lucky Jack. Lucky Jack hit it rich up in the Balloong Valley. He found gold, you see. Not just a small bag of dust but proper big nuggets. Lucky Jack built himself the finest house in Croydon. And Lucky Jack had a wife and that in itself was something of a novelty in a gold mining town like Croydon. But Rosy wasn't just any wife, she was the prettiest girl in the colony and Lucky Jack loved her and she loved him and they wanted for nothing. The other gold miners, though, oh they were jealous. They were jealous of Jack and his luck, his house and his gold and especially of beautiful Rosy Sutton. So they devised a plan and they asked Lucky Jack to help with a seam in a cavern and when he was underground they killed him with a pickaxe and buried him under a pile of rock. They went to his house and they took Rosy and bound her to the bed. They drank Jack's wine and ate his food, and then they took turns with beautiful Rosy Sutton. And her heart was broken, so down she went, down to the cold deep river and she threw herself into the torrent. And if you go to the Balloong at night you might see her wandering the banks, calling for her husband, Jack.' Chris finished the story and stubbed out the butt of the spliff.

'I'm scared,' said Amber.

Warwick tied the laces firmly on his soft canvas shoes, tightened his belt and pulled on his brown hoody. He glanced quickly around him, but the only people who were up were Chris and a few young punks talking around the fire. They took no notice of Warwick as he hurried off in the direction of the Rat Camp toilet, a pit with a wooden platform placed on top. He flashed his torch around, locating his pack which he had hidden in a patch of dense fern. He unzipped it just to check that he had everything he needed – the big plastic bottles he had collected from the recycling, the long piece of hose he had discovered among the Rat Camp emergency supplies and a hammer he had nicked from the central camp.

Warwick set off in the direction of Front Watch, but he didn't go along the main trail via the logging road, but instead he followed the damp, fern covered valley through the bush. When he got close to the parking bay he switched off his torch and began to climb up the steep slope which separated him from the carpark. A light came from the Front Watch hut and Warwick did his best to move without making a sound, but this was hard because the ground was slippery and he had to keep grabbing onto ferns, roots and bushes to stop himself from falling. He had nearly reached the road and seized hold of a sassafras branch to haul himself up, but the branch snapped. Warwick tumbled back with a crash and just managed to stop himself from sliding down the slope by grasping hold of some ferns. He lay silently in the dirt. The sound had alerted the Front Watch crew and he saw a torch turn on and flash around the trees close to where he lay.

'What is it?' A female voice asked.

'I heard something.' It was Lauren, and she sounded close.

Warwick stayed perfectly still, bit down on his sleeve and prayed that he wouldn't be seen. He heard a scrabbling in the branches above and sounds of two possums hissing as they fought.

'It's all right,' Lauren shouted back in the direction of the Front Watch hut. 'It's just a couple of possums.'

Warwick waited for a long time after the sound of her shoes had ceased before he climbed up the slope and onto the parking bay. Keeping low to the ground, he moved through the cars to the contractor jeep and he saw with relief that the fuel tank door had already been smashed open, he wouldn't need the hammer. The diesel filled his mouth with fumes as he siphoned it, and he watched as the brown liquid fuel flowed into the plastic bottles.

As Jane stared at the sky above, she began to dream, vivid dreams. She dreamed that Grey lay on a wooden sleeping platform in his high walled tent, lit with whale oil candles. He was covered with a thin white blanket. He was pale and sweating as he tossed and turned on the bed. While beside him the black-robed priest sat on a stool. His fleshy face was solemn and his hands were pressed together in a demonstration of piety.

'Bring me the New Zealander,' said Grey.

'Sir,' replied the priest, 'You are delirious. You are overcome with a powerful fever and are beset by foul humours. It is my duty to decline you. The black woman is a pagan worshipper of false idols, a specimen of an uncouth cannibal race. The men whisper that she has the power of the Devil and her presence can damage your immortal soul in its moment of weakness.'

Grey reached his hand down on to the floor beside him, drew up a pistol and pointed it at the priest's throat. 'Quiet you fool. Bring me the woman. If God has forsaken me, the Devil must suffice. Bring her before me, or I'll send you on an early voyage to the street of gold as clear as glass.'

The priest hurried off and returned shortly, bringing with him the tattooed woman and she stood inside the tent, her head bowed. The priest stood at the entrance, shifting nervously from foot to foot.

'Be gone with you.' Grey waved the pistol at the priest. The man looked like he wanted to protest but moved off into the darkness.

'Come closer.' Grey addressed the woman.

She shuffled over to stand at the foot of the bed.

'Closer.' His voice was hoarse and low.

The woman moved closer so that she knelt beside him.

'What is your name?' he asked her.

'My name is Whore,' she replied.

'But what was your name before?'

'Tairi a kohu.'

'What does it mean?'

'Woman of the mist, wife of the rainbow.'

'Wife of the rainbow,' murmured Grey. 'I have been bewitched, by black sorcery, my skin is burning. I am dying. Even the priest says that you know magic.' Grey reached out and grasped the woman's arm. 'You can help, you can drive away the pestilent bewitchment. You must know a way. I'll let you be free, I'll send you home, and I'll give you gold.' Grey coughed and rolled on the bed in obvious agony. 'Help me.'

The woman stared at the sweating man. 'The makutu entered you. The lizard eats in your belly. I can not help.'

Grey pointed the gun at the woman's breast. 'Work your magic, or the Devil take you.'

The woman held up her hands showing the chain that held fast her chafed wrists.

Grey placed the pistol beside him on the bed. Breathing heavily, he reached into a wooden chest on the floor, pulled out a key and unlocked the chains around the woman's wrists. She knelt beside him, her arms outstretched.

The woman began to stroke his feverish face brushing the sweat soaked hair from his forehead. And as she tenderly caressed the man she began to sing, a low melodic chant. The sound was both sweet and sad. The woman's voice touched something in Jane's heart and she began to cry. The interior of the tent seemed to change, becoming filled with blue light, the air felt thick like water. Jane looked up at the ceiling which appeared to shimmer like the surface of the ocean. And she watched as the body of a shark, black and silhouetted, circled above her. Jane forced her eyes back to the bed and slowly the vision returned to its former clarity.

Grey had fallen asleep, and his handsome face, though pale and wet with perspiration, displayed an expression of peace. The woman had stopped singing and in her hand she now held the loaded pistol and in a slow and graceful movement she placed a blanket over the sick man's face, pressed the muzzle of the gun against it and shot him through head. Jane turned and saw that the priest stood at the tent's entrance, Grey's long rifle in his hands.

The woman stood and turned to face the cleric.

'Go and cry unto the gods that you have chosen; let them deliver you in your time of tribulation.' With these words the priest lifted the rifle's stock to his shoulder and shot the woman through her heart. Somewhere an animal howled and Jane awoke. She was back in the rainforest nestled between the roots of Old Gnarly.

Chapter 13: Friday Morning

Sergeant O'Connell steered his car along the winding road as he drove into the depths of the temperate rainforest. The early morning mist flooded from between the trees, shrouding the terrain in a white curtain, choking his vision, as he looked into his rear view mirror at the convoy of vehicles behind him.

It seemed like it would be a fairly basic operation. All he had to do was keep an eye on the search and rescue team as they unhooked people from the sits and some of his boys gently persuaded others to move out of the way, arresting those who put up resistance. Those activists who hid in the bush bothered O'Connell, but so long as they did not impede the removal of the blockade, he intended to ignore them. A quick in-and-out job, arrest the troublemakers, fill the paddy wagons, disperse the rest and get back to Port Town ASAP.

The thing that bothered him was the size of the operation. As well as his contingent of local police, he had the search and rescue crew and a squad of out of town police, trained specifically in riot control under the dour Sergeant Logan. Not only that but David Johnston had insisted on accompanying the operation, bringing with him a crew of private security, and then there were the contractors. And so O'Connell had found that he was nominally in charge of what had become, in his view, an unnecessarily huge operation.

The mist hung in dense swathes around the tree ferns as O'Connell approached the Balloong blockade. The first thing he noticed was a banner hung between two swamp gums. It spanned the width of the highway and must have been at least ten metres long. Save the Balloong, it read, and was subtitled, logging ancient forest is a crime. It was adorned with pictures of wedge tailed eagles. It was certainly impressive and he could not help but admire the logistics involved in hanging such a banner. An air alarm sounded its shrill call in the still morning. The activists would be prepared.

O'Connell felt the pull of his bladder as he exited his car and breathed in the cool air. At some point the activists had dug a deep trench across the road, which could only be crossed by a narrow rope bridge. Around the trench more banners hung from trees, which were cabled together. O'Connell realised a lot of work would need to be done before the contractors could begin logging, they'd have to fill in the trench to allow their vehicles to move forward, and the trees would have to be uncabled by the search and rescue police who had the skills to climb. O'Connell knew that in America uncabling, and removing sits, was done with cherry pickers, but here the terrain was too rough and the trees too high. The police would have to climb just like the activists.

More of the convoy pulled into the parking bay. Police exited from cars and paddy wagons and began to form up near the trench or stand near the edge of the parking bay. The contractor trucks pulled in, and men wearing yellow hard hats and orange high-vis vests hopped out. They had three trucks, one was loaded with long chainsaws, ropes and scrub cutters; the second truck carried a couple of prefabricated offices; the third, a grappler, and a bulldozer. The men stood around their trucks waiting for the police to do their job. The private security were bringing up the rear and O'Connell didn't wait for them but turned to face the blockade. Flanked by two junior sergeants, he strode to the edge of the rope bridge.

On the other side O'Connell saw his welcoming committee, and his heart sank; it seemed the activists had their own press presence. There was a woman with shaved hair and tight black jeans standing in front of a respectable group of people. On her left was a young woman in a red dress with long brown hair, and a large press ID. Beside her was a tall blond holding a high quality camera, also with a press ID. On the shaven haired woman's right was a well dressed African man and beside him a brutish-looking bull necked man. He was dressed in an old suit and leant heavily on a pair of crutches.

O'Connell crossed the bridge with the two sergeants behind him, dressed in high-vis vests, and sleek blue trousers. The shaven haired woman walked to meet him, they met in the middle of the bridge and she extended her hand.

'Good Morning officers, my name is Nalia Hunter. I am the practicing barrister on behalf of Save the Balloong Coalition. Am I speaking with the officer in charge?'

O'Connell grimaced as he extended a hand and he heard the click of a camera. Goddamn, nobody had told him that he would have his hands bound by lawyers and hostile press. Oh well, he was within his legal rights to use force if necessary to break an illegal blockade. He had the legal high ground. 'I am the officer in charge.'

'And what is your name and number?' asked the shaven haired girl.

'Senior Sergeant Michael O'Connell, 4254.' It annoyed him how the woman had somehow gained the initiative.

'I would like you to meet Jeanette and Holly, journalist and photographer.'

Christ, thought O'Connell, it was getting worse.

'I'm sure,' continued the shaven haired woman, 'that we would all like to see a swift and peaceful resolution to the blockade.'

'Certainly,' replied O'Connell. 'The blockade violates section six of the Summary Offences Act and section six of the Trade Practices Act.

Disperse the blockade immediately and no charges will be pressed.'

'I'm sorry, Sergeant. The situation has become far more complicated. A homicide has been committed and the body of a young girl has been found in a logging coupe. We have photographic evidence of the body being hidden and eyewitness statements. Those statements implicate the forestry and Woodchip companies in covering up a first degree murder.'

The woman indicated the thuggish man in a suit. 'This is John Thompson, a forestry contractor. He will testify that a lobbyist, David Johnston, employed by Woodchips Ltd, paid him a considerable sum to dispose of an unidentified body. It's your immediate duty to investigate this crime.'

The blonde pointed her camera at the sergeant and snapped another shot of him.

O'Connell felt himself sweat. He was a cop not a lawyer and this was turning out to be one hell of a lot more complicated than he could have imagined. 'I'm a senior sergeant, not an inspector. I'm here to disperse this blockade. We can follow up these allegations with an investigation back in the city.'

'Don't be ridiculous, Sergeant.'

'Give me a moment,' he said, and instantly he felt his authority begin to slip away. This was moving beyond him, he'd have to call the superintendent.

Jane woke to the sound of the air alarm, but the Green Cathedral seemed not to have noticed, and the spring morning brought with it the chirps of fairy wrens and the chattering of rosellas. She rose and stretched, folded her sleeping bag and tarp and sat with her back against Old Gnarly to watch the forest wake. She heard the rustle of leaves and Chris emerged through the tree ferns.

'Chris, you startled me.'

'Oh, I'm sorry.'

Chris gazed down at Jane, as she sat on the moss. Her nails were long and dirty, her clothes ragged and the lines around her eyes showed more sharply. Her hair was entwined with white cockatoo feathers, and he felt in awe of her.

'I was looking for you —'

'Chris,' she cut him off, 'I need you to do something for me.'

O'Connell crossed back over the bridge to talk to the shaven haired woman, who rose from her sitting position to again meet him halfway. They stood facing each other on the narrow rope bridge. He noted that two people crouched with saws at either end of the bridge ready to cut the ropes. He glanced back at the parking bay. The contractors had begun to set up the prefabs, two large white rectangles that would serve as the offices for the operation. O'Connell could see David Johnston standing at the back surrounded by private security. The lobbyist had somehow managed to get a coffee, and he stood out among the other men, tall, suited, wearing a hard hat, and staring straight at the sergeant. O'Connell turned away, not meeting his gaze. Did the activists know he was here?

'I've spoken with my superiors,' said O'Connell, to the shaven haired lawyer. 'They're dispatching an investigator. He should arrive in the Balloong this afternoon. In the mean time you must disperse from this illegal blockade unless you want to face arrest. I feel that your concerns, and allegations have been taken seriously, however, we cannot negotiate with you while you continue to flout the law. We are giving you ten minutes to disperse.'

The blonde with the press ID snapped another shot of O'Connell, and he winced.

'Careful, Sergeant,' said the lawyer. 'You're on the edge of wrecking your career.'

'Ten minutes.'

'I'll see you in court.' The shaven haired girl turned and marched to the beginning of the bridge. 'Cut the ropes,' he heard her say.

O'Connell barely made it back, before the bridge collapsed, the trench separating the police from the activists.

Sergeant Logan dressed in his padded glow-vest flexed his baton and gave what seemed to be a snide look as O'Connell hopped off the bridge more quickly than dignity would normally allow.

O'Connell didn't wait for ten minutes but went to talk to Collin, the contractor boss.

'Yeah, shouldn't take us more than half an hour to fill in the ditch,' said Collin.

Half an hour seemed like quite a long time, and he told the contractor boss to, 'Get a move on then.'

Chris, hurrying back from the Green Cathedral, and accompanied by Johnny Vegas, arrived at the log that crossed the logging road in front of the yurt. The lock-on crew had assembled themselves preparing to lock on to the fallen swamp gum. Holes had been drilled into the log and then plastic piping had been concreted inside. At the back of the hole was a steel loop. The lock-on crew had dog lead clips attached to their wrists. They would place their arms down the holes up to their shoulders and clip on to the steel loop. Lauren was clipping and unclipping her lock with what was probably nervous tension. She was talking to Moth.

'Lauren,' said Chris.

The tall, long limbed, tattooed girl turned to observe the North Sider with trepidation. 'Yes?'

'Where's Lui?'

Lauren pointed to the line of swamp gums, which bordered the edge of the proposed coupe. 'Over there. But you'd better be quick. He's about to get up to his tree sit and lock on.'

'Cheers, good luck.' Chris gave Lauren a quick hug before he and Johnny Vegas ran off in the direction of the sits.

When Chris got there he found Lui, and the half dozen other climbers assembled, their ropes and climbing gear attached to them. Lui had attached one of his ropes to an arrow, and as Chris and Johnny Vegas approached he fired it into the air from a composite bow. The climbers cheered as the arrow sailed through the air, and over a lower limb of the swamp gum. The rope could now be attached to the branch with a slipknot, and, with prusik knots tied to the bottom of the rope, the tree could be scaled.

'Lui.' Chris and Johnny approached the climbers.

Lui turned to face the newcomers. His brown hair hung lank around his stubbly cheeks. 'Yes.'

'I need a quick word.'

The misty morning had become a clear day and from his position in the sit, seventy metres above the ground, Lui saw everything. The vehicles were blocks of white and yellow, the people were tiny multi coloured dabs, and the forest was a rolling mass of green. The police and contractors filled the parking bay and spilled onto the main road, but kept behind the ditch. He watched as the welcoming committee disappeared into the trees, and as the digger and bulldozer filled in the ditch while search-and-rescue police slowly uncabled the trees. He watched as the fluorescent-yellow police line eventually moved up the logging road to the fallen swamp gum, where the lock on crew had assembled. So it had started. He gazed at the sky, and saw a hawk circling and he wondered what had happened to Jane's friend, Salt, the big guy with his gun, and he gulped back some water.

As Sergeant O'Connell approached the blockade a weasely young man wearing a hoody ran in the direction of the forest. He briefly considered sending a few constables to pursue him, then thought the better of it – focus on the task at hand. He eyed the blockade; it was a line of activists, their arms shoulder deep in a fallen log. On the centre was a lanky brunette. On her right was a bearded rough looking man. An old man with long wild hair and a bush shirt was on the far edge, where there were also weaker younger people. One girl had rainbow coloured hair. One guy wore a tie-dyed shirt. It looked like an easy bust but it felt like a trap. O'Connell spoke the ultimatum to the Blockade.

'You're flouting the law and will be arrested for trespass and obstruction of infrastructure. Hand yourselves over now and we won't charge you. Resist arrest and we will use force to remove you.'

The blockade was silent.

'Get a real job,' shouted the brunette.

O'Connell was losing his patience. They'd wasted enough time by the trench and he wasn't going to mince words with these people any longer. He squatted down and picked up a handful of gravel and threw it at the nervously grinning and stoned-looking face of the boy wearing a tie-dyed T shirt. He turned away to avoid the hail of rock, but not fast enough, and the stones smashed into him. Mud splattered into his eyes. It seemed like he was about to cry out and maybe unlock himself.

'Move!' roared O'Connell.

'Don't listen to the bullies,' screamed the brunette.

O'Connell moved up to her and kicked her in the ribs.

She gasped.

'The longer you stay locked on the worse it's gonna get,' said O'Connell. 'Do the smart thing – get up, now. Act like a grown up.'

'Somebody's filming us from the bush, Sergeant,' said a constable.

'Well stop them filming,' he snapped.

The sergeant hurried off in the direction of the trees.

'You,' O'Connell turned to another officer, 'get back to the cars and bring some bolt cutters.'

'Is it the job of the police to do the dirty work for private companies?'
said the brunette. 'I thought the police were here to protect the interests
of the people. But I see you're just bully boys for your corporate masters.'

'It's our job to enforce the law and you're breaking it.'

'And you do such a good job that you let killers run free. Then you go
throw stones at boys who can't move, and stop people documenting what
you're doing. You're a joke.' The girl spat at O'Connell.

'See if these greenies feel like moving with a bit of pepper spray in their
faces,' he said to the squad.

Sergeant Logan grinned.

After what seemed like a long time and continuous harassment Lauren felt
she was starting to break. Her mouth was parched, her ribs were bruised
and she was tired. She needed food, water and comfort, but the line held
strong. She was proud of the blockade for despite being kicked, beaten,
abused and told to move, everybody had held strong. She was particularly
proud of Rainbow, her loose Indian clothing was covered with mud and
she was bleeding from the lip where she had been hit by rocks, but she
hadn't moved. Another man in the blockade was cursing, swearing and
clutching his stomach where the police had hit him, and Old Mad Mark
screamed. He'd been screaming for a while now, and the sound he made
was so loud, high pitch and unsettling that it put everybody on edge,
especially the police, who left the old man alone, but still he howled like
a thylacine. The sergeant approached her and crouched down to speak at
her level. He spoke softly.

'See what you're putting these people through. There's no need to keep
it up. We'll get you some warm food and blankets. Even now, we won't
press charges if you unhook yourselves.'

Lauren barely heard him. She looked back along the road and saw trucks driving slowly toward her, flanked by private security. They were going to log the Balloong, and this was her home. The pain in her heart, as she thought of the ancient trees reduced to smoking debris, was far greater than any pain the police could inflict.

'You'll log this forest over my dead body.' She sounded braver than she felt.

Then came the pepper spray. A constable walked down the line, spraying it in their faces. Lauren buried her eyes in her left elbow, but breathed some of it in through her nose and mouth. The pain was unbearable like she was inhaling fire. It burned the inside of her nostrils and throat. She gasped, her body trying to pull more oxygen into her lungs but only drawing in more gas that dried her mouth. Her eyes began to sting like there were nails being hammered through them. She began to dry wretch, and it felt as if her skin was burning. She felt strong hands on her arms. She had to get out. She released her lock and allowed herself to be dragged through gravel. She didn't mind the grazes or the plastic handcuffs or the man reading her her rights, all she wanted was air.

Lui saw that even as the police dragged away the lock-on crew through clouds of pepper spray, the contractors had finished filling in the trench and had moved up the road, while three search-and-rescue police had moved to the bottom of the first sit. There were five sits, three of them in a line and one to either side, forming a semi-circular ring around the end of the road. The proposed coupe was, according to Nails, scheduled to be to Lui's right as he looked forward toward the blockade. He'd therefore decided to place the least experienced climber, a young guy Joel to the left. It was also the lowest sit. This was the one that the police now approached.

They used the same climbing method as the activists, firing a line over the lower branches and ascending with a metal prusik, repeating the process branch to branch until they climbed into the tree's crown.

Lui heard revving, followed by the whir of chainsaws and saw that the contractors were beginning to saw the fallen tree that blocked the road, and that they'd already unloaded the grappler. He looked over to Joel's sit and felt frustration and disappointment. Joel had already unhooked himself, and the police were helping him off the tree. Lui had seen it before in inexperienced blockaders, so excited to be on the frontline, and full of big talk, only to turn to jelly, when actually confronted by the police. Oh well, they weren't going to get him out of his tree so quickly.

Joel was arrested, hand cuffed and marched back to the paddy wagons. The contractors finished cutting the log and the grappler moved it to one side. Lui watched as a bulldozer pushed over the yurt. He saw people emerge from the bushes to defend the building, but the police and private security were ready for them and charged. Some were pinned to the ground and arrested, but most were able to flee back into the bush. The yurt and the kitchen were demolished and pushed onto the side of the road. Lui felt like screaming as his home was being destroyed, but instead he cried and his tears moistened his wind-dried face. He looked down and saw that the search-and-rescue police emboldened by their easy removal of Joel had split into groups, and a pair were now approaching the base of his own tree.

The search and rescue officer prusiked slowly and carefully up towards Lui. The cop wasn't a bad climber, but he was more ponderous, less practised and he didn't appear to be as at home in the branches as the activist. As he neared the sit a gust of wind swept from the south. The tree swayed, the platform creaked and the officer rocked on his rope. The eucalypts were not bushy, more like a collection of, sparse, slippery branches and Lui had positioned his sit so that it blocked a climber from reaching his position. The cop settled on a branch below Lui, and called up to him.

'You're under arrest for obstructing infrastructure. Come off your tree house and we'll help you to the ground.'

Lui forced himself to laugh and the sound was carried by the fresh biting wind. 'Infrastructure? It's a twelve hundred year old tree, mate. If you want me off this platform you'll have to do better than that.'

The officer looked uneasy, as the gum rustled its leaves as if in agreement with Lui, and he peered down at the sixty-metre drop to the land below. 'Don't be ridiculous, mate. Come down now! You're endangering human life and you're making things a lot more difficult for yourself.'

'Making things more difficult for you, you mean, you wanker. What's wrong, Search-and-Rescue afraid of heights?'

The cop rested on his branch and eyed the possibility of approaching the sit.

'If you throw a line to any of my branches I'll remove it,' said Lui, 'and if you try and forcibly remove me, well then there will be danger to human life.'

The cop considered for a long time before replying. 'You won't save the bush, you know. Get off that tree hut, and stop acting like an adolescent. You pricks just do this for the attention.'

'Do you think I care what your opinion of me is? I don't recognise your corrupt laws.'

Time passed and neither the cop nor Lui moved but the wind blew and with it a sprinkling of rain. The officer was becoming uncomfortable. 'I'm getting paid a lot more than you to be here,' he yelled out.

'So you love money, then?' Lui called back. 'Would you kill someone if I paid you enough?'

Lui felt the sweet moment of victory. They couldn't remove him and he could stay in the sit until he ran out of food, and even then he knew he'd be resupplied in the night. He was here to stay. But the moment didn't last long. The contractors were moving to the bush on the left where no coupe had been scheduled. Leaving the swamp gums for later, they cut into the smaller rainforest trees with their long chainsaws, and Lui felt sick as he heard the snap of breaking trunks. Tree ferns, sassafras, celery topped pine and myrtle crashed to the ground as the contractors worked quickly stripping the forest of its lower canopy, and there was nothing he could do.

Salt, his face and body smeared with mud, crouched among the grass and pampas of the wetland. He had remained still for so long his limbs were going dead and his boots had sunk, past his ankles into the mud. He grasped his rifle in both hands and watched as a flock of cockatoos flew, screeching, overhead, alighting in the branches of a swamp gum. They were waiting for him, He was sure of it. There were men in the bush with long range accurate silent weapons, watching for a sign of movement.

But he couldn't stay here forever. He had to move. So he crawled on his belly, snake-like, through long grass toward the deeper water. Mosquitoes, damselflies and water skaters buzzed around his face. While long legged spiders scuttled out of his way and frogs disappeared into oily pools as he approached.

He didn't hear the first bullet that hit him. But he felt it as it tore through his left bicep, opening the muscle, and staining the grass red. The second bullet ripped through his ear, spraying blood across his face. He felt his wounds sting as he dragged himself into the cold water of the swamp.

Rat Camp was a cauldron of emotions when the chainsaws started. The activists were upset, angry, frightened, excited and sad, but there seemed to be nothing they could do. The rush to save the yurt had been a disaster and the private security hung close to the contractors as they cleared the rainforest, while the remaining activists had gathered at Rat Camp.

Nails had tried to persuade Johnno to go out and talk to the contractors, to try and stop them from working, but he had appeared uncharacteristically bashful. He'd not met her eyes, and made some lame excuses. The only thing she could think of doing was to try to convince the pig-headed sergeant to call off the bust, but that wasn't looking very hopeful.

'He's here,' said Warwick, breaking Nails out of her depressed revere, 'I saw him. I'd recognise him anywhere.'

Nails observed Warwick. His skin was sallow and his hair had grown longer so that his fringe covered his eyes and he had to keep brushing it out of his face, he had a racking cough and was raving.

'Who?'

'David Johnston.'

'What does he look like?'

'You can't miss him. He's tall and he's wearing a black suit.'

'What can I do to help?' asked Moth. The drug dealer was clearly agitated, biting his nails and looking nervously over his shoulder, as he joined the cluster of people around Nails.

'Well, you tell me.' Nail's tone was harsh. 'What can ya do?'

The drug dealer looked around as if he expected to see cops listening to him and then lowered his voice. 'Well, I've got a truckload of LSD.'

'Have you seen Holly?' asked Jeanette.

Nobody had time to answer and tell Jeanette that they hadn't because somebody was shouting, 'cops, cops!' Nails barely had time to wonder how the police had found Rat Camp but they had. And dressed in black, blue, and fluorescent yellow, the police and private security emerged from the rainforest and charged. It was chaos. People grabbed things and ran in all directions while others stayed to argue or fight. Nails saw Jo the commie trip up one cop with a stick before he was brought down, hand cuffed and arrested. Nails turned and ran.

As the contractors cut through the forest they got closer and closer to the Green Cathedral. From where Jane sat, her back against Old Gnarly, she could see them through the gaps between the trees. She watched as a myrtle fall, and perhaps it was her imagination, but she thought she heard it scream. The loggers were slowly but inevitably drawing closer to the grove of swamp gums. Normally, the Green Cathedral was alive with birds, insects and lizards. What would happen, she wondered, to all the sleeping mammals? But now it was silent. The tree to her back seemed to shiver like it was speaking to her, trying to tell her something.

Sitting in the protective roots of the ancient swamp gum, Jane began to daydream. She imagined that she was a terrible forest demon with magical powers, which could storm from the trees bringing lightening, thunder and floods upon the people who were about to destroy the Green Cathedral. She imagined the men dropping their chainsaws and fleeing in fear before her superhuman power as she sent swarms of birds to attack their faces. She dreamed that she commanded armies of savage thylacine tigers that ravaged the police. While she was in the spirit form of a huge gnarled demon she crushed the vehicles like they were toys. She imagined the men, the contractors, the cops suffering, dying slowly, and feeling remorse for what they had done. While she, the demon of the wilderness, stormed on toward the city smashing and destroying all in her path.

But Jane's thoughts were only fantasy, for she was just an ordinary girl, and the forest had no vengeful demons, for in truth, she thought, if there were such beings they would be gentle and even in the face of destruction they would still love humans. Jane cried, the chainsaws came nearer and she closed her sodden eyelids.

'Wake up.'

Jane opened her eyes and saw a tall blonde girl, standing over her, she knew the girl. Her name was Holly. She was the photographer, the friend of Jeanette's, and she was holding a gun.

'Where is the notebook?' Holly asked.

Jane felt so miserable she felt she wouldn't even care if she was shot. She could die here in the Green Cathedral and go with the spirits of the trees. She simply stared at the girl, and realised that there was something faintly familiar about her, the shape of her face, the angle of her nose, the blondness of her hair. It reminded her of the man from her dreams.

'Who are you?' she asked.

'That's not important, you feral bitch. Where is the notebook?'

'Shoot me and you'll never know.'

'You've got a cousin, don't you? Called Sky? Do you know where she is right now? I think she'd like to talk to you.' She pulled out a phone. 'It's handy, isn't it, that satellite phones can be so small these days?' She pressed a button and threw the phone to Jane.

Jane felt her world collapsing. Everything she and Salt had done would come to nothing, and with a feeling of dread she picked up the phone.

'Jane.' She heard Sky's voice on the other line, her voice shook slightly, and she detected a hint of terror in it.

'Yes, Sky, it's me.'

'Jane, please, it's so good to hear your voice.' It sounded like she wanted to say more. But stopped abruptly. 'Just, Jane, please do whatever they tell you. Please just do it.'

'The notebook?' said Holly.

'Sky,' Jane said, 'I love you. I'm going to do what they tell me. I have to go now, be strong for me. You'll be ok.'

Jane unzipped her pack, pulling out the notebook and showed it to Holly.

'Light a fire,' the blonde demanded, throwing Jane a packet of matches.

Jane, always in the sights of the gun, gathered eucalypt bark, while all the while the sound of chainsaws tearing wood filled the air. She lit the bark with two crumpled leaves of the notebook and soon the fire was crackling, the flames growing as they burned the oil packed bark.

'Burn the notebook carefully.'

Jane watched as the notebook burned. The flakes of ashen paper made light by the fire, and lifted by its rising heat, fluttered like moths around Old Gnarly, the words still visible on the charred sheets before they disintegrated. When the last page had been consumed by the flames, Holly, her golden hair flecked with ash, turned her narrow face to Jane.

'Give me the camera.'

Jane felt despair rise through her. The camera was her most valuable possession. It was her life and it contained the only evidence of Anya's murder.

'Give me the fucken camera.'

Jane slowly took the camera from around her neck and passed it to Holly.

'Run.' Holly fired the gun at Jane's feet, and Jane ran just as she heard another tree crash and snap.

Chapter 14: Friday Afternoon

Chief Inspector Jonathon Piper, accompanied by a junior detective, drove toward the upper Balloong, leaving behind them the farmland and plantations of the lowlands. He rounded a bend in his unmarked car and slammed on the brakes. A rolled logging truck blocked the highway. The cab had twisted forward so that it lay on its side, its lights staring directly at Piper. The long double trailer, also on its side, had spun diagonally across the road from which the logs fanned out in an impenetrable barrier. Accidents involving logging trucks were common on the roads leading from the Balloong, but up here at the beginning of the highlands there were no alternative routes.

Piper got out of his car and met the driver, who was standing by his vehicle. He seemed nonchalant about the fact that he'd been in an accident and he was unharmed.

'Nah, I've told the clean-up mob,' he told Piper. 'There'll be no getting into the upper Balloong tonight and possibly not even by tomorra.'

Piper gazed up at the hills and wondered what was happening up there, He'd have to contact the officer in charge of the Balloong operation, Sergeant O'Connell. It'd be up to him to respond to the allegations until Piper could arrive.

It was three in the afternoon when the police and contractors finally broke for lunch, and Johnston surveyed their progress. It'd gone fairly smoothly. The police had removed the blockade. The trench and fallen tree had held them up, but Collin's contractors had worked quickly and the road was now serviceable. The sits blocked the route to the coupe they'd mapped out, but why bother going the hard way when there was perfectly good lumber on the other side, cutting into that had been Johnston's idea.

Holly, Patterson's agent, had done her job. She'd destroyed the incriminating notebook and located the activist camp. The police and private security had promptly raided it, bringing back more ferals for the paddy wagons, and more importantly their food and medical supplies. He doubted the ferals would last long without them. The military contractors had shot down the terrorist, Salt, and if he lived he'd be tried by a court martial. Everything was in order, Johnston breathed in the clean air.

Environmental extremists have links with armed and dangerous terrorists, that'd make a great headline for his newspaper buddies. The front page would probably be unsuitable; there was no need to draw more attention than necessary to the day's events. Maybe the third page of The Australian, next to something boring like an analysis of Labour's new fiscal policy. That could work.

They'd won, the sun shone, the bush would be logged on schedule, and the money from each of those big gum trees would help line his pocket. It was time to get another coffee. As he headed toward the prefabs he remembered the one thing that had been bothering him. The cop, Sergeant O'Connell, had been avoiding him. He wouldn't meet his eye, and Johnston wondered what the shaven haired lawyer had told the efficient sergeant. Johnston dismissed his fears by reminding himself that he was due for a holiday. A nice hotel, a tropical beach, a dry martini, and a well-tanned hooker, that was his destiny. There was nothing that could be pinned on him.

Jane wandered through the forest in no particular direction. She felt broken, lost. They had lost. Sky was held captive somewhere, having been tortured, and it was her fault. She no longer saw the beauty of the spring flowers, the white fluttering butterflies or the iridescent birds. All she felt was shame and despair. She trudged through a grove of tree ferns, lost in miserable thoughts, then she stopped. She thought she could hear voices off to her left, the voices of friends. She hesitated, wondering if she should follow the sound, or go and get lost in the woods so she could be alone with her guilt. She stood for a moment undecided, and watched as a fairy wren landed on a branch beside her and caught a small green beetle in its beak. She turned to her left and pushed her way through a dense patch of myrtles, tripped on a root and fell, catching herself on her hands in the moss.

'And look what the wombat dragged in.'

Jane raised her head. It was Nails who had spoken.

The lawyer stood with her arms folded, while her mouth cut a thin straight line across her face. Chris lent against a tree fern, smoking. Johnno stood nearby, leaning on his crutch, and Moth was rolling a joint.

Nails walked forward and helped Jane to her feet. 'I'm glad you could make it,' she said. 'There's not many of us left. But they,' Nails pointed in the direction that Jane assumed was the road, 'are in trouble. They're logging areas that were not allocated as coupes, and a friend of ours, a lobbyist, David Johnston, has come to the Balloong, and we're about to take the fight to the enemy.'

Jane surveyed the dirty, motley survivors of the raid. They were an unlikely team – a drug dealer, a lawyer, a logger, and a few young punks –

but the sight of them raised her spirits, and she grinned.

``Let's do it!' She said the words so loudly and with such enthusiasm that the group actually cheered.

Back at the prefabs Collin stared at the tits of the journalist in front of him, while he sucked on an instant coffee. He was the boss of a logging crew and times were tough but the government subsidies kept him in the lifestyle of drinking and eating in pubs, while providing for a family of pudges. He had lost his most dedicated team leader, Violent Johnno, and his labour force seemed diminished without him, but his machines, covered by expensive insurance, were good to go. To Collin, old growth trees were money, and he wasn't ashamed to tell that to the press. 'Each of those big eucalypts should give me a couple of grand.'

He shuddered inwardly as he considered his debts. He was completely bankrupt owing over half a million to banks and loan agencies. The gums wouldn't cover much. But they might allow him stay afloat for a month or two. 'And I thought you were with the greenies.'

'Oh, god no,' said the journalist, 'I'm so glad you're finally here. I've felt like a virtual prisoner with those ferals. They smell.'

The journalist, Collin appreciatively noticed, did not smell, at least not of BO, but she did have a fine scent. And she was properly dolled up, wearing a flowing blue dress while her hair was tied in a Japanese topknot. She was even wearing lipstick and makeup. It was good to see a fine example of the female sex out here in the bush and he couldn't help but feel aroused.

The sexy brunette leaned forward to reveal her cleavage, and she ran her delicate fingers down the inside of her thigh.

'What's your opinion on climate change?' she asked.

'Well it's a lot of greenie nonsense isn't it? It's just a theory. No scientific consensus, the planet's been warming for thousands of years. I'm providing jobs and there's a whole lot of bush out there.' Collin swept his arm toward the hills indicating the evidently infinite amount of timber. He took another sip of his coffee; it was good, and the journalist had offered to make it herself.

'Shall I,' asked the journalist suggestively sucking her finger, 'make coffees for your whole crew? I would love to meet them all.' Was it just his imagination or had the brunette winked at him.

'Yeah, come meet the boys. We'll have a coffee all round!'

Holly clicked the safety on her gun, and slid it into the pocket of her jeans. She opened a GPS app that allowed her to navigate in the bush. Her phone bleeped, warning her of a low battery. She had done her work. It was time to get out, finally, head to the prefabs, drink a hot coffee, get the first car to town and never look back. Holly hated the bush. It was cold, wet, dark and the trees unnerved her and made her claustrophobic. She could see on her GPS that one of the activist tracks leading to the road was not far and she made for it, picking her way through the dirt, sticks and moss.

She brushed past a wet celery topped pine, and suppressed a shriek of disgust when she saw that a big black leech had attached itself to her arm. She tore it off, ripping her skin and flesh. Her phone bleeped again, battery dead. Holly cursed under her breath. Jeanette, the little tart, had always been using the car to charge her computer, so inconsiderate, and Holly hadn't wanted to draw too much attention to herself by turning on the engine just to charge her phone. Well, it didn't matter now. She was close to the track so, no problem. She pushed her way through ferns and moss covered branches, but the undergrowth seemed to be getting thicker. A branch caught in her hair and she pushed it wildly out of her way, showering herself with droplets of water. Had she come this way? It didn't look familiar to her. Where was the damn track?

Then she heard the unmistakable noise of a chainsaw revving, the noise came from off to her right, and sounded close. She'd just make for that and the safety of the contractors and private security. The blonde pulled down the bottom of her blouse to conceal the handle of her weapon, and plunged through the bush to her right. Scratching herself on branches and tripping over roots, she headed straight for the noise. She waded through a sea of light green ferns that came up to her chest, and arrived at the trunk of a mighty swamp gum. Perched on the buttressing roots of the giant tree was a bird. It had long, elegant, striped tail feathers. It had a bright red neck. The bird threw its head back, opened its beak, and to Holly's horror and surprise, it made a sound identical to that of a chainsaw, even loud enough to be one. The bird then swiftly changed its song emitting a series of clicks and whistles. Holly stared at the canopy above, and then at the twisting shapes of the trees all around her. She was lost.

Warwick walked out onto the logging road. He had not been arrested during the raid on Rat Camp and had escaped into the bush. He knew what he had to do and the activists wouldn't like it. He was alone, Warwick understood that now, and realising that he belonged neither with Johnston or the activists, his mind had become clear and his course of action set out before him.

As Warwick approached the grappler, parked on the road where the fallen log had been, two security guards moved to intercept him on the road.

'I'm with you.' Warwick managed a sufficiently haughty and confident tone. He pulled out of his pocket his still valid security company ID. The security guards looked at the photograph that matched his face. 'I've been under cover and I need to see Johnston.'

The security guard nodded. 'You'll find him down at the prefabs.'

Warwick thanked the security guards and moved past them and out of their sight as he stepped behind the grappler. The big yellow machine loomed above him. The cab was placed on a set of caterpillar wheels and the long arm was held up so that the claw at its end dangled high above the ground.

Warwick pulled the bottles of diesel out of his pack. He unscrewed the lids and began to pour the fuel over the tracks of the machine. He stepped back from his work, poured the last of the diesel onto a rag, wrapped around a stone. He lit it and threw it. The fuel ignited with a woof. Flames swept across the engine and leapt up around the cab.

As Warwick watched the grappler burn, he experienced the same thrill he had felt last Saturday night when he'd started a riot. He thought of Goldy. She'd loved the forest and he'd done this for her, something that not even Tom would have dared to do. He felt the heat on his face, and elation and emotion flowed through him. He whooped. Then he was tackled to the ground.

The remaining activists, with Jane in the lead, were walking single file down the forest trail, toward the logging road, when they heard a sharp whistle coming from a patch of ferns to their left. Jane stopped to look in the direction of the noise, bringing the group to a halt.

'Good to see you're still at large, snot face,' said Salt as he emerged from the ferns.

'Salt,' Jane hopped off the trail to greet her friend, 'what happened?'

The big man was a mess. His left arm was tightly bandaged with a torn piece of his T shirt and it hung in an improvised sling. A piece of cloth was duct taped as a bandage to his right ear and it was red with blood. He was covered in mud but still had his gun.

'The sons of bitches nearly sent me to the pearly gates,' Salt spoke low so that only Jane could hear, 'but I swam my way out. I'm not dead yet and water don't bother an AK.'

The activists watched as Jane approached the old soldier, took a spare blouse from her pack, and gently wiped the mud from Salt's face. 'You need to get your injuries treated,' she whispered and she stroked his cheek, the skin of which was as rough as sandpaper. She looked up into his small eyes and scarred chin. 'Hide somewhere and rest,' she told him, 'we'll try and get you some proper medical stuff.' But the words sounded hollow even to her. They had no medical equipment; the police had taken everything from Rat Camp.

'Too late for that,' said Salt. 'Give me something to do.'

Lui watched from his tree sit as the fire engulfed the grappler, and he heard the engine explode with a resounding bang. Red flames licked the machine's arm and a column of dirty black smoke poured from the burning cab. A group of police and security had gathered around, watching the blaze, but curiously they didn't seem to be doing anything about it. Whoever had set the grappler on fire was a maniac and a damn fool. Despite it being a typically wet spring it was a clear and windy day, all it would take would be strong gust blowing the fire in the direction of the sawn swamp gum to start a forest fire. Swamp gum bark and wood was packed full of flammable eucalyptus oil. If the big trees went up, starting a fire storm, everybody, police, loggers, and contractors would most likely die. Lui felt himself sweat as he imagined the fire sweeping through forest, incinerating everything. From the neighbouring tree sit Tom the anarchist cheered.

Collin looked out at the trees as they morphed, bent and warped. The broken landscape of the coupe appeared suddenly to be a seething mass of hissing snakes. Collin peered around him and the vision vanished. He stared up at the maelstrom of the sky, the universe receding infinitely back in time toward the big bang. He felt waves of elation roll over his tingling body. He was struck by a moment of lucidity, and realised that something seriously weird had happened. The police and contractors stood or sat apparently transfixed by everything around them. He saw that one of his contractors was on all fours, running his hands through the gravel. The contractor looked up at Collin, and he saw that the man's face was flushed and out of proportion with his body. He opened his mouth and spoke but there seemed to be a delay between the shaping of the lips and the sound that they made.

'What's happened boss?'

Collin's own mouth seemed dry and strange to him as he replied. 'We've been drugged.'

The sound of his own voice echoed in his mind, drugged, drugged, drugged. Somewhere in the forest a bird was singing and he felt he'd never really heard a bird sing before. The bird's voice quavered and tremoloed, and Collin was distracted from everything else as he listened.

'Is it difficult being a lawyer, do you have to do lots of things?' Amber asked Nails, as the group drew near to the road.

'Not really, you just tell people they're being ridiculous until they do what you tell them.'

'I don't think I'd be very good at it,' said Amber.

Despite her brave words, Nails felt a nervousness gnaw at her stomach. She didn't really know what she was going to do once she got there, and she had an increasingly unpleasant feeling that they were walking toward certain arrest.

Two burly security guards, wearing fluorescent vests moved to intercept the group as they gathered at the edge of the forest.

'This is private property,' said the security guard. 'You can't be here.'

'Yes I can,' said Nails. 'I'm a lawyer. A murder's been committed and I'm here to see Sergeant O'Connell immediately.'

The security guard looked unsure, and their motley crew was beginning to attract attention from of the police.

'Immediately.'

'I'll just check with my superior. Wait here.'

'Don't be ridiculous, man. This is murder, not a freedom of information request.'

The activists, staying in a tight group, walked onto the middle of the road. It was a clear space between where the yurt had been, and the Front Watch trench. Behind them the grappler still burned and the northerly breeze carried with the scent of toxic smoke. Ahead of them was the carpark, the prefabs and the police vans. Jane turned to observe the burning machine and wondered what had happened. There was something ominous about the red flames and black smoke and she began to feel fear.

The security guard, who'd seemed unsure of what to do, now spoke into his radio, and Jane saw a group of police and private security moving swiftly toward them from the burning vehicle. This was it. They were going to end up in a paddy wagon, and Nails was crazy if she thought any other outcome was possible.

'Come on,' said Jane, and she began to walk to meet the police. The others followed, the two security guards walking on the flanks. As the police drew near she could see that there were three police, two private security, and a third man, a tall guy wearing a suit and a hard hat, the security guards walked on either side of him.

'Johnno!' Johnston's voice cracked like a whip as the two groups met on the road. It was a bleak place, exposed to the wind and sun, the ground was covered in sharp grey rocks and there was nowhere to sit.

Johnno seemed to flinch at the lobbyist's tone.

'There you are, man. We've been worried about you. You're in time to help with the operation. Sergeant,' Johnston turned to one of the police officers, 'arrest these troublemakers for trespass.'

'Don't be absurd,' said Nails, cutting in 'I'm a lawyer, and —'

'I don't give a damn who you are.' Johnston's voice was sharp and saturated with anger.

It would seem that the police didn't care who Nails was either because they and the private security moved to restrain the ferals, five guards to seven activists. They spread out around the group which drew close together like a knot.

Chris stood next to Jane. 'Link arms,' he whispered, and in what seemed like a futile gesture they locked arms at the elbows and formed a tight circular knot of bodies. Only Johnno stood outside the group, leaning on his crutches.

Jane did not resist as the police moved in to break the knot. A cop grabbed her by the hair and pulled her roughly away from her friends.

'Well don't just stand there gawping,' Johnston snarled at Johnno. 'Move man and get yourself cleaned up. You look like shit.'

A security guard stood near Johnno ready to guide him back to the prefabs.

The contractor didn't move, and it seemed to Jane, as she felt the hand cuffs clamp around her wrists, that he was having an internal battle between the orders of his superior, and, something else.

Johnno dropped his crutches, and with unexpected speed and agility, lashed out at Johnston. Keeping his body low, he leapt forward on his good leg and delivered a powerful uppercut to the lobbyist, twisting his hips into the punch. The blow hit the lobbyist on the side of the jaw, he staggered backward and fell, seemingly concussed. Johnno turned to the security guard who had come up behind him, grabbed him in a bear hug, and head butted him in the face. The security guard fell on his knees, bleeding from his nose. Johnno winced as he put his weight on his bad leg, and turned to face the remaining police and security. He licked the man's blood off his lips.

'Any more of you lads wanna give Johnno's fists a bruising?'

The police released the activists from their holds and moved to surround the heavy, pub brawling contractor.

The dark haired, pale skinned and broad shouldered sergeant, Logan, stepped forward. 'I don't normally fight cripples,' he said as his lips curled in a sneer.

'And I don't normally fight before a drink.'

Johnno fell onto his knees as the police closed in on him. He grabbed one of his crutches from the ground and rammed it upward at Sergeant Logan's groin. The cop screamed and fell backward clutching the seam of his pants. Johnno raised his head to look up at the police and roared at them. The sound was throaty with a hint of bloodlust.

Chris watched as Johnno's fist decked David Johnston then brought the arsehole sergeant to his knees. His arm ached where the same sergeant had ripped it behind his back and his chin was grazed from where he had hit the gravel. He felt his own anger boiling inside him.

'No justice, no peace,' he shouted, and sprang at the nearest cop, aiming for the back of his knees. The cop fell forward catching himself on the ground, swearing as he fell.

Johnny Vegas ran forward, jumped at the nearest officer and knocked off his hat, quickly dodging away as the policeman swatted at him like a mosquito. While he was distracted by Johnny Vegas, Amber stole his handcuffs, and threw a thermos of lukewarm tea at his face. There were now only one policeman standing, and one of them wet and hatless. As the confrontation turned into a chaotic melee, nobody took much notice of another security guard, who arrived, helped the dazed Johnston to his feet, and assisted him to walk in the direction of the prefabs.

O'Connell surveyed the area of prefabs and vehicles. It was chaos. He had been in the force long enough to recognise the symptoms of a strong LSD dose when he saw it and half of his officers, as well as all of the contractors, were high in the sky with Lucy and her goddamn diamonds. That journalist who'd obviously slipped them the drug was nowhere to be seen. She'd made a fool of him. Meanwhile some damn punk had set the grappler on fire and Sergeant Logan had made a complete balls of arresting the protestors up the road. A riot had broken out, and the police had lost control of the situation. It was a mess.

O'Connell rounded up his officers who were still clearheaded, not giggling hysterically, staring at the sky or picking spring flowers. They assembled in front of the trench, and armed with pepper spray and batons headed in the direction of the scuffle. As he passed Collin he heard a snippet of the contractor's conversation.

'Do you see that? The ground is covered with bugs. They're everywhere over the ground,' said a contractor, sounding terrified.

'I see them,' replied Collin, 'don't worry we're nearly at the vehicles. We'll be safe there.'

O'Connell rested his fingers on his revolver. He'd deal with this fiasco later, and have the people responsible in cuffs.

When O'Connell reached the location of the fight the two groups drew apart. The officers had their hats knocked off, and one of them was drenched in liquid. Sergeant Logan looked miserable, bent over, holding his crotch while his own cuffs secured his hands. As O'Connell drew up to face the activists he couldn't help but feel a sense of glee at seeing the arrogant sergeant and the aloof lobbyist so humiliated; he had to stifle his own snicker.

The activists were similarly dishevelled, and he noted with satisfaction that the shaven haired lawyer had nasty looking grazes on her arms. The thuggish man who'd been introduced to him that morning as John Thompson stood, flushed and exhilarated, clearly ready to take on more police.

'Assaulting police officers is a serious crime.' O'Connell's voice was harsh and grating. 'You'll all be going to prison for it. Along with possession of LSD.'

A skinny guy in a hoody giggled.

'You won't be laughing when you're locked up. You're all under arrest for inciting violence. Make it easy for yourselves and come quietly. There's always room for a few more in the police vans.'

'One minute, Sergeant,' the girl who'd spoken was small and with long dreadlocks entwined with white feathers, and not somebody he'd noticed before. 'We'll come along peacefully, but first, please, hear my statement.'

O'Connell considered telling the girl that she could give her statement in custody, but he didn't want any more chaos and it was probably easier to hear her out if it would mean the greenies would come along quietly. It wouldn't do any harm and she was within her rights. 'Make it quick,' he snapped.

Jeanette watched from the bushes as Sergeant O'Connell and the remaining sober officers left the parking bay. She waited till they had passed a bend in the road before she slid down from her hiding place, and walked with feigned confidence through the prefabs, to where the police vans were parked. The police and contractors may be tripping but they were still all big men, and Jeanette watched with apprehension while two contractors, laughing uncontrollably wandered up the road toward the smoking grappler.

Jeanette reached the police vans and could hear the muffled sound of the activists packed inside, banging to get out. One officer sat on the ground and she approached him. He looked up at the journalist through pupils the size of twenty cent pieces. His appeared to be young, and he was crying.

'What's wrong?' Jeanette felt for the cop, he'd no idea he had been drugged and was probably going through some emotional turmoil. She sat down beside him and put her hand on his shoulder where it rested on the blue cotton of his shirt.

'I don't know what's happening; I think I'm going crazy.' Tears tricked down the officer's face.

'It's ok,' she told him. 'You've been drugged. It's just an LSD trip. It'll be over in a couple of hours. Try and enjoy it. People take it for fun you know. It wasn't your fault that you took it. And I'm sure lots of other people feel the same.'

The officer gazed at Jeanette and his face had a look of wonder in it. 'You're so kind,' he said. 'You're so beautiful.'

Jeanette sat on the ground with the cop and talked to him. She comforted him with gentle words and massaged his shoulders. He gradually began to smile, cheer up and relax. 'Now,' she confided, 'I actually came down to see my friends. But they're locked up inside those vans and I don't know what to do.'

'We were on our way to see you, Sergeant,' said Jane. She looked O'Connell straight in the eye as she spoke, her arms folded and her voice level. 'We have further evidence regarding the murder of Anya Ivanova. I feel my life is also in danger and we were coming to you for safety, but we were detained by David Johnston, a corporate employee with links to the murder.'

'Rubbish.' Sergeant Logan, who'd had his handcuffs unlocked by one of O'Connell's team, stepped forward mace in hand. He was flushed with anger. 'These protesters attacked the police. I don't see any need to negotiate with violent criminals.'

'Hold it,' said O'Connell. 'I make the decisions around here.'

Logan stopped in mid step.

'I want to hear what the girl has to say.'

'About an hour ago,' said Jane 'I was threatened at gun point by an undercover corporate employee who threatened my cousin. Anya was an underage prostitute, a girl from North Side that no one cared about. She worked for a high class establishment in Man-O-War Bay, and did call work for very special client who liked young girls. But Anya was becoming a problem; she ceased working for the club and set up a private arrangement with the client. She began to probe into his business affairs. She discovered his identity and threatened to reveal it to an advocate, Mateen. But Anya made a mistake, she returned to visit her patron at the house she had always visited him. 302 Dead Horse Road. Here Anya was killed and her body taken to the old woodchipping plant on the same road, where her body was dumped in a discarded Roundup drum. David Johnston, who had a close relationship with Anya's patron, and evidently has vested interests in forestry, knew of the murder because when he instructed Johnno to clean up the plant, he directed him not to take the rubbish to the tip but to a logging coupe scheduled for a burn off.'

'How do you know all of this?'

'I followed her trail. First to the club, then to the house on Dead Horse Road. There's also witnesses.'

'Fancy yourself detective, do ya?' O'Connell did not sound impressed, but he had questioned enough people in his life to have an instinct for bullshit. Incredible though the girl's story was, he felt he couldn't dismiss it. But she was holding back something. She hadn't told the whole truth. 'Logan,' he turned to the scowling sergeant beside him, 'where is Mister Johnston?'

Johnston looked over at the security guard who was helping him back to the prefabs. He was only just starting to recover his senses after the blow Johnno had dealt him. The damn contractor would pay for that. He would never get a job again. He felt vaguely grateful to the security guard who'd had the presence of mind to take him out of harm's way. He needed to lie down somewhere, and it was getting late. He wanted to get away from the bush and back home. The guard was an ugly brute of a man, but Johnston supposed that made him good at his job. But where was the man taking him? This was not the way to the prefabs; this was a track leading into the bush.

'Where do you think you're going?'

The security guard let go of his waist, and Johnston stumbled, still groggy from Johnno's upper cut. His shoe slipped in the mud and he fell hard on his bum in the dirt. The security guard turned to look straight at Johnston, and he recognised the ugly scarred face of Jack Salt. Johnston felt his bladder discharge with fright, soaking his briefs with warm urine.

'Pretty nice fiddle boxes ya got there,' said Salt, pointing to Johnston's Italian leather dress shoes. 'But pretty damn loopy to bring them to the bush. Now shut ya pie hole, or I'll shut it for ya, and come along nice and quiet with old Salty. I got a few questions to ask ya.'

Lui could not believe his eyes, as he sat perched on his sit and watched the scene unfold through his binoculars. The police, contractors and private security seemed to have lost their minds. A pair of contractors had driven the bulldozer into a ditch. Some seemed to be wandering aimlessly in groups while others had gathered around to stare at the grappler which had started to burn less fiercely. Meanwhile, Jeanette was calmly opening the paddy wagons and letting the arrested activists loose. He watched as Old Mad Mark leapt from the back of the paddy wagon, grabbed a dazed police officer by the waist and began dancing around. He watched as Lauren, Herb the commie, Rainbow, Jaxon, Goldy, Mateen, Joel and others streamed out of the police vans, and began to mill around in the parking bay. He watched as Jaxon jumped into his brightly painted hippy van, and he fancied he heard the bassy sound of reggae blasting from its stereo. While this was happening a group of police and other activists seemed to be involved in some kind of negotiation further up the road. Lui had the sensation that a bizarre miracle was taking place. He turned to look at his neighbouring sit, and waved to Tom the anarchist. The black clad climber waved back and whooped, the sound carrying in the now still, late afternoon.

Johnston sat on the moss, his legs splayed out, his back to a celery topped pine, and his hands tied behind the tree with his own shoe laces. His face was bruised and swelling and his clothes were wet and muddy. And he looked over at Salt who squatted on the ground cleaning the dirt off an old assault rifle.

'What do you want from me?' He spoke with an unwavering confidence that had made him rich. 'Do you want money? How much? Ten grand, twelve grand? Name the sum and I'll tell you what's possible.' Johnston's voice became cajoling and matey. 'I could make you a rich man, rich and powerful. I like your ability. You're a resourceful bloke. I admire that. You could work for me. We could clean your record, blank slate right now. How does that sound? No running and hiding and living out of your pack, always looking over your shoulder. Think about it for a minute. All you'd have to do is get me off this damn tree, get us back to the cars, help us round up the ferals, and then we can shoot on out of here and start the new life. You could live respectably. You could have a flat in the city, women.'

Salt paused in his work and watched the lobbyist.

Johnston held his gaze. 'Think about it, mate. What're the bush and the greenies to you anyway? You've been around long enough to know that if you've seen one tree you've seen them all. So what're you say? Cut me loose and let's cut a deal.' Johnston's tone had become animated; the idea of cutting a deal had excited him.

Salt stood up and turned his back on the lobbyist.

'Or we could always cut the deal first.'

'A deal eh? Well, I could do with a bit coin, a hot bath and a shave. And it's been a long time since any lady graced this ugly mug with her lips. But how do I know you're not all piss and wind? How do I know you won't just hand me over to your mercenary mates so they can dump me cold corpse in the bush and leave me for dingo tucker?'

'You don't have any damn choice but to trust me,' said the lobbyist. 'You can't live out the rest of your days in the bush with one eye over your shoulder, you've got to take a chance on me.'

'Trust ya? I'd sooner trust a fox in chook pen. Na, ah, I like your offer but I'm gonna need an insurance policy.' Salt reached into his jacket pockets and pulled out an old phone. 'Now I've been on the trail of some piece of jail bait. Some Russian immigrant orphan who turned up dead in a logging coupe a couple of weeks ago, and your name keeps cropping up. You leave a message after the beep, spit out your confession, I have me insurance, and we got a deal.'

'I don't what you're talking about.'

'Oh come on now, Davo. Who're ya trying to fool? We both know that ain't true. Neither of us are bloody angels, so stop giving me that face like you're Mary mother of God. Ya wanted a deal and I'm giving it to ya. I just need a bit of collateral. Go on, tell me about the girl. Or I could just strip ya and leave ya here to freeze.'

'So you want to know about the little blonde slapper?' Johnston's tone had turned from jocular to spiteful. 'Well I can tell you one thing. She's caused more problems dead than alive. I hardly know much about her, and I really don't care. A friend of mine he has an unhealthy taste for that kind of thing, thinks sex with young girls will stop him from ageing, and she was his exclusive little elixir. I don't know the details, and I don't want to find out, but she was getting out of line, found out something she shouldn't of, so her body turned in up in an old woodchipping plant, a plant I was involved in decommissioning. I just did a favour for a friend.' The lobbyist's mouth curled into a sneer. 'She was just a whore after all.'

Salt turned to look at Johnston and there were tears in the corners of his eyes. His fingers closed on the trigger of his Kalashnikov and bullets smashed into the ground between his captive's legs. 'What friend?'

Salt heard a twig snap behind him, and turned his back on Johnston to aim his rifle at the man who emerged through the dense tree ferns. He wore standard issue camouflage pants, and shirt, over which he wore a black bullet-proof vest. He didn't wear a helmet and the hair on his head was dark and closely shaved, much like it was on his chin and cheeks. A long scar ran down the left side of his face. He held a Glock, elongated by a long silencer, aimed at Salt's head.

'I got ya, ya murdering traitor,' the shaven headed man said. 'What happened to the men I sent to bring you in?'

Salt's finger gently stroked the trigger and he watched the man unflinching, staring hard into his face. 'They were green and you were a fool, Captain Lionel Breck.'

The man showed no emotion. 'You know me?'

'Logar province, Afghanistan, you soulless mercenary. Give me one reason why I shouldn't fill ya chest with lead, I've yet to see a flak jacket stop a Kalashnikov.'

'Logar province,' repeated the mercenary, and it seemed that he was distant. And Salt knew that for a moment he too was reliving the heat, the death, the madness, but it was only for a moment.

'What are you waiting for, Breck?' Johnston shouted. 'Shoot the son of a bitch and get me off this tree.'

The first silenced bullet tore through the top of Salt's shoulder as he dropped to the ground, and struck Johnston in the neck. The second bullet took Salt in the chest at the same time as his fingers closed on the trigger of his gun, sending a spurt of bullets through Lionel's groin. As the three men lay dying in the forest a funnel web spider emerged from its hole, beneath a rotten log close to Johnston's foot. The spider was large and black with a smooth abdomen, hairy legs and long spinnerets. It stood at the edge of its hole, completely still, observing the scene before it moved swiftly across the mossy ground to a patch of shade beneath the dead fronds of a fern.

When, drawn by the sound of the shots, Nails, Jane, O'Connell and the police arrived on the scene with pistols in hand, they found the bodies still warm. Johnston was bound to a celery topped pine, his head slumped forward, his jacket drenched in blood. Salt, his hands still gripping his weapon, lay face down on the moss. Lionel lay on his back, his insides spilling from his wound.

'Sergeant,' said Nails to O'Connell, 'It's time to call off the bust.'

The clean-up crew had worked efficiently, and Chief Inspector Jonathan Piper was able to drive past the rolled truck and on to the Balloong Valley. It was late afternoon when he pulled into the Balloong blockade parking bay. Piper and his assistant sat in the car and stared in amazement at the young police officer who, carrying an activist placard walked barefoot across the parking bay singing. Some kind of ethnic-trance fusion played from a large sound system in the back of a hippy van. Feral characters were taking banners from a police car, hanging them on vans and tying them to trees.

Piper exited the van. 'Hey you!' he called to the officer.

The policeman turned to look at the inspector with a flushed, grinning face.

'What is going on here? Where is O'Connell?'

The policeman giggled. 'Is that a real moustache?'

'You'll find him up at the crime scene,' said one of the ferals, a tall brunette girl with a goblin tattooed on her arm.

Lui watched with glee as the old banners were rehung. A great wind roared up from the south and shook the tree on which he sat, while in the distance he saw clouds and fancied he could smell the spring rain. He saw an eagle ride the wind, and a flock of rosellas rise from the forest. He realised he was thirsty, and remembered the tea thermos that Chris had given him from Jane. Lui let the rope, attached to the branch above, feel his weight. He swung around to where his pack lay on the solid plank of the sit, opened the zip and pulled out the thermos. Chris had been very insistent about Lui taking it, probably pre-bust emotion. He unscrewed the lid, and saw that the plastic stop had been removed and the thermos had no tea in it at all, but a roll of pages torn from a notebook.

Epilogue

Johnno finished his breakfast of bacon and eggs and stroked the neck of his Jimbo. He was a Rottweiler cross something, a mongrel and a fine pup. He rolled some choof into a joint. Moth had dropped the baggy off to him last night. He had acquired a taste for the green during the time he'd spent in the bush with the ferals, and it wasn't bad stuff. He'd given up the drink and taken to choof, and he was calmer for it. His leg was healing and he would soon be good to go. He passed Jimbo a scrap of bacon fat and the wee puppy licked his fingers. The now unemployed contractor pushed his plate away and spread the newspaper out on the table. He sipped his cup of tea and read the paper. He read it slowly and carefully, following the lines of print with a big a callused finger. The front page read:

Murder and Mayhem Mar Forestry Operation
Three men were discovered dead after a shootout in the upper Balloong two days ago. The bodies were discovered by Sergeant Michael O'Connell, who was on the scene to oversee the removal

of an illegal protest blockade. The circumstances regarding the shootout remain unclear.

The Detective in charge of the investigation, Jonathan Piper, said that it was 'too early to be sure of anything, but at this stage it looks unlikely that there was a fourth party involved. What we probably have here is a contracted killing gone wrong, with a civilian hostage caught in the middle.' When asked if he believed there was a connection between the shootout and the protesters, Piper replied that 'the blockade and the deaths are being treated as separate incidences, but we're also not ruling anything out.' Several protesters are under house arrest for questioning, and others are facing charges under the Summary Offences Act.

Sergeant O'Connell said he was 'unaware of any connection.' O'Connell discovered the bodies after he was alerted by the sound of shots in the forest. He then called off the operation, which he described, 'as fairly peaceful and straightforward until that point. It was lucky that I was there and nobody else was hurt.'

Nalia Hunter, spokesperson, for Save the Balloong Coalition expressed regret at the tragic events. When asked if the protesters had any connection to the killings, she dismissed the question as, 'deeply inappropriate. We have been and always will be a group committed to non-violence.'

Johnno chuckled as he pushed the paper away from him, and took a puff of his joint.

The cafe was a trendy little place in the student part of town. It had a colonial theme and the walls were covered in an impressive collection of nineteenth century Port Town photographs. Lui and Jeanette sat in the beer garden at a small wooden table, beneath a blooming magnolia. A waitress appeared bringing two frothed and glossy coffees. Lui took a sip of his flat white and forced himself to look at the beautiful woman in front of him and saw that she was fidgeting nervously with a newspaper rolled in her hand. The two smiled at each other.

'You did really well,' said Lui. 'That whole thing you pulled off with the acid and getting everybody out of the vans. That was legendary.'

Jeanette smiled even wider and flicked some strands of hair out of her face. 'Well I did my best. Have you seen this?' She pushed the rolled up newspaper across the table to Lui. He slowly unrolled the paper and read.

Leak Reveals Widespread Corruption

The anonymous disclosure of hand written documents, seen by The Pigeon, confirm that considerable cash sums and other kickbacks were paid by a slush fund, to local and federal politicians in exchange for favourable contracts and policy initiatives. The documents paint a picture of a political system saturated with corruption and private interest...

Lui skimmed down the page.

The disclosures have thrown into doubt a number of lucrative government contracts, which have been awarded with a clear conflict of interest. Among the largest are controversial forestry contracts, which include millions in taxpayer subsidies to the forestry and woodchipping industries...

Lui stopped reading. 'This is incredible,' he said.

Jeanette blushed and looked down at her black coffee 'What are your plans now?'

'I don't know. I guess I should take a break from the Balloong Blockade, but,' Lui's voice faltered and his eyes flicked across the journalist's face.

She reached across the table and slipped her hands into Lui's. 'Lui, I got a solid commission for the leak. Is there anywhere in the world you want to visit?'

Sky drove the cream Toyota away from the city and Jane, sitting in the passenger seat, watched the shimmering Pacific Ocean recede into the distance. Roofus sat curled in the back seat, lost in dog dreams. They drove through orchards and passed by dairy farms, and through a small town, until they came to a picnic place by a stand of eucalypts that bordered the river.

Here in a spot of soft grass they drank white wine and juice, ate fresh bread rolls with cheese and hummus, and talked about the things they had been through. Roofus chased the butterflies, and a kingfisher preened itself on a branch. Jane watched the brown winding line of the river as it curled though the paddocks and rolling hills dotted with daisies, dandelions and sheep until it disappeared among the dark green hills of the upper Balloong. The sun disappeared behind a cloud and a cold wind blew up from the pacific, shaking the silvery leaves of the stringy barks. Jane closed her eyes and lay back on the blanket. She ran her hands through her knotted dreadlocks, her fingers brushed against the hairy stump where one of her locks had been. Gradually, the sounds of the world around her became distant and distorted and she slipped into a dream.

Jane stood in the logging coupe. It was night and the piles of smashed vegetation towered over her. The trash was there, the broken asbestos panels, the rusted razor wire, the tin drums, the plastic sacks. And as her eyes adjusted to the waxing moon she saw the body of Anya. It was just as she remembered it – naked, half wrapped in a black plastic bag, the white peeling skin blotched with bruises and covered with black veins, her matted hair, her open torso, the smell of death. Jane heard snuffling and scratching among the debris and watched as four devils emerged into the moonlight. They were the size of small dogs with black fur and white markings on their neck and shoulders. They had short heavy tails. Their ears were pointed and their strong jaws were filled with sharp teeth.

The four animals tore at the body, pulling it out of its plastic wrapping, and dragging it onto a clear space amid the debris. One devil began to bite chunks of flesh off Anya's leg, slicing through the pale marbled skin, pulling at the strings of fat. Another devil bit through her arm crunching the bone and licking at the marrow. One devil fed on her guts, pulling her intestines from her open body and chewing through them, while the fourth devil pulled the meat away from her face. As Jane watched the devils feed, she became aware of another presence. Looking up, she saw that the woman from her visions also stood beside the corpse.

'You live,' said the woman, 'but a part of your wairua lingers in the world of the dead. Let her go.'

'It's not right,' said Jane. 'Anya's body will never be found. Her killers are free and will seek out new victims. She never knew that her father loved her and now he's dead too.'

The woman pointed to where the devils had begun to drag away what remained of the corpse. 'She nourishes the children of the forest, and her spirit belongs with me.'

www.ingramcontent.com/pod-product-compliance
Lightning Source LLC
Chambersburg PA
CBHW021420110726
47901CB00008B/2240